JACQUELINE HART
CITIZEN

EDDIE SHORT

ISBN 978-0-473-61788-2 (Hardcover - POD Amazon)
ISBN 978-0-473-61787-5 (Softcover - POD Amazon)
ISBN 978-0-473-61789-9 (Kindle)
ISBN 978-0-473-61790-5 (Apple Books)
ISBN 978-0-473-61791-2 (Epub - Googleplay edition)
ISBN 978-0-473-61792-9 (Epub - Kobo edition)

Edited by Jaimee Short [v1.2].

Made In New Zealand.

God Defend New Zealand

JACQUELINE HART
CITIZEN
PART ONE

EDDIE SHORT

Prologue

By 2040, our world had arrived on the cusp of a technological revolution. The constricted internet had been freed, and the planet's resources unbridled, precipitating the greatest renaissance of engineering the world had ever known. Every intellect that wanted to be, was perfectly represented, and every hand that wanted to be, was generously equipped, until the world's greatest moment of industry had been initiated.

Endless skyscrapers were erected rapidly to spread out all the cities and innumerous islands were reclaimed swiftly to spread out all the homes, while an epiphany of innovations and new technologies were poured into the markets. Personal transport for the masses was transformed in an instant, and personal gadgetry upgraded multiple generations, before a succession of medical advances began to reveal the possibility of a life being lived without permanent pain or old age. But it was for an even greater reward that the moment had been initiated, to materialise the promises that would come with the longly awaited, 'Third Space Age'.

And that age was a success, quickly producing a new generation of rockets that could transport more cargo into orbit, and manufacturing a new grade of shuttles that could follow them in and out of that same orbit more freely. It brought about several new internationally-funded space stations and a host of diversely qualified astronauts trained to populate them, before a miracle of chemical and physical engineering propelled the world permanently from off the cusp and into the revolution.

In 2045 the 'Ziolkowski Thruster' was invented, along with the 'Light Fuel Cell' that would power it, and together ultimately help materialise the greatest reward the world had been working so hard for, to visit and inhabit another world. Or simply make it, and let it float out in space by its contained-self indefinitely. By embracing a revolutionary yet familiar form of energy, sunlight, but that had been captured without a filter or atmosphere, and seized inside a frozen case to produce a magnificently efficient battery, our space industry was transfigured forever.

The Moon suddenly became a lot closer, due to the multiplying thrust our rockets and shuttles had to travel from the Earth to its surface in mere hours. Mars suddenly entered into the world's backyard, due to the reducing costs required to ship to it and power the foundations for a new academic haven. And the asteroids were suddenly given to the masses, for them to explore and exploit with their private spacecraft, and subsequently start the greatest era of hope and prosperity the less qualified and privileged of the world had ever known.

But it was a false start, with another deadly war breaking out in the East that resulted in the collapse of much of the world's financial markets. Funds diverted from the burgeoning space corporations back into the spurring military industrial complexes. Academies that had been dedicated to training astronauts began training in their place, foot soldiers, as the ideological causes of the 'Unification War' became, virtually overnight, the world's new industrial moment.

But not everyone was united by the war, nor even had a care to end it. There was a passionate few in the West who were already far too determined to draw the world instead along a path towards a technological evolution. With our technology having reached the level required to turn a computer into a human, they aspired to obtain 'The Singularity' and turn many humans into a computer. And it was this that they demanded become the new industrial moment because it was this, they believed, that would heal the disparities in our world and consequently end its lust for war forever.

But the markets wouldn't let them, nor the engineers and biologists inventing their future, because they had already committed to fighting in the war. And so the passionate few became the 'Breachers' and decided to fight them, and everybody else who wouldn't put the war aside and give them what they wanted.

By 2050, our declining world was on the verge of a permanent destruction. Being gripped by an intense war in the East and terrorised by the Breachers in the West, it was in need of a new resolution. After rekindling our hope in the technologies we had developed to expand us during the Third Space Age, we resolved to build a new world again, though this one would need to be built in a hurry. And with less money, as there was still much needed to be spent on pushing back the lurching front of the war. And with less skilled people, after some of them had been killed by the Breachers, who were still trying to bring us to our knees.

And so came the constrictions, to crush those who selfishly wanted to evolve us, and the bridling, to secure our resources so that we could protect our world while desperately trying to build a new one. And then the poverty, precipitating uncontrollably into our financially receding societies, and the promises, made by a rising oligarchy, that the Great Stations we started funding would eventually reward us.

Now, that we have arrived in 2063, we are on the cusp of a very curious and uncertain tomorrow. We are waiting, for the first of our Great Stations to emerge from their complexes in just about any coming day now, and hoping, that after submitting to so much of the oligarchy's control, we can finally emerge from our complexes with them. But we are cautious, because the ruins in the East and memories of the West are still smouldering, and worried, because there are eleven billion of us who want to leave, and only one million spaces to go.

Chapter One
Tuesday, 5th June 2063

'I cant talk about this rite now, biik about. P.S. did u get the J10 caps? Uncle not happy capless. Wont leave his whchair -T.'

After examining the latest alert message to flash in the lenses of her HUD, Jack slowed along the path for a moment to dawdle inside the shadow between two amber-glowing streetlamps. She warily looked up at the uneven facades of the area's tall tenement buildings and exhaled a nervous mist into the wintery evening air and groaned.

Someone, somewhere, within the surrounding wall of cold, damp and serrated concrete was likely studying her, or perhaps preparing to lunge out at her from one of the pitch-black nooks beside the path. And someone, somewhere else, possibly inside another of the rundown residencies, was listening to them, while peeking out through a pair of mouldy curtains, or maybe while just slouching in one of the parked cars that were numerously packing either side of the road.

Unable, however, to spot any dim silhouettes staring down at her from above the grimy sills, or sense any coherency from the few lone loiterers the recent icy shower hadn't dispersed, she reluctantly held her nerve and pressed on.

Like all information wardens, Jack was never welcomed wherever she went in her dowdy uniform. And, though, she was only wearing the pants this time, their overt black and white-lined authoritarian design made sure she was still obvious to all who could simply look.

'And that's why I hate them,' she mused, pulling the hem of her black coat down with her hands to cover the council logo embroidered into the top of her left thigh as she squeezed in between two parked cars to cross the road. Shivering then at the prospect of being run over by the guy who was possibly just slouching in his car, she attentively checked both ways for any vehicles erratically driving off the network and paranoidally picked up her pace. 'This is *Topher*, after all,' she fretted, double-checking the road both ways again.

After already having walked along the suburb's relatively dead, cobbled streets for the last hour, Jack had become increasingly worried about the content her HUD had been intercepting. It had been increasingly *derogatory*, bearing more and more references to an information warden roaming the streets, and seemed to be intensifying the closer she approached a ten-storey cluster of buildings surrounding the head of the next street she was going to turn right down. Though a commonality everywhere else in a city serving up derogation and tall buildings for the wardens every day, the increase in derogation here, in Topher, mixed with the suburb's infamy did make her feel quite a bit more afraid. Wardens had been hurt in the area multiple times before. And, though, having occurred elsewhere, Jack had been threatened multiple times and hurt before as well. It also didn't bring her any solace to admit that she was starting to feel quite lost in an area she only knew by the electronic map overlying the data listing in the lenses of her HUD.

Suddenly, while coming to the head of the next street, it was her privilege to observe a great deal more of the derogatory interceptions begin flooding into the background of her lenses. As if being deliberately poured into her device to overload its software with Topher's charm, they began listing uncontrollably as a torrent of mean messages, nasty voices and a complete channel of dirty videos. Jack witnessed a ream of new alerts appear vividly in front of her eyes while watching her device's frame rate begin to plummet, jar and then freeze, causing her an isolating moment of distress. A recent order given sternly to all, by her supervisor, threatened punishment for those wardens who fell far behind their data, and Jack had become averse to punishment, now that she had been punished so much already.

In order to keep above the lowest acceptable report ratio reported to her employer by the hour, she hurriedly reached into the left pocket of her pants and pulled dutifully out her coder. She gave it a stern whip while holding down the corner button, abruptly unfolding its stack into a taut eleven-inch display, and observed it autonomously synchronise with her frozen HUD as she turned right into the next street and diagonally stepped out onto its road. She then began pressing against its screen and swiping with fervour to offload some of the gushing data into her cache, for slower processing, before efficiently dumping the rest of the overwhelming stream into the city's bottomless junk servers.

As she stepped up onto the left-hand footpath and dawdled with her eyes glued to her screen, she attempted to select a few of the alerts that had stacked up as the frame rate of her HUD improved significantly. 'Give me a report,' she quietly stressed, starting a triangulation on the first one before being distracted by an abrupt change in the building a door down.

"What?" she warily lipped, noticing its newly darkened windows and entrance blend suspiciously into the night's dark.

Comparing it unfavourably to everywhere else in the street that was still reliably powered on, she cautiously decided to step back out onto the road and steer away from the tenebrious tenement when a small glimmer of light coming from one of its higher windows caught her eye. She dipped her frenzied HUD and watched the small object fall onto and clang against a parked car's roof and bounce into the empty space behind it. Observing it nestle into the gutter ten metres ahead of her, she then paused for five disgusted seconds to sneer at Topher's relaxed attitude to littering.

Suddenly a bright light and crackling fizzle exploded from the object, bleaching her vision with a flash of bright white, causing her to stagger, spin away and curl over to shield her dazzled self from an unexpected attack. She then stumbled over a divot and fell frightenedly to her hands and knees as her coder clapped against the cobbles and HUD awkwardly slipped from one of her ears. "Ow!" she groaned, watching the brightness quickly recede into a blackness. "Ow," she repeated, kneeling back to compress her panging hands and wait a few seconds for the silky glimmers of the wet evening light to return.

Seeing them return much darker, however, due to all the nearby streetlamps being somehow turned off, she skittishly grabbed her coder to stand up, wipe from its screen some moisture and rub her dampened knees. 'Was that *a flashbang?*' she wondered, circling warily about to find the suspicious tenement's neighbouring buildings now also blending into the night's dark. 'Or was it *an EMP?*' she considered, noticing that the lenses of her HUD had also become perfectly clear. Jostling them gently over her nose and reattempting to enliven her dead coder, she subsequently shrank as she saw others begin to open their windows right in front of her and indignantly moan.

"*Who, did that!?*" an old lady hanging a bent arm out over a third-storey windowsill rasped.

"Ohgh!" a middle-aged women, stepping out from the front entrance below whinged, barking, "would yous *stop doing this!*" with a ungrateful glare toward someone living further down her street.

"*Hey!* Who's chucking those things around here again!?" an angry man leaning out the second storey complained above a number of others leaning out of their own windows to complain just like him.

Spotting a few of those others then naturally begin to glare indignantly her way, Jack took in a very deep breath of the evening's brisk air to repress an incoming memory she didn't want to have, and brace for a brief spell of demoralising public castigation.

"INFO WARDEN!" a man frowning down from the fourth storey furiously yelled.

"INFO WARDEN!" another repeated, pointing very directly at the obvious authoritarian pants covering Jack's nervously shaking legs.

Walking backwards *immediately* to create a more substantial amount of deescalating space, Jack proceeded to leave the indignant to their inconsiderate neighbour so that she could just concentrate on tracking back along the way from whence she came.

"YOU *PIG!* GET OUT OF OUR TOWN!" a disgusted lady peeking out from the second storey shouted directly at her.

"YOU *PERVERT!* GET OUT OF MY MESSAGES!" another loiterer approaching from the head of the street berated.

Keeping in the middle of the road to avoid confronting any of the other loiterers collecting along the paths, Jack anxiously turned up her coat's heater to thirty-seven to help warm up her muscles a second before starting a capitulating jog straight back out of the indignant residents' decrepit suburb. "Stuff this," she steamily stated, taking in a large breath of the cooling winter air, "I'm *never* coming back here."

After twenty long minutes of jogging on and off through the suburb's silkily lit streets, Jack finally arrived at the local transport station for a timely boarding of the 8:32 pm train to Grafton. Choosing for herself inside a near-empty carriage, a rear-facing, green-patterned vinyl seat, a little on from the doors, she threw her tired body down so she could dejectedly wallow in an overheating and embarrassed heap. Feeling the carriage begin to move as the buildings of Topher started to accelerate forward out of her right-hand window's view, she then lowered her coat's less-than-accurate thermostat down to twenty-four and relievedly panted.

'I hate my life,' she thought, managing to lower her heartrate a dozen beats, as her mind inevitably started to reflect on the displeasing situation that she had worked herself into with her job.

She had been assigned to patrol the evenings in Topher as a punishment for her consistent tardiness and general absence from work. And, though, it had been a better deal than being simply fired and left for the economic vultures to devour, it had only really been assigned as a cruel punishment by a supervisor harbouring a cruel desire to make her quit. Because it would be cheaper for her that way, as she, the cruel supervisor, could avoid a small, insubstantial severance pay, and any improbable inquiries that could come from someone employed higher up inside the council. 'And she probably just even enjoys *toying* with me,' Jack speculated in angst.

'I mean, what's wrong with working a few less hours?' she whined silently while watching the city pass outside the window. 'No one even *wants* info wardens.'

"Oh, and *the uniform!* " she quietly lipped to herself, spreading her hands out in despair. Looking disappointedly at her conspicuously designed dichromatic pants, she subsequently then shook her head and reflected on her lacking finances that were keeping them there, before sighing and more maturely reflecting on the ever-descending state of her employment.

It wasn't in good shape. She wasn't wanted where she was, and had no skills or clout to make a move up to fast food. And all the other jobs in the city were filled with endlessly long waiting-lines of would-be employees anxious for an opportunity to earn something insignificant or even just work for free. What she found hardest of all to bear, however, was the overwhelming attention to the sciences that had been going on in society. Because she wasn't a scientist, and with the massive new space stations being built around the world, and the excessive hype around all their yet-to-be realised promises pumping, it all together made her feel like she might not have a place in the future. 'Nor even have a place, perhaps, in the *near* future,' she worried.

Becoming aware of a pair of eyes that had glued themselves to her left side as she calmly sat on the now wobbling train with her feet rested against the back of the seat in front of her, she then disappointedly rolled her head and made eye contact with a hobo. Being something of a common sight that she had seen so many times before while working, and more so when commuting, she had come to appreciate their presence to some obscure degree because they always hoboed about her so respectfully and never called her names.

And this one was no different, sitting across the narrow aisle from her, all curled up with his legs and feet on his seat while gripping between his hands an obviously outdated coder that he was holding defensively against his chest. Using his torn grey trench coat, open ended-shoes and ruffled blue and grey Tomcat rugby beanie and scarf to compose a mental image of the man's character, she proceeded to paint a picture of a timid man who had once lost everything and now owned virtually nothing.

'And the Tomcats don't even have any All Blacks,' she pitied.

While remaining largely absent from the CBD, hobos and other homeless people could still occasionally be found rummaging through the outer suburbs, and evidently, travelling on public transport. Being seemingly regarded more as pets, in those places, than people, the bulk of them were continuously ignored by the government's hard-nosed police and border patrol so long as their numbers were kept to a minimum.

Feeling that one day soon she too may end up all curled up on her own seat while gripping an outdated coder defensively between her hands, Jack obligingly held up her HUD and coder to submit a wounded smile across the carriage. "They're broken," she said, pleasantly watching her future neighbour consequently ease his grip and submit a tiny, respectful nod back as he slowly relaxed his posture upon his seat. "Go Tomcats," she mildly added, steering her eyes back down so she could glumly look over her broken work kit she returned to her lap.

Still recovering from the last council coder that she clumsily dropped into a public toilet and ruined two months earlier, she fretted the idea of fronting up to work with another damaged kit. Giving out a sigh and a quiet whimper, she wondered how she could ever get ahead in life as an information warden. She didn't expect her supervisors to go easy on her with this newly compromised hardware and assumed they would just find some way to blame the damage on her. *'You shouldn't have been there,'* she imagined them saying, *'you shouldn't have been so careless.'* She could only wonder what the new kit might cost her to repair. 'Hopefully it's fixable,' she thought while reflecting back on the last moments with her previous coder.

Slightly entertained by the unfortunate memory, she chuckled, 'I should have pulled it out and cleaned it instead,' and then finished with a downward, *"damn."* She had endured a reduced pay for the last eight weeks to pay off that device, and was now looking at a possible eight more, and so flopped herself deeper into her seat.

"Could things get *any worse?"* she thought aloud. Her dead coder then slid off of her lap with the carriage's sway to stand sideways on the seat and rest against her right thigh. Its light but sure weight pressed against her right cargo pocket, causing her to remember the compacted stinger that was concealed inside it. Its hard, metal body could be felt pressing horizontally into her leg and it prompted her mind back to the stories that had led to its adoption.

In previous years, info wardens had been attacked severely leaving one deceased, some injured and many frightened. An increasingly paranoid public had begun objecting openly to the use of public spies and a heavy intolerance had ensued. Even Jack, far more recently, had come across brazen individuals who had confronted her and demanded her kit in exchange for nothing less than a hiding. It was only then that she had ever revealed her stinger, let alone waveringly threatened to use it.

Images of previously injured wardens shown in safety meetings, and the past injuries of her co-workers then filled her mind. Finally recalling her own injuries inflicted upon her during one unprovoked attack in the CBD, she remembered her appreciation for her stinger and sighed gratefully for her current wellbeing.

"I suppose it could get *a lot worse*," she contemplated.

After disembarking at the Grafton transport hub and strolling for a few minutes in the moist air around the inner-city blocks, Jack arrived in the grassy park across from her forty-storey apartment building in Charterton. While walking onward along a curving path, she beheld her home across the road from the park's right corner and palpitated gratefully at its beauty and cleanliness.

Nestled in between two taller buildings to its right and behind, respectively, and a shorter commercial one to the left on the street corner, the apartment building had a modern and rousing design. Three glassy archways stretched from the ground up to the penthouse on each of its sides. Four heavy white structural pillars and arches bordered and capped each window with a stylish bevel right the way around. And a numerous array of concealed lights lit the shape of the structure with a gentle garland of royal blue light that shined well amidst the typical inner-city activity. It stood out amongst the other high-rises and skyscrapers of Charterton, and Jack was always grateful to come home. Especially to her twenty-second-storey apartment sitting high above a footpath many of the city's wealthy usually strolled along well below.

'Because twenty-two is where the most successful people live,' Jack chuckled to herself, forcing a blustery mist of breath into the air.

After a pause at the park's corner to appreciate the relative calm of her neighbourhood, Jack cleared her throat and proceeded to cross the road towards her home. Upon entering its spacious off-white foyer, she was prompted by a familiar warmth to turn off and remove her coat, where she could then move on comfortably while enjoying the calm obliviousness that had recently become normal among her building's fellow residents.

As the result of a public rally two years ago, wardens were now prohibited from working in their immediate neighbourhoods. And though Jack's neighbours knew she would never spy on them anyway, they still eased up another notch around her once the law was relaxed. Jack was also grateful for the change. It meant she could officially avoid developing any personal conflicts with those who knew where she slept, even though she knew other wardens still operated in the area. It also meant that Jack had a healthy relationship with the few tenants that bothered to notice her.

As she neared the elevators and made eye contact with one of them, Douglas, the evening security guard, she nodded her head and happily acknowledged him. With the same silent gesture, he reciprocated while expressing a critical but friendly smirk.

Middle-aged and always dressed in his azurite blue uniform, and technically not a resident, Douglas had been a friend to Jack ever since he had started working at the building a year earlier. While standing and leaning against the back wall with his coder at his waist, he cordially looked into her eyes and queried, "they've got you working out late again?"

"Pssh," Jack expelled disappointedly through her lips as she passed through the threshold of the elevator and reached for the twenty-two button, "you know it. You still finishing making that video game?"

"Pssh," Douglas replied as he watched the elevator doors begin sliding shut, "you know it."

Jack waited peacefully for the marbled elevator to glide up the building to where, after a short trip, it eased its subtle downward pull on her body and gently parted its doors. "You have arrived on level twenty-two," its pleasant male voice informed to its rider's well-versed mimicry.

Jack stepped out with a cheeky smile into the twenty-second-storey hallway and walked the few steps over the bright grey carpet to her apartment's door with her keycard ready. She entered inside and waited for the latch to click behind her before calling out, "Ebee?" and walking on from the entrance. "I'm back."

After balancing her coat on the dark wooden entry table to her right at the edge of the lounge, she looked over the quiet open-plan apartment to find everything just as she had left it before she went to work. The three-metre screen affixed to the right wall was still turned off, remaining just a semi-decorative translucent film. The three cerise couches arranged in a U-shape in the navy-blue carpeted lounge's centre were still empty, appearing like no one had sat in them for a whole day. Her snowboard was still out between them, standing vertically against the edge of the coffee table above her wax block and iron that had been untidily left out upon the small table's surface. And finally, her morning's crumbs were still out, being left upon the wooden dining table standing directly across the tiled path from her, where she had sat earlier in the day and not finished her toast while staring out the adjacent panoramic windows.

"Ebee?" Jack called again.

Proceeding to place her broken work equipment atop her coat, she cautiously pulled the contracted stinger from out her cargo pocket and prepared to set it safely down for the night. While gripping the fifteen-centimetre handle tightly and pointing it well away from her, she squinted and braced for the ever-uncomfortable next step. Squeezing the handle with force violently sprang the weapon's shaft from within, causing a startlingly hollow snap and vicious mechanical jolt to surprise Jack and tweak her elbow hurtfully.

"Ooh!" she winced at the pinch. "Ow," she expressed in displeasure.

Holding the extended device away from her to avoid contacting the electroshock component housed at the distal end, she separated its now exposed battery and cautiously placed the components together with her kit.

Shaking her head as she reviewed the glossy black sixty-centimetre-long baton, she genuinely considered, "how do we even *have* these things?" Despite understanding well the need for a deterrent, she couldn't help but wonder how an information warden could be trusted with an electroshock device that could melt through plastic. 'Some of the wardens are really bitter,' she thought with concern.

Moving across to the dining table to collect her mess, Jack quickly noticed that the morning's crumbs that had fallen down onto the alabaster tiles below hadn't been cleaned up by the vacuum.

Scheduled to work twice each day at 10:30 am and pm, the small round gadget had begun skipping shifts since a couple days ago due to a prohibitive build-up of sealed vacuum bags that hadn't been removed from its waist-high charging station.

Jack sighed with a moan and dropped her shoulders while recalling her duty to clear it.

She then chose to skip that duty, once more, and ignore the build-up, and instead simply collect her plate and peer out into the evening street through the lightly blue tinted windows.

While staring out at the small urban park to the right where she had stood earlier and looked up, her mind momentarily contemplated on the people she had been observing while working in the poorer confines of Topher.

'They probably skip emptying their vacuum stations too,' she thought, reflecting on the constant state of untidiness and lethargy throughout their suburb. 'They are probably just very good at skipping in general.' Jack had watched them skip their duties, skip their work, skip their children, health, and largely skip their life. There was so much skipping that the collective depression of it all distressed her quite sorely from time to time when she was there. Their economic difficulties were all so plain to see that it reminded her often of the even more economically difficult past she had endured at times, and could endure again, if unlucky.

A deep feeling of hollowness opened up above her stomach again just thinking about it. She put her plate back down and breathed in deeply while running her hands through her hair and rubbing her face and eyes. She then steadied herself as her mind began to wander downwards.

Born at the end of the mid-2030s ahead of the last real financial boom, Jack only ever remembered seeing her natural family from her youth get unbelievably poorer. While her mother stayed at home to care for her and her sister in the otherwise growing work climate, her father lost their inherited finances to too many foolish business decisions. Consequently, they were driven out of their modest wealth into that which became the rusted and rotted confines of the southern metro squatters to live amongst the country's poorest and sickest. Jack was old enough to remember the incredible change down and young enough to have to endure it for a time, before her best friend, Ebee, was able to reach out through her more affluent family and rescue her.

Suddenly snapping out of her gloomy state, Jack cleared her throat and combed her hair back behind her ears with her fingers. Grabbing her plate again and turning to take it away, she asked aloud, "where's Ebee?"

Upon approaching the kitchen cubicle, situated back toward the entrance opposite the lounge, she spotted a message that had been digitally fingered onto the refrigerator's side. 'Having night with workmates, dinner on the bench,' she read from it. Humming a chuckle at Ebee's recognisable fingering and smiley handprint signature, she then looked along the kitchen's dark granite benches for her best friend's offering. Seeing a plate covered in a reflective foil that concealed an obvious heap of food, she put her morning plate back up into its pine-green drawer and set it to clean before approaching the new one.

Lifting up the stiff foil revealed a neatly prepared lamb roast with scooped mash potato, long green string beans, crinkle-cut carrot slices and large soft pieces of kumara. 'She must have got it from a restaurant,' Jack deduced from a rather immaculately sauced presentation that was contained inside an unusually thick, recyclable plastic plate. After taking a second to relish the warm aroma, she hummed pleasantly and thought graciously of her friend.

Being only a year older than Jack, Ebee had looked after her ever since they were together in primary school. With no siblings to call her own, she had quickly adopted Jack as a sister and carried her along a more privileged path where even until now at twenty-six, she still made sure Jack was privileged. She paid the rent for their expensive apartment and covered most of their food and bills, all without a hint of disdain for Jack's lack of success and general disposition toward laziness.

After savouring the roast at the table while watching out over the late urban activity outside, Jack got up and rinsed her dishes before returning them to their washer drawers. She then moved on quietly around the lounge into the bathroom so she could ready herself for bed.

While standing in front of the white porcelain sink and running the warm water, she lowered her hands beneath the stream and looked forward into the mirror. Her eyes wandered between her reflection and the various advertisements playing colourfully around the mirror's glass and read one displaying an item that they were low on. 'Taylor and Taylor's velvet soap. On special this week at Ngahere Kai,' Jack senselessly regurgitated in her mind, 'Contains four times the antioxidants of the other leading brands.'

After collecting some of the water in her hands and washing it over her face and massaging her tired eyes, she leaned in toward the glass and looked deeper into her complexion.

Her shoulder length, dark brunette hair had become frizzy in the cold, wet air outside. In locks, it both hung in bundles around her ears and wrapped around her cheeks making her look like someone that hadn't been to a hairdresser in years. Her green eyes were glazed, her lips were lightly chapped, and her skin looked like it needed to be scrubbed with a tub of Ebee's manuka honey exfoliator. "Another eight weeks," she quietly uttered with regret, ineluctably thinking of her broken work gear.

Straightening back up while leaning with her left hand on the side of the sink, she reached back behind her right ear and gently peeled the inch-by-inch HUD articulator patch off her skin. She placed the silvery sticker-like device on the side of the sink and opened the mirror's cabinet to pull out a new articulator from a half empty box of thirty to place it above the old one. She then cleaned and dried behind her ear with a handtowel and warmed the new articulator beneath the hand dryer before placing it behind her ear and rubbing it against her skin.

Proceeding to clean her teeth with the excessively bent bristles, dwindling foam whitener and dying blue light battery of her three-in-one toothbrush, she also started multitasking with a swipe across the mirror. Skimming through advertisements to her favourite toothbrush's reorder link, she spat out her toothpaste prematurely and gasped, *"four hundred and eighty dollars!?* Last month it was *three-eighty!"* she whined, considering whether a follow-up was worth it. Having to include an unfair fee she might have to pay for her broken work kit into her considerations, she hesitated but ultimately sided with her desire to have at least a few of life's luxuries.

After difficultly confirming her purchase and exiting the bathroom, she heard the toilet start its evening cleaning cycle and automatically acknowledged, '10:30. Bedtime.' As she walked past the lounge screen to her bedroom, a loud beep suddenly alerted her to a build-up of vacuum bags prohibiting the vacuum from working. "Oh," Jack moaned, dropping her head back to lazily declare, *"tomorrow!"*

Chapter Two
Friday, 8ᵗʰ June 2063

Unscheduled to work the following days, Jack let the time pass with little input. She woke up each day after Ebee had left and spent the morning lounging in her apartment due to her prohibitive budget and poor motivation. To avoid boredom, she waxed her snowboard and played socially constrictive videogames that helped her to pretend her life was better. Using her own HUD and electronics, she drowned out the need to leave her den with more games, ads and updates about the lives of other people. In the evenings, she played more and ate alone as Ebee was always busy with her job and always obliged to participate in her employer's evening entourage. During her break, Jack's greatest exertion was cleaning the dust from another faulty vacuum bag that ruptured while being jiggled out of the vacuum station. Her second greatest exertion was placing her broken work equipment into the hands of a council contractor that came to her door.

The following Friday morning, Jack returned to her day shift, reporting first, as per usual, to the city council building located deep in the middle of the central business district. As a ninety-storey, tubular chrome skyscraper with a pointy peak falling short of the corporate aerial village suspended above, it brought a bit of shame to Jack every time she approached its entrance. From all her intercepting, she knew the general public held the entire council and much of their workers in contempt, especially their information wardens, and it troubled her sometimes to see her face on the building. The local body politicians working inside, that she never saw, were also always so desperate in the news to be glamorised and associated with the mega-wealthy floating higher up above, and the public hated them for it. The mega-wealthy couldn't stand them either, but Jack could only surmise that from their workers, since the mega-wealthy always had the latest encryption and erasure routines employed in their communications, or were quite simply out of reach.

Jack was also embarrassed by her lowly position among the more cheerful council workers who she saw every day passing through or working in the front of the lobby. Dressed in their more stylish business wear and holding cafe-bought beverages in their hands, they would smile at her courteously while giving her a wide birth and holding their breath.

"Hmhmm," Jack could only snigger, however, as she walked through the vestibule onto the marbled tiles where she observed that behaviour once more.

'I'd do the same,' she admitted, glimpsing at someone turn their passing gaze quickly from her and exhale.

She then turned immediately left a few metres into the lobby to reluctantly approach a single crimson exit door labelled with a white paper sign declaring, 'OTHER-EMPLOYEES ENTRANCE.' Effortfully pushing it open and descending the concrete stairs behind, she went down beside three levels of car parking and valet offices and into the council building's absolute basement where the information wardens' quarters were situated.

Darker and colder, and distinctly very drab, the cave-like quarters were surrounded in black painted concrete walls covered in maps, protocols and demanding schedule planners. Besides the space around the lockers and a small central black lounge area with a circular coffee table, the floorspace wasn't particularly generous nor the presentation welcoming. There were cages and cages of arbitrary inventory stacked one upon another due to an overflow always pouring out of the neighbouring Archived Assets Department. There were two large mobile blackboards, a couple too many displaced mobile cabinets left to bang into and a twenty-metre-diameter no-go zone of terror that surrounded Jack's primary supervisor wherever she went.

Able to be felt on the other side of the freestanding row of lockers or even through the restroom walls, the no-go zone was unrelenting. There was barely anywhere Jack could place herself to avoid feeling unwanted, or in trouble.

Ultimately, the vibe of the workplace was of a department discarded and a bunch of reprobate wardens swept from the public's disapproving eye. 'They don't even give us descent markers,' Jack criticised of the council while moving beneath a giant smudgy whiteboard bolted to the wall before the toilets.

Walking on to the front of the Archived Assets Department, a square hole in a diagonal wall adjacent to the toilets and linearly opposite the whiteboard, she approached a faded, pastel yellow counter presided by Bob.

Being a well-fed Turkish man, rounded in shape and stuck on a stool for the most part of the working day inside the confines of a basement burrow full of junk, Bob wasn't a particularly formal man, and dressed accordingly. He often wore a casual pale-yellow polo shirt with the top unbuttoned and bottom pulling up, like today, indifferently revealing his moderately hairy chest and navel from his slouched posture.

Sitting beneath a small hanging light that illuminated his receding hairline and helped him work, Bob brushed sweat off his forehead and spoke, as Jack approached, with his thick Turkish accent, "your new equipment is here." He picked up from below and pushed forward across the counter a new HUD and black vinyl-backed coder that resembled her previous kit. "Your old one was fried," he said with a discerning face, "did you get hit with an electromagnetic pulse?"

As something of a technician, he was assigned to look after the wardens' expensive equipment while keeping a running log of the council's least important assets, and Jack was never really sure how to take him. He was in Archived Assets, so was always bored, but considered a part of the wardens' team and so was always disgruntled. He was either a friend or a creep, and his accent prevented her from understanding most of his probable banter. He also spoke with a staunch and rather loud voice that often drowned out Jack's pre-empted thoughts, leaving her confused after their brief conversations.

"Yep. I think so," Jack replied slowly, while averting her gaze from his overhanging midriff, "it was down in Topher. There was a flash too, with it, like, you know."

"Hmmm," Bob mumbled, "this happened to Julie the other day, about a week before you. In Greenhithe." He began speaking more quickly, outing an English that Jack failed to fully translate.

During a break in his rhetoric, Jack reached and grabbed the kit and interestedly diverted the dialogue toward their mutual working conditions. "Have you ever thought of moving up to valet?" she asked, before adding over his reply, "I mean those guys are always laughing and they get tips for cleaning all those flash cars, like the Mayor's Ferrari."

In a defensive manner Bob replied with a staunch retort, "those guys get all the council cars and trucks to clean and repair. I get to sit here and do very little while getting more money. Why would I want to switch up to their backbreaking job, e?"

Jack mumbled a short, "uh" before being interrupted.

"I get twenty dollars; one-hundred-twenty-dollars more than them per hour to do what I do here," Bob ranted.

'That's not much,' Jack thought while Bob continued to explain, "I don't need to do more work, I just need to get paid."

As his difficult English loudened into a thick Turkish English, Jack thought she heard him explain that his wife needed the extra money for her, "drone refurbishment business?" she mumbled with an uncertain brow.

Bob stopped for a second before shooing Jack away. "You go," he said with an expelling flick of his wrists. "You're working in the Viaduct now. Off you go!"

As Jack pulled away with her gear and turned to leave the quarters, Bob called in displeasure, "put your clothes on. And your hat!"

Deliberately ignoring his instruction to change into her uniform, Jack picked up her walking pace and called back with a hand to her ear, "wha? I don't. What?" she feigned. Seeing Bob give up counselling her as she approached the exit to the stairs, she chuckled and called over her shoulder, "see ya Bob."

Later that morning the sun was out in Jack's newly assigned area of the city, The Viaduct, an upmarket apartment and cafe area nestled deep within the metropolitan between the Viaduct Harbour wharves and the towering heights of the CBD. Jack was as grateful as always to work in the cheery area, especially in mufti, and enjoyed the light commercial atmosphere much more than the dreary lethargy of the suburbs. The people here walked pleasantly along the footpaths and sat on fanciful furniture outside artistic eateries eating brunch while enjoying a maritime view. Birds flapped between dotting evergreen trees in the unusually warm winter weather and chirped amongst the branches, swooping down intermittently to fetch the crumbs left by shoppers. Even the beeping from cars pattering along the mosaic stone roads did little to disturb the cheeriness or interrupt the chinking and chattering of porcelain and gentle plashing of water.

Sitting at one of the tables by herself outside Rioux Café, a small French bistro situated by an intersection decorated with bare deciduous trees, Jack was fiddling with her new work coder in a peaceful mood. Every time she would look up and about between swipes to see if anyone was staring at her, she would happily find no one taking any interest. With no conspicuous uniform to warn the public, she had been able to potter along for the last two hours without the unsettling, silencing stir that usually accompanied a warden wherever they went. And though she had been in trouble in the past for not wearing her uniform, and could be again if caught, the absence of ostracism was sometimes just too good to resist.

With her new HUD already set up and reacting to the environment, picking out cues from the surrounding tables and dishes, and generating a list of interceptions, she finally finished toying with her coder and put it aside. She switched to her HUD and slipped it over her eyes to find the time, '11:14 am,' and her order of two friands and a hot chocolate nearly ready. 'Menu,' she thought, dutifully looking over some of the most recent data intercepted. In response to her trained brainwaves, the HUD reacted, and she proceeded to think, 'Interceptions,' according to the title of one of the coloured links. 'Enter,' she thought while looking over the 'Most recent' tab.

HUDs and share-powered coders had become a way of life for the people in the city. With technology reaching a cultural plateau in the late 2040s, the brainwave-reading HUD and share-powered, collapsing coder had become a staple among the population. It would be completely unusual today to find someone technologically naked and absent of the hyper-connected devices.

'Add to prepared reports,' Jack thought while looking over an instant message about Anupam Ramakrishnan, one of the city councillors. Someone had referred to his heritage when demeaning his political agenda for improving freshwater access to the Western Squatters. Looking to start an unsanctioned petition to overturn the plan, the person's communication had showed up as an alert on Jack's HUD, highlighting the ethnic slur and the potentially illegal petition.

Often undecided about whether what she was doing was truly right or wrong, Jack just continued to file interceptions and use her kit to identify and record as many relevant people she could at the time, within the legal radius. Political slander and protests didn't interest her very much except when info wardens were mentioned. In the past, she had come across much more provocative topics such as the breaching of anti-singularity laws and citizens-initiated culling. She had even intercepted the broadcasts of an illegal, makeshift humanoid robot but usually her days were long and boring. People mostly just hated the heavy-handed government and kept using alert words to express it, or were simply communicating with their loved ones and colleagues on legally monitored devices.

With the cafe order timer on her HUD going into overtime, Jack became a little disappointed. Her food wasn't delivered yet and due to a custom-integrated live stream camera and GPS built into all of the warden's HUDs, there was the smallest of chances that her supervisor might notice that she hadn't moved for a while. They didn't normally watch the streams or live GPS reports because it was boring, and due to a clause in the laws around public spying, recording them from the council terminal was prohibited, so they couldn't save it for later. 'But still,' Jack pondered with mild concern as she continued to wait at her table, 'I'll have to move soon.'

While taking a moment to review another interception, a commotion spontaneously erupted across the street. Piercing shrieks of smashing glass etched into the air followed by a discord of angry growling. As with everyone around her, Jack sat up from her slouch and extending her gaze up above the heads of the other cafe goers and traffic on the road. On the edge of her seat and looking over to discern what was going on, she noticed a man scramble to his feet on the footpath outside a small gift shop and start sprinting rightward, towards the CBD.

A retailer then exited the same shop and yelled into the street's pedestrians with his finger pointed at the runaway, "*stop that thief!*"

The heated call suddenly aroused Jack's thoughts and her mind began to process. Info wardens were not only tasked with intercepting data but also in assisting police in their area. While staying out of trouble, they were supposed to record evidence and be a temporary liaison for the council. 'Just what I need,' she opined, reflecting momentarily on the much-needed kudos she could get from snapping a shoplifter.

Without another thought, she leapt forwards, bumping over her chair and jolting her table. She clasped her HUD and coder in her left hand and bounded into a sprint. While whizzing past curious pedestrians, she scanned the parallel footpath with her eyes and saw the runaway shaking out of a random person's tackle a number of shops down. Taking only a few steps on her side of the street, she skipped out onto the road through an opening in some decorative railing and skewed in front of the moving traffic. Knowing that the cars' systems would automatically detect her, she sped on to the heavy braking of vehicles and the skidding of tires. Glancing at aggravated faces behind windscreens only enlivened her more to the chase.

Skipping up onto the next footpath, she began putting more force into her step as she spotted the fleeing thief at the head of a wake he had created in a group of perturbed pedestrians. Worried she would be mistaken for a fleeing accomplice, or even an info warden, and be tackled too, she held up her kit and sped toward them. *"POLICE!"* she yelled as she neared. *"POLICE!"* she assured as she whizzed through with a cheeky grin.

Hearing the calls from further up, the fugitive turned around at pace to inspect but collided backwards into an elderly lady, knocking her down onto the pavement. Avoiding a complete stall, he glanced at Jack again and hastily left the dishevelled lady to continue his flight towards the CBD. Conscious now of his attentive pursuer, he began evading the public more skilfully and started manoeuvring through and around obstacles to escape.

Adjusting to the heightening challenge, and acknowledging the aching elderly lady, Jack placed on her HUD and carefully slipped her coder in her pocket. She trailed the fugitive's evasive path above the gutter through large bright holographic signs visible on her HUD and dashed by bins and over benches. She sped through a long, animated skit revealing new milkshake flavours and darted through interspaced posters assigning her coupons for sushi and paninis.

Drawing stamina from her innate athleticism and seven years of school and club rugby, she accelerated but the broadcast of information began to confound. Advertisements interrupted each other repeatedly and intercepts built up as she determinedly pressed on until an offer for paua coasters caught her attention. 'Two for one at Sails City Souvenirs,' her mind autonomously recited.

"Argh!" she instantly exclaimed and refocused, gazing forwards through the shrinking gaps in her lenses.

Pulling off her HUD and suddenly realising the thief gone and the coasters far too expensive, she slowed to a halt upon an intersecting driveway and released a breath of frustration.

She then turned her sights left to a kerfuffle of rubbish and a desperate pant to find the thief struggling to scale a large brick wall at the end of a short, shaded alley she was at the head of. Relieved she hadn't missed her opportunity, she slipped back on her HUD and pulled out her coder and called, "oi!"

The thief turned around and shouted anxiously up the dozen metres to his pursuer, "leave me alone!" After an intense few pants, he added with an awkward, upwards inflection, "you don't know me!"

Jack breathed through her lips to try and calm her pulse. "Nope," she replied, holding up her device and its camera, "but this will."

Then through the instrument's reticule, she noticed an unusually scruffy appearance. The thief's hair and skin were excessively oily, and his brown bomber coat was well worn and stained. His frayed black pants were too wide, hanging baggily from his waist, and his dusty black shoes were creased beyond form.

After a nervous whimper, the thief wavered, "I don't want any trouble. I'm not even supposed to be here." He reached inside his coat and pulled out a fuzzy soft toy with his right hand, holding it up for Jack to see. "It's for my daughter," he stated with a shaky voice and wobbly posture, "I don't, I don't want it anymore."

Jack lowered her coder a few inches and peered through her HUD at the white teddy bear clothed in a pink dress.

With a pink bow set between its ears, it stared longingly in her direction with its plush limbs ready to hug and silently broadcast its worth.

Automatically receiving its cue with an incidentally confirming gaze, Jack read off a simple diagrammatic box that appeared in her HUD as if floating beside it, 'Margaret, from the Cuddlebunnies range; $1,200.00. Exclusive to Baker's Toys. $5.00 from every purchase will go to Save the Children.'

Figuring the man now a confused simpleton, or a squatter that had wondered in from behind the city's walls, she relaxed a little and ineluctably queried, "where're you from?"

Lowering the bear, the thief replied, "from Sunnyside... Homes."

The words made Jack sink into a gutted slouch.

Sunnyside Homes was an old dilapidated housing project that had long been forgotten and was now behind a portion of the city's armed border wall separating, there, the tormented Western Squatters from the city. Jack had witnessed so many people in her early years endure a horrible life amidst the anarchy of those particular shanties that she had come to pity those from there who tried to do anything but wallow. While basking bitterly in the reflected radiance of the city and its developing Great Station across the Manukau Harbour, most of the people dwelling in that sprawling slum had given up trying to be civilised. The crime there was constant and their conundrum complex; the fortune on the other side of the wall was a world away, and they were never going to partake in it. Even Topher and Charlemont, the city's two most malnourished suburbs, were immeasurably advanced compared to the corroding and crumbling shanties of the squatters.

As with all the hobos and drifters that somehow meandered in and out of the outer suburbs of the city, Jack felt bad dealing the thief any ill will. Figuring that her efforts could condemn him to a life even harder than the one he was likely suffering now, she swiped across her coder and deleted the footage she had recorded of him. After folding down the device and sliding it into her left pocket, she removed her HUD and powered it off. She cleared her throat and nodded her head silently while beginning to turn away.

"I was supposed to meet some coffee dealer," the thief then desperately exclaimed, "these guys, dropped me, off, in a van."

Feeling the man wanted an emotional acknowledgement of his troubles from anyone who would listen, Jack stayed a moment longer to satisfy the small ache of sympathy she had for him.

"They wanted, me," he earnestly appealed, "to meet someone, and get some coffee. I was gonna go out... It was gonna go out on the street."

Jack's mind then began pondering on the last time she heard the word coffee said in such terms.

A wide sweeping, syndemic blight had plagued much of the world's vegetation nearly two decades earlier disturbing the growth of a number of the world's plants. With coffee among the biggest hit, its prices soared until it became a completely regulated substance. Many people complained of depression and others began stealing what they could get their hands on. Now, with the natural beans reserved only for the privileged, man-made versions had become the norm among everyone else, while those who wanted authenticity turned to the black-market where the natural product was more available and for a lower price.

Jack snapped out of her thoughts when she heard the thief lament out loud.

"I just wanted to make my daughter happy," he wept, burying his face in his hands while beginning to sob tearfully. He then lowered himself to his knees to rest in front of the alley's rubbish bags and discarded boxes to begin crying to himself in obvious regret.

Now feeling even more uncomfortable with the development, Jack dipped her head to avoid watching the broken father suffer and turned completely away. 'I better go,' she told herself. Peeking back one last time to consider giving advice about returning the bear, she was unexpectedly interrupted by a deep whizzing sound growing in the air. Advising about that instead, she uttered, "sounds like a— "

A loud bang then abruptly shuddered through her skull, causing her to stumble into a group of rubbish bags and clutter lining the alley. She braced her head tightly, to alleviate a sudden panging on the top left of her crown, and moaned with her eyes and jaw shut tightly, to express her discomfort. After a few seconds upon the craggy rubbish, she rolled sideways onto some softer bags and looked up to find out what exactly it was that had hit her.

"Halt, resident!" a multi-timbred mechanical voice abruptly exclaimed from above, "remain calm. Police officers are in attendance."

With her hands compressing a likely cut, Jack spotted through her elbows a large pentagonal, white and blue drone hovering steadily above the alley, flashing an integrated set of red and blue lights. She watched it proceed down and repeat itself loudly at the mewling father while she shuffled off the bags to sit on the concrete and prop her back against the rubbish. As she quickly tried to gather herself, she was interrupted by the arrival of heavy footsteps and aggressive yelling.

"*POLICE! POLICE!*" a man shouted.

"There he is!" proclaimed another.

Two blue uniformed officers suddenly trampled past to confront the thief, leaving a third officer to stand over and intimidate Jack.

"Hold it right there!" the third growled as Jack tried to get up.

Jack's shoulder was subsequently shunted by a heavily gloved, blue palm, forcing her back to the ground. "Argh!" she moaned while continuing to compress her head with her left hand. After steadying her posture with her right hand, she assertively exclaimed, *"I'm an info warden!"*

"You're a warden?" the third officer gruffly asked her aloud.

To the sound of the other officers shouting at the thief, Jack nodded her head and replied aloud, *"YES!* Warden 5-6-2-0. Jacqueline Hart." As the officer stood up straight and began reporting through his semi-transparent HUD covering the top of his face, she looked over at the other officers and saw them approaching the father slowly with their disruptors out.

"GET UP! Get off the ground!" they shouted at him.

The father rose up his arms and stumbled to his feet. Keeping his hands out towards both the aggressively posturing officers that were dressed for confrontation, he tried to calm them. "It's ok," he submissively called with a nervously enfeebled stutter, "I'll, I'll come along... You don't, need those. Here," he appealed, offering them the stolen teddy bear, "I, I don't want it."

The father's sudden submission to the officers' pointed disruptors alerted Jack to the disruptor in the hand of the officer standing over her.

Used as tactical EMPs for humans, the plastic grey handguns invented a decade ago had become a mainstay for modern law enforcement. With only an LED on the end to indicate their activity, they used intense electromagnetic radiation to selectively disrupt the electrochemical signals inside targeted nervous systems. But being individually ineffective, due to regulation, multiple disruptors were employed by multiple officers from different angles to immobilise a target for minutes.

The sound of the father abruptly collapsing onto the concrete and moaning in humiliating submission redrew Jack's gaze.

"Get up! Get up!" the officers shouted at him as he groaned with the now soiled teddy still held in his hand.

"Please?" the father begged them as he propped himself up with his left hand and right forearm, "I, I don't want it— "

"Get up maggot! Get up!" the officers dictated, "or you'll spend the rest of the day at the bottom of cell eight in a pile, with the other squatters. *Unconscious!* "

Absolutely convinced of their threat, the father leaned his upper body forward and curled his left leg to stand. With a limp right leg, he exerted with just his left and partially occupied hands to raise himself when his disrupted right arm suddenly gave way causing him to awkwardly dive back into the ground headfirst.

Grazed by the concrete and clearly trapped with three opportunistic bullies, and coming to a realisation that he wasn't going to see his daughter again, let alone give her a gift, he gave up his remaining strength and uncontrollably cried.

"Get up dummy," one officer heckled, causing the other to snigger. They then began pridefully nodding and giggling while mocking the downed man, "you must've thought today people would be nice to you and give you stuff.

Bet you could have just bought that teddy bear, but instead you just bought a fine."

The drone then suddenly backed off and returned to the third officer to enter into a mid-air standby and power off its flashing lights.

Being careful not to incite the processing police, Jack adjusted herself amidst the rubbish and pulled her feet away from the reinforced soles of the third officer's intimidatingly armoured boots. She hesitantly relieved her left hand from compressing her throbbing head and lowered it slowly down to check its colour. "Eergh," she squeamishly expired at the sight of her rich red blood being smudged across her palm and fingers.

Hearing her fuss, the third officer questioned her aloud, "what's your problem?! What's in your hand?" He suddenly elevated his voice and pivoted and raised his disruptor to point at Jack. "Show me your hands!" he demanded.

"Your drone," Jack replied timidly while showing her palms, "it hit me. I'm bleeding."

The officer sneered through his HUD in disgust and leaned down towards her and subsequently interrogated, "you got a HUD, warden? And coder? You *are* a warden, aren't you?"

With the father still weeping down the alley and the officers over him preparing to take him away in handcuffs, Jack nodded and dutifully complied, "yep."

The third officer held out his left glove and gestured for her to pass him the equipment to which Jack quickly handed him her HUD before reaching into her right pocket to pull out her coder. Holding it up, she assured, while continuing to compress her crown, "this is it. Do you want my stinger?"

Snatching the coder from her hand and swearing disapprovingly, the officer slipped the second device into another pouch on his blue bulletproof vest and exclaimed sceptically, "you have *a stinger?*"

"Yeah," Jack quietly admitted with an assuring nod.

"Pass it," the officer ordered her and asserted, "evidence. This is all evidence," he stated as his peers dragged the sobbing and crippled father up the alley towards the road.

Jack caught a glimpse of the father's grazed face as he was brought past and began to feel a deep sadness swell inside her. Her limbs began to tremble nervously as she handed over her stinger, and her temperature picked up an uncomfortable degree. She watched on as the officers dumped their catch into the back of a police car that had silently arrived and then secured their large drone to its roof racks.

"It's getting flat," she listened to the third officer exclaim to his grumbling peers before adding in displeasure, "and it's got a big dent in it."

She then watched them leave in their car before drooping back uncomfortably onto the rubbish bags.

"*My kit?*" she shakily lamented, ineluctably letting her declining emotions run free.

Chapter Three
Friday, 8ᵗʰ June 2063

Later at home, Jack had been relaxing quietly for a few hours when the icepack on top of her head had warmed into a slush and the pain it had been chilling had significantly subsided. She was feeling better after a period of sobbing and felt clearer inside after letting some time pass. She had been able to let go of things, the thief, the teddy and the heavy-handedness, and had been able to decide with some hopeful optimism that her kit would show up tomorrow at work somehow.

While lying across her favourite firmly puffed cerise couch, situated opposite the large screen on the lounge wall, waiting for something peaceful to happen, the front door opened and the home console greeted with its feminine voice, "good evening Elisabeth. You have no new business."

Jack smiled gratefully and recalled, 'I still haven't set that up for me.'

"Hi Jack," Ebee greeted radiantly as she walked in from the entrance and looked on at the pair of bare feet resting on the closest lateral armrest, "you look relaxed."

The comment coaxed a giggle out of Jack.

Ebee's peppy personality had been a regular comfort to her since her childhood and it still was today. Due to twenty-six years of good parenting, an unbelievably innate humility and life unbeknownst to misfortune, she was always happy, and her words well pointed. Even when speaking in relative nonchalance, while entering a front door, her perpetually positive attitude ensured her words always lifted Jack up.

Her appearance too was always warming. With her thick blonde hair tied back for work to display her bright magnetic face, she graciously bathed Jack with her infectious smile while removing her glaucous-blue business jacket. Revealing more of her matching skirt and chic white blouse, she removed next her glaucous-blue dress shoes before letting out a deep de-stressing breath through her pursed lips. A follow-up smile and light-hearted contraction of laughter in Jack's direction made Jack respond in kind.

Ebee was more of an angel in Jack's perspective at times, and effortlessly so. She was intelligent, spoke eloquently, and being an inch taller than Jack at six-foot-one, could be looked up to, even if only slightly. She was also lighter than Jack somehow by a number of kilos while bearing a more rounded profile, and was easy to hug. It was as if, even after a long day of working at her desk and fatiguing for her boss, Ebee's ever brimming light could cast a shadow from Jack, even on Jack's most excited days.

Ebee pleasantly moved on from the entrance with her jacket tidily folded over her arm, passing the kitchen towards her bedroom located opposite the apartment from Jack's. Leaving her garment on her bed and personal effects on her dressing table, she peered out through her great panoramic window to the street and hummed. She then returned to the living room to enter the kitchen but stopped short. Standing behind the seatback of Jack's couch with a straight face, she undid her blouse's top button and looked down at her best friend. "Did everything go well at work today?" she inquisitively asked.

Jack held the icepack in place as she turned her head and looked over the back of the couch.

Before she could reply, Ebee inquired, "is that an icepack? What happened? Did you hurt your head?"

Knowing that Ebee was one to make an unnecessary fuss over her as she always had, Jack tried to dull the conversation early. "It's my inverted pillow," she said, "it makes my head comfortable, like on top. Like a pillow."

Ebee smiled and sniggered.

The two then laughed another contraction at each other and seeing that Ebee was going nowhere, Jack proceeded to describe her day.

"I went into the council this morning and picked up my new work kit," she spoke, "I was assigned to work in Viaduct Harbour— "

"Oh, how was that?" Ebee asked.

Jack thought for a second and subsequently realised, "whoops!" She slapped herself on the forehead and exclaimed, "I didn't wait for my food! I took off after this guy and I left my table. I paid for a hot chocolate and a friand!"

"What guy?" Ebee asked with a sceptical brow, "and also, I thought you didn't like almonds."

"This guy robbed a small toy shop down by Rioux Café," Jack went on to explain, "so I thought I should chase after him, you know, for my job. And I hate almond *icing*. I wanted to try the friand because they looked yummy."

Ebee spoke up with concern, "I'm pretty sure they taste the same. Was the man dangerous? You really shouldn't be chasing these people down Jacqueline. You could get hurt."

Jack responded to Ebee's advice, "it's just my job though. They know where I am because of my HUD and if something happens, and I don't do anything about it, I get in trouble."

Ebee paused for a second to gaze piteously down at her less fortunate friend. She leant down onto the back of the couch on her elbows and contemplated, "oh, do you think you could go back for your food? Maybe they'll refund you or give you a credit?"

Jack breathed out with a sigh and arbitrarily eyed the matt cream of the ceiling. "I wish I had it now, you know when you get like that?" she longingly said, thinking of the space left in her appetite for something yummy.

Ebee smiled and got up off the couch and walked into the kitchen. "You should stay away from those bad people Jack," she advised, "if your employers tell you otherwise, I'll have *words* with them!"

Jack smiled. Ebee wouldn't have *words*, but she would get someone else to. Last time something bad happened to her, Ebee asked her own employers to call Jack's boss. Jack wasn't sure how that communication went, but the contemptuous look her supervisor gave her afterward, followed by isolation made her think it went awkwardly. 'Or at least *I* felt awkward,' she chortled through her nostrils.

After opening the fridge and pine-green cupboard doors in the kitchen, Ebee spoke aloud, "there's nothing. Do you want to go out for some friands? I bet you won't like them," she joked with bubbly warmth.

Jack declined, "oh ah nah, yeah, nah, I'm ok." She was happy to stay at home and rest. The last time she went out, she was cut by a drone and shouted at by police.

"Ok," Ebee submissively replied with an agreeable bob of her head and suggested, "I'll do something with this. You just keep talking."

Used to seeing Jack down or depressed by her job, Ebee was always accommodating. And though she understood the privacy constraints, she often encouraged Jack to air her frustrations to her so she could let things out. But Jack wasn't so easily persuaded. She hated her job and believed that its monotony was a cancer. She felt that if she brought too much of her work home in her attitude, she would ruin the peace there and she didn't want to upset Ebee, though she couldn't if she tried. Ebee's career was always on the up and it was obvious from her perpetually positive personality.

Unlike Jack, Ebee had always lived in relative wealth and had good fortune. She had always had a good relationship with her parents, and she had always excelled. She had believed that since her parents had been successful, she too would inherit a high paying job and through her confidence and skill, did earn it. After graduating from the University of Sails with an MBA four and a half years earlier, she took up a position in the CBD with the multinational corporation, RF Space. Working as an assistant to one of the regional managers, she had established a good work ethic and had developed a good rapport with her company over the four years she had been there. And unlike Jack, she didn't work out of a basement.

Situated a few floors down from the exclusive, floating quasi-village, Babel, Ebee's office looked out from the eightieth-storey windows to the other glossy facades of the CBD. To her, the ground had become just a means to get where she was going, while to Jack, the ground was the place where she was stuck. Only at home did Jack feel successful, but even then, she felt as if she was only really a guest.

Though Ebee was an amazing best friend and an eternal big sister, Jack recognised that one day Ebee would grow up and begin to take upon her the responsibilities of motherhood. Ebee wasn't currently dating and spared no time for it but would sometimes express a desire to do what her parents did and settle down. Jack would definitely have to leave at that point, possibly by her own volition, to get out of Ebee's way, but would always be ready to come back if needed to bring her male into line, if he slipped up. Until then however, she was extremely grateful to live with Ebee, even if just as her guest.

"Even if just her lazy one," Jack conceded with a degree of disappointment.

"What?" Ebee questioned from the kitchen. "Are you ok?" she asked sincerely.

"Oh," Jack responded while coming out of a state, "nothing."

While looking into the empty shelving with the doors opened wide, Ebee stated, "you know how you stand in front of the cupboards and there's no food in there, and then after a few minutes there's still no food in there, but you just can't look away?" After a short pause, she gestured for a result and quipped, "but you wish it would just be there, so you could eat it."

Jack chortled and replied empathetically, looking over her seatback into the kitchen, "yeah. Is it like that is it?"

"Yeah, it's like that," Ebee assessed. "Let's just order something in, something fast. And maybe I'll get some shopping delivered tomorrow."

Jack turned around on her couch to place her feet on the carpet and sit up. She then leaned forward to the black glass coffee table in front of her and swept the objects on it to one side before holding down the power button along the right edge.

"I've got it," she told Ebee.

Acknowledging her presence, the table lit up a cool, neon-blue grid upon its surface with a concomitant dimming of the living room lighting. A blue Windows logo then appeared vibrantly in the air above the grid followed a few seconds later by a polite male voice that addressed and asked, "welcome back Jacqueline. Do you wish to resume your previous session?"

Jack accepted the prompt with a simple, "yes," and observed a few holographic boxes and tablets float straight up from the table's surface to the height of her shoulders. Looking into the three-dimensional displays to find a paused game of Space Flight Simulator, an unfinished Rubik's cube, a recipe for butter chicken and a snow report, she waved her right hand through the holograms and reset her space. "Find food," she enunciated.

Samples of websites popped up and suspended in the air. Coloured 3D samples of extravagant dishes and common fast food hovered gently, trying to entice. Jack's arms, hands and fingers manipulated the immaterially viscous light display, as she tried to discover what most tickled her fancy. She sieved out exotic recipes and supermarket ads to reveal more food samples and ogle at interactive nibbles she could daydream of eating.

Using the holotable was always a pleasant experience when searching for something or learning about how things worked. It most often brought a smile to Jack's face when ordering food that would materialise on the other side of the front door or was used to examine the coverage of Ruapehu's snow fields. It was also a delight to simply toy with it at times.

Placing physical objects upon the table's surface, that were sizeable enough, would block a column from processing causing a simultaneous shimmer of holographic water to fall down from the ceiling unit and surround the obstruction. Splashing onto complementary appearing rocks at the bottom, it would create ripples three centimetres above the table that could be further impeded with a mere finger. It wasn't the most capable home holotable on the market, but no one Jack knew other than Ebee could afford one. And while using a HUD was easier or whipping out a coder like an accordion satisfying, interacting with the holotable was simply magical.

Originally a gift from Ebee's parents for her new apartment, the device had to be installed by the manufacturer. Being composed of two extra-heavy parts, the table and ceiling unit, they both had to be vertically aligned to perfection and permanently fixed into place. Once synchronised and configured, the two units could create a deep and vivid yet warm hologram within the pillar of air between them. Due to its seriously power-hungry nature though, exacerbated by the apartment's high ceiling, the girls typically kept its use to a minimum but relished it each time they had it on.

"What do you feel like eating?" Jack asked as Ebee walked past the assembly.

Placing floating advertisements for Jonburger, Hemi's, and The Flower Pot into the centre of the space, she watched them mutedly clamour for attention and waited for Ebee's response.

"Keen for some Jonburger?" she then cheekily exclaimed while twisting around an unrealistically good-looking burger in the air with her fingers. She knew Ebee wouldn't even consider it.

"It's too fatty," Ebee dismissively replied while entering the bathroom, "and those images are inaccurate. When you get it in real life, all the lettuce is falling out and the patty is flat. I'll just have some sushi from The Flower Pot. Maybe, just one of those assortments. Or lamb."

Jack hummed a chuckle and approved, "ok." She then proceeded to order lamb sushi for Ebee on one floating tablet to the left and a kea burger combo for herself from Jonburger on another tablet to the right.

Ebee then returned and sat down next to Jack on the couch and began swiping things with her in the play space. "So, why did you need that icepack?" she asked.

After a second of waiting for a two-player puzzle game to load, Jack moved it into the middle for Ebee to reach and apathetically answered, "I got hit in the head by a police drone."

The next morning, Jack was feeling better at work while preparing for her day in the info warden's quarters. While standing in the small gap between her locker and one of the black couches in her uniform's black and white-lined pants and top, she was slipping on her uniform's thick matching jacket while reflecting on how upbeat she felt despite the terrible day before.

Having enjoyed playing videogames the previous night with Ebee, an increasingly rare activity, she had slept well on a full stomach of richly flavoured fast food. She had arrived this morning to work on time, and was immediately relieved to hear that her HUD, coder and stinger were back in Archived Assets, waiting to be released.

She was a little concerned however with her supervisor, who was in a particularly odd mood. The much older, wiry ginger haired woman, half a foot shorter than Jack, and a few decades of presumable loneliness bitterer, was moving around the room sternly motivating the other preparing wardens for work. Barely sending a glance Jack's way, she seemed as perturbed as usual, but was today, a little standoffish and a lot less accusing.

Ensuring to change into her complete uniform, mostly to please her present supervisor, and also because it was the law, according to that same supervisor, Jack plucked her odious black and white-lined hat from her locker's top shelf and closed her locker.

She then moved around the lounge area to Archived Assets, where after a relieved sigh, she addressed Bob over his counter and uttered peaceably, "hey! Uh, I'm ready to get my kit back."

Bob ignored her, however, to stand up off his stool, poke his head out from his den and gruffly call across the quarters, "Gelena! She's ready."

Jack suddenly felt saliva build up at the back of her throat. She looked away from Bob and his counter to feign obliviousness and after swallowing the detested build-up, cringed at the sound of her name being specifically called out by her supervisor.

"Jack," Gelena squawked like a set of fingernails running along a blackboard.

With the nerves down her spine penetrated and tingling in disgust, Jack turned to see the obstinate lady eyeing her directly. She tried to ignore the red wandering perm on her head that stood out as if trying to escape and forced her eyes to meet with the one's beadily lodged behind Gelena's thickly framed glasses. For the second she could bear it, she replied respectfully, "uh, yes?"

With a grouchy face, Gelena declared while gesturing with her index finger to follow, "I want to speak to you. Privately."

While usually fussy with the other wardens, Gelena was constantly discontent with Jack. She was always sceptical of her performance and was always ready to scold. Jack found it easy to assume it all out of jealousy for her youth and sporty good looks, but had to admit it very typical for her performance to be under par. But then, Jack didn't like being a warden and only wanted to work *sometimes*. She especially didn't want to be an *overt* warden and most especially didn't want to work under the uncompromising cross-eyed stare of Gelena, nor her pungent perfume or hairspray. The only solace she could take from the situation was that she barely ever saw or smelt the stiff-necked supervising, "witch."

"What!?" Gelena scoffed and glanced back at Jack, on her way to the warden's offices.

Quickly, Jack repaired her slip, "which, area, am I assigned to today?"

"What?!" Gelena exasperatedly retorted, and flung her hands dismissively, "how should I know, I gave that job to Bob to sort out. You know that. Ask him."

While walking through the doorway to the offices with Jack close behind, she coarsely asked over her shoulder, "did you know that your HUD streams a live feed back to us!?"

Gelena walked into the warden's short, windowed conference room and pointed for Jack to stand on the nearest side of the room's short wooden table. Stopping on the opposite side, she turned to look at Jack but found her stalled in the room's doorway.

Jack looked on from there with a deliberately blank face to feign ineptitude.

"What were you doing in The Viaduct yesterday?" Gelena grouchily stated into the entire premises, "you were supposed to be across town, in Topher.

You were in trouble, for leaving your duties early. You are meant to be working in the evenings. You haven't shown up to meetings."

Jack wanted to point out Gelena's contradiction from a moment ago about Topher, and wanted to protest having to attend needless meetings and trainings outside of her shifts, but held her tongue instead, as she always did.

"You never, show up for afterhours trainings," Gelena ranted on in passionate disapproval, "you're not even six-B-plus certified! You're not even operating in the right area!"

As Gelena continued to stab her with her words, Jack took a moment to try and surmise what 'six-B-plus' was. She then attempted to explain what happened in Topher, with the EMP, that lead to Bob's resultant orders, but Gelena finally got to her point.

"Bob was watching your stream yesterday," she said to Jack's concern, "he watched you run clumsily after a squatter down Market Place, towards town. And there, down some alley opposite Pakenham Street, you were about to let him go."

Jack knew that the warden's HUDs fed back to the office, but she was under the impression that no one ever watched it because it was completely boring and unproductive. Bob also happened to have a wife he could watch instead.

"And we know he was a squatter," Gelena then continued to lecture, "because the police told us when they dropped off your equipment this morning. They also told us you interfered with police equipment and impersonated a police officer. And now they've put all our wardens on notice. They've put *me* on notice! *How do you think that makes me feel!?*"

Before Jack could lie about Gelena having feelings, the supervisor began again, "how did you delete the recordings you got of that squatter and how did you access the city's junk servers? You do *not* have authority to delete things or access those servers. *Who* gave you that access? *Who* gave you those passwords?"

Jack was stuck but fortunate that Gelena's incessant love of dictating and hearing her own voice meant that Jack couldn't really reply.

"We want to have a disciplinary meeting with you on Thursday," Gelena condescendingly diverted to her ultimate point, "is eleven o'clock good for you?"

Jack nodded quietly and turned around to exit the room.

"Oh, and Jack?" Gelena called.

Jack turned half-way around to look back when Gelena jabbed in displeasure, "the officer told me that those on duty said you were not wearing any uniform."

A little shocked inside from the public rebuking, Jack remained quiet and her eyes looked around arbitrarily to try and dispel her supervisor's brashness. With a satisfied look of smugness on her face, Gelena then finished her fusillade, "see you Thursday."

Chapter Four
Thursday, 21st June 2063

During a peaceful mid-morning in the centre of the CBD, Jack was sitting back on a green wooden bench seat in the middle of Haven's Park, a small patch of grass situated amidst the city's tallest skyscrapers. Dressed correctly in her full uniform and on her first break of the day, she was enjoying a moment of relative calm, off the busier footpaths, and clearing her head from all the intercepting.

Having been moved recently from off the private wharves and into the neighbouring office buildings to work, she had begun stopping in at the park for her breaks to distance herself somewhat from the busied public and enjoy the winter breezes. Though lacking her more comfortable Huffer coat that comprised a heating system and some style, she could appreciate the cool climate enough without numbing in her warden's coat, and could hide herself from the public eye in the park so long as everyone was looking elsewhere.

But no one ever looked elsewhere, not at least until they had looked at Jack first, in contempt. Then they'd swivel their sights to their peers and murmur in revulsion.

The mounded shape of the park didn't help that either. It elevated the central bench seat half a metre higher than the four close, bordering footpaths, making Jack slightly more visible. The park too had little cover, with just a very tall statue at its centre, behind the bench seat, and a few artistic, waist-high contraptions placed closer to the four corners.

Jack couldn't help but imagine there was a giant curse word of dollar signs, hashes, asterisks and 'at' signs hovering above the park in everyone's HUDs, just a bit in front of the statue, because she certainly had picked some up in the morning's intercepts. The thought of it saddened her a little, because she was just feeding the pigeons her dry, leftover cereal from breakfast, and the park had a lot of meaning.

According to Jack's HUD, the park's namesake, Jonathan Haven, was a hero who died trying to save people trapped in the great fire of 2048. Pro-singularity activists had set alight the mall that used to occupy the site along with some of the surrounding buildings in protest. After an explosion and some bullets, Jonathan saved fifty innocent lives and later lost his own in hospital due to the wounds inflicted upon him by the fire. His heroic story made him a national icon which resulted in the tall statue of him behind Jack and helped push anti-singularity laws forward in the country.

Fifteen years later, the grassy patch was now a relatively quiet attraction with various skyscrapers surrounding the small square spot like sentinels, protecting its memorial from the outside world.

One of those sentinels also happened to be of great value to Jack as well. Across the street to Jack's left, standing majestically and stretching high up into the elevated village above, was the hundred-and-ten-storey, sky-blue chrome Zen Building, the tallest building in the CBD and place where Ebee worked. With its lofty peak towering more than twenty storeys over Babel, the suspended village of bridges, landings, platforms and penthouses, Jack couldn't see its top from her simple bench seat down below. Even the tops of the other towers that surrounded the park, and all those a block out in every direction, were equally obstructed by Babel's lofty foundations.

She also couldn't make out most of the air traffic that hovered above the city that was so evident from outside the CBD. From there, it looked like a loose network of flying insects moving around a lustrous bouquet of windows and towers. But from where Jack was sitting, the traffic was simply cars and people, and a couple quietly whizzing delivery drones, all moving around in an artificially boosted light that made Haven's Park feel a little bit plastic.

While reluctantly reflecting back on the disciplinary meeting she had attended a week earlier with her supervisor and manager, Jack's mind began to shift from the pleasantness of the park back to the demands of her job. Her bosses had made sure during that meeting to express what they wanted Jack to do to sustain and reinforce her employment with them. They wanted her to show up to work on time, every time, and they wanted her to work the full shift.

They wanted her to wear the correct uniform and drilled into her the legal requirement for information wardens to wear that uniform, to satisfy government regulation. They told her she was forbidden from accessing the server side of the council network for private use, and that she should keep away from police equipment. They also went over council etiquette; that when one enters a room for a private meeting, they should close the door behind them. The list of demands they dictated just went on and on while Jack just nodded and agreed with everything they said.

But she loathed it. The general public didn't like information wardens at all, and so, Jack preferred to disappear into the people when she was monitoring them so that she could go about her business without being scorned by them. She preferred moving around her assigned areas however she felt like too, and appreciated the sense of freedom. And she loved leaving when she got bored so she could return to her apartment and laze or plan her next snow trip she couldn't really afford without Ebee's help.

Jack then exhaled a deep despondent breath into the park's morning air while the pigeons plucked the last of her cereal from the grass. She was starting to see the thin ice beneath her good fortune. 'The apartment is *Ebee's*,' she introspectively determined, 'not mine.'

While she was adamant Ebee would never think of upending her life and would never hurt her, Jack felt like she might hurt Ebee if she lost her job and became completely dependent. Ebee's life was on the verge of change and Jack becoming dependant would put a strain on that progress. And Ebee had already rescued her from poverty and kept her life sheltered and clean and organised, and full of resources to exploit for her good use. But Jack couldn't think of anything she had done to help grow that good fortune or reinforce it; Ebee didn't really enjoy the snow as much as Jack and didn't really like spending a lot of time playing videogames.

Jack let out another deep despondent breath, pausing her declining thoughts in their tracks, to summarise, 'I really don't want to let her down.'

Sitting forward and preparing to return to the footpaths, Jack took a moment to watch the pigeons waddle away when a council notification suddenly vibrated her coder and came up on the lenses of her HUD. 'New assignment for Jacqueline Hart,' she read, 'Warden 5620 - XO123748.B - Report to council.'

A peaceful smile came to Jack's face. She enjoyed the infrequent and short assignments that were sent her way. They paid double her regular pay, becoming a decent wage, and always instructed her to wear mufti. She also appreciated the fact that assignments were run by a slightly different department which meant spending some time away from Gelena and her gang.

'Even if at least for a day,' she mused.

Later, after a commute back to the council building, Jack returned into the wardens' quarters and fetched her casual attire so that she could quickly decontaminate her image in the restroom. Coming out in her grey marl track pants, opened black Huffer coat, visible black thermal T-shirt and her warden's clothing happily crushed under her left arm, she approached and stuffed her open locker. She then paused to examine her warden's hat in her right hand. "Ergh," she murmured in disgust.

Jack hated the information warden's outfit but by far and away mostly hated the hat. Being something of a cross between a black fedora and a bowler with a short two-inch-brim, a bright white reflective edge and two white bordered insignias on the front and back, it was an ugly piece of gear and made everyone feel uncomfortable.

None of the wardens liked wearing it because it wasn't warm in winter and made them sweat in summer. It also made them stand out like a signpost, for taking verbal abuse, or sometimes like a target, for being spit at or getting hit. The public hated it because it represented the authoritarian bullies ruling their communication and could often be observed walking by where they ate their lunch, and later, by where they relaxed with their loved ones in their homes.

Exhaling another deep breath, Jack placed the hat on the top shelf inside her locker and shook her head in a moment of contemplation. "I hate that hat," she mumbled, picturing it sit in her apartment by the entrance after work and then on her head in the reflection of the buildings she walked by during the day.

"Miss Hart," a deep, manly voice from behind then made her jump.

Turning on the spot to address the source of the call, Jack replied, "oh, hey Gerry," and expressed a bright, thankful smile.

"How's it going?" Gerry smiled back.

As the Assignments Department's supervisor, Gerry was the person Jack was about to go looking for and the one about to make her day a lot less painful.

With an office established elsewhere in the other half of the basement and a small team of undercover wardens that could legally go out without a uniform, Gerry was a boss of whom Jack could respect. The assignments he handed to her every once in a blue moon were always specific and came with targets. They usually took a day or two to complete and sometimes required a report that Jack could write on a following day as thoroughly as time would permit.

Jack also appreciated working in a department where no one was weird enough to watch the live stream of a warden without clearly telling them first.

"So," Gerry addressed her as he neared with a big warm smile and document folder tucked beneath his wrist, "are you available?"

Dressed in a massive, casual white polo shirt and very long, deep dark slacks, Gerry approached Jack as politely as a sturdy, six-foot-eight man could. He grinned appreciably and bobbed his head as he came into her space and towered over it with his head humbly hanging.

Likely an imposing figure to anyone who had never spoken with him, or to those that had resisted arrest during his brief time as a police officer, Gerry was an all-around nice guy in Jack's opinion and a great friend. With a phenotypically Maori appearance, deep velvety voice and very short, dark straight hair, he was also a rather attractive man to Jack's eyes and ears, though not quite enough to win her over. Despite his clear fancy for her, higher class in society and sweet, woody Brut smell, she felt a more big-brotherly bond with him but never made that known lest she would lose her appeal as a friend and occasional employee.

As the two walked out of the information wardens' quarters and on through the offices towards the Assignments briefing room, Jack cheekily asked about the hourly rate for the upcoming contract, "are you guys still paying sixteen-hundred?"

Without looking, Gerry replied while continuing to walk, "seventeen-ten."

"*Seventeen-ten!?*" Jack mimicked in astonishment, "are yous paying out *seventeen-ten now? Per hour?*"

Gerry slowed to a dawdle and turned his shoulders to answer with an agreeable hum, "mm." After a second, he opened his mouth and asked, "what are they paying you in Info?"

"Seven-ninety," Jack said in discontent.

Gerry opened his eyes wide and mimicked, "seven, *ninety?* Not *seventeen-ninety?*"

Jack shook her head and replied quickly in displeasure, "no. It's always been seven-ninety."

Gerry breathed out a sigh of pity and began discussing about his small team, "Jack, I would hire you if I could, but the council hire these guys. Mark might be able to pull some strings, but Gelena has him wrapped around her little finger and I don't, I don't know if I would want to put a strain on Mark. He's, uh, I don't know. He can be— "

"Yeah, I know," Jack eased Gerry's concern as they entered the slightly dimmer light of the Assignments Department and approached their window-blinded briefing room.

Mark was the manager of the Assignments, Archived Assets and Information Wardens departments. He was a nice enough man, though rather weak, and the very manager involved in Jack's recent disciplinary meeting. She understood well just how wrapped around Gelena's little finger he was.

"I'm truly sorry," Gerry continued to unnecessarily apologise with a calming gesture of his palm, "my job, *only*, is to give my wardens something to do, and on the odd occasion we can't keep up, and they let me, Council, Mark— I come and get you."

After a short few seconds of disappointed contemplation, Jack asked, "did Gelena make it hard this time? To get me out?"

Gerry watched two of his passing wardens move across the end of the mint-cream corridor as a grin developed across his face. Entertained by his thoughts, he replied to Jack while nodding, "yep. She certainly did."

While he chuckled about it, Jack asked again hesitantly, "did, she, tell you about our meeting?"

Laughing under his breath and looking Jack straight in the face, he politely altered the truth with an upwards inflection, "you know Gelena really loves you? You know? She just doesn't really know how to say it."

Bemused, Jack shook her head with a smirk and retorted with a guess, *"you're fired?"*

The two then giggled together in pity.

"Yeah nah, that's it," Gerry agreed in amusement.

Interrupting their otiose banter, he then cleared his throat and paused them with a stopping gesture, stating, "oh, before we get too carried away, I've just gotta— "

Holding up a pink warrant paper in front of Jack's face with his right hand, he light-heartedly repeated the same drone he had to give each time he offered an assignment, "Jacqueline Hart. Council warden 5-6-2-0. In order to accept this assignment, you will need to sign your name and signature on this court order form where indicated along with the time and date. You will need to leave a handprint on the specified terminal within the Council Warden's quarters."

Swapping the pink paper for a stapled set of white forms, he continued, "you will need to go over all the protocols required to follow before leaving the quarters as the council will not defend you in the event that you go outside the legal limits of your assignment."

As Jack pulled the papers from out of his hands, she insouciantly distracted him, "why do you still have paper? Where do you get it from?"

"Thank you," Gerry replied.

He then proceeded to introduce the assignment, "we've had a report from Council Tech that Alex, Hazelwood's, HUD was hacked or distorted by a jammer, or something, down near the Port Pascoll docks yesterday. It didn't last long and with all the activity going on there, Alex found nothing that could explain it. Now, Tech looked over Alex's feed, and a film he recorded with an unaffected device, uh, and also his kit's source code, and are certain the jamming, or whatever, was a bit too complex to be ignored. They sent a report to Police about it— It was *very* complex, and then Police sent the report back; they don't think it's suspicious and aren't going to do anything about it."

With Jack still listening, Gerry nodded his head sideways toward the briefing room door next to them and entered inside while continuing, "but a couple in the council have decided it *is* suspicious and— "

"Now I get paid," Jack inserted.

Gerry nodded and chuckled, "yeah, yeah."

With a large thirty-inch coder lying flat upon on a large mint-cream table displaying a satellite map of the port along the Waitemata Harbour, below the CBD, the two sat down on either side of it and began examining.

"They said it interfered with Alex's monitoring and communications software," Gerry explained, "blocking not just his reception but also the use of his camera, and he couldn't send a feed back to Info. And being an information warden, he just moved on with his patrol, and it went away."

While Jack looked over the map and read the papers she had been given, he went on, "Alex said he didn't see anyone suspicious; it was just the jamming and it only lasted about ninety seconds."

Jack then interestedly inquired, "was Alex in uniform?"

Gerry smiled and replied candidly, "yes, as is the, *legal*, requirement for all information wardens when on duty. But you Jacqueline, we're sending down to the docks in camo. You'll be in street, because, as is obvious, you are in Assignments today, and we have a warrant. You'll also be operating in double-secret."

After clearing his throat, Gerry continued to explain, "so, you're being specifically tasked with going down to the Port Pascoll docks to find out if the jamming, or whatever, is still in effect. You'll also need to try and identify any equipment and people that are responsible for it. Now, jamming equipment like this isn't illegal in internationally operating premises. Businesses like Port Pascoll, the spaceport, the UN campus and the various embassies around the city are completely within their rights to inhibit local body interception. Heck, even regular private businesses are doing it in various ways, and that's fine so long as the streets are clear. But this complex interference, which did spill into the street, has made a couple in the city council nervous and that is where this assignment comes from. Fang Sima, one of those two councillors, has a stake in Port Pascoll through his extended family and got in touch with me late last night after talking with Tech. Apparently, this jamming has been picked up before by others on site with similar scanning gear— Not wardens, and he reckons the style of jamming is definitely unique and not something anyone respectable would be using."

"This is private property, right?" Jack interrupted casually.

"Yep," Gerry nicely responded to her curiosity, "since about five years ago, but Alex was actually going along Quay Street when he came across this. He was in the public sphere."

"So how do they know it came from the docks then?" Jack queried.

"Well I, said that," Gerry reminded her, "Councillor Sima believes this is happening inside the docks, because of internal reports there, and has spilled out onto the street. It's this spill that has granted us a court warrant to go in and surveil."

"And, the fact that Sima owns this," Jack tried to deduce.

"No, he doesn't," Gerry clarified, "it's his extended family and they only have a small stake."

Gesturing with his hands to emphasise, he summarised with a chuckle, "look, I don't get too interested in the bureaucracy behind these assignments, and you probably shouldn't either. Someone wants to keep trade secrets; someone wants to know those secrets. Or someone wants to hurt someone, and some councillors and a politician get involved; on which side I don't know. Look," he paused with his palms, "the jamming wasn't knocking out everything; someone or something was interfering specifically with monitoring equipment and a couple councillors want us to take a look."

"And I get paid," Jack said with an appreciative nod.

"And you get paid," Gerry agreed.

After a second, Jack eyed him directly and innocently proposed, "I'm gona dawdle."

Bursting out with a hearty chuckle, Gerry adjusted his posture in his seat and concurred.

With the simple briefing finished, Jack stood up and went to exit.

"It's probably nothing," Gerry stated from his chair, "or it could be some guys trying to hide something. Either way Jacqueline, you're not a cop, ok. You're not to get into any trouble. And if things look serious, you just walk out of there. Ok?"

With a pert smile, Jack feigned conformity beneath the doorway and replied, *"serious.* Got it."

Chapter Five
Thursday, 21ˢᵗ June 2063

After a period of preparation and a follow-up with Gerry, Jack left the council basement with her kit in her pockets and a security pass to Port Pascoll in her hand. She moseyed in her mufti to a quaint food court a few streets closer to her destination for lunch, and then eventually made her way down to the harbour.

Coming out on Tamaki Drive, the eastern portion of the contiguous solar road bordering the port with Quay Street, she crossed an elevated T-intersection covering a rail line and walked rightwards along the footpath. Able to see clearly into the vast complex over its continuous red-orange, ten-foot-high metal fence from her higher position at the top of a grassy decline, she moved on in the direction of the eastern entrance and quickly became confounded.

Port Pascoll was a conglomeration of constructions, containers and endlessly operating machines. Stretching westward for more than two kilometres along the harbour from its eastern entrance, it bore an uneven profile, comprising many different parts, and was subsequently difficult to discern without a map.

The far western wharves abutting the cruise ship and ferry terminals, that had been obvious in the overhead view of a coder, were completely concealed behind the gabled roofs of great enamel-white warehouses. Through a space between a closer row of multicoloured container towers and another row of warehouses arranged inside the fence further east, four of the site's giant white gantry cranes could be seen in busy operation. Standing dominantly over the central area of the port, they were conveying cargo effortlessly over the high brim of a huge inland-facing container ship while a small flock of seagulls larked about their girders.

A large neighbouring safety-orange quadcopter could be seen too, impressively hovering high in the air further along, above another container tower it was building with its winches.

Jack breathed in a slightly bemused breath as she paid attention to the buzz of sawing, beeping and driving labouring over the grounds. She saw containers whip past on the suspended ends of booms through narrow channels and watched a number of workers gather together around a slowly moving autonomous trailer to guide its improperly loaded frame into a clearing.

She then set her sights further east to the complex's roadside corner, where above the next set of warehouse roofs, she could see the teal and taupe top floors of the site's main office buildings. Expecting to find the main entrance there and a security scanner with which to use her pass, she deeply inhaled a breath of salty sea air and diligently pressed on.

Descending with the footpath to circle around one of the two grassy knolls guarding the perpendicular, busy, four-lane road into the complex, she beheld the multistorey main offices standing erect on either of its sides and their interconnecting skybridge and began to wonder.

Jack had never been inside Port Pascoll before and wasn't sure how her presence would be received. She was a little worried as well about the countless drones operating on the ground and in the air behind the offices, and could only hope they would notice and respect her small and pulpy frame amidst all the steel. The port was also very noisy and so made her quite worried about missing a warning before being hit by an autonomous truck, or container ship.

Unsure then of how things would go, but more than happy to be off the streets with all their disdain, Jack attentively gave way to a car entering the taupe high-rise car park she was passing and slipped on her HUD.

A couple dozen metres on, she entered through the main office's vestibule and set foot inside its black and grey-weave carpeted lobby.

"Ah," she quietly expressed while pausing to observe the latest interceptions in her HUD corrupt before her eyes. Stepping on to see her device's connectivity icon disappear, an orange icon for interference display and the battery icon come on in red, she looked up to a polished wooden mezzanine where white-collar workers ate nonchalantly, and then back to two conspicuous six-foot bollards on either side of the entrance. 'Are those, jamming nodes?' she curiously presumed.

Likely responsible for the abrupt killing of her connection to the council's internet provider, and resultant switch to a very scant backup of battery power, the bollards looked deliberately placed in their solid, black matt presentation and rather assertive. They both stood erect one foot in from the front windows and beamed an oscillating, electric indigo gaze at anyone passing between them through a narrow, horizontal strip set close to the height of Jack's eyes.

Jack attempted to recall what memories she had of that category of devices from the few work meetings she had attended while moving across the lobby to exit past two more bollards.

Coming back out into the port's noisy exterior, however, caused her to cease recalling when clean interceptions began listing once more in her lenses.

"Hmm," she scoffed while crossing a transverse delivery lane to an unattended security kiosk guarding the red-orange fence. 'Maybe the problem's management?' she opined, thinking back over her co-worker's experience.

She then waved her coat's left wrist by a scanning panel affixed to one of four tall, galvanised turnstiles neighbouring the kiosk. Promptly entering as its cylindrical cage unlocked and opened, she pushed through the circling gate to find her internet connection killed once more by another pair of purple-gazing bollards standing at either inside-end of the gates.

"Oh," she disconcertedly expired as the time in her HUD ticked over to 2:00 pm. 'Surely not for three hours?' she silently moaned about the disconnection hampering her remaining time at work.

Stepping on into an empty car park between a row of small drivable vehicles, she readjusted her coat over her torso and proceeded to read a simple linear collage of differently coloured tabs painted onto the concrete ahead of the cars. 'Western Port Pascoll,' she perused from left to right, 'Bledisloe Wharf, Jellicoe Wharf— '

"Ooh! Sorry," she apologetically reacted to a politely beeping vehicle attempting to return into the car park she stood occupying.

Quite embarrassed by her obstruction, she hopped out of its way and ineluctably read a corrupting cue floating in the air beside the driver identifying him as either a forearm or foreman. Spotting a bright yellow safety vest, hard hat and operational HUD on the man through his windows, she hurriedly, and anxiously, pushed on into the yards following a right-bearing violet line to the Fergusson Wharf.

'I'm going to need a hard hat and vest,' she reluctantly told herself before very shortly arriving at an intersection in the violet line that split in two perpendicularly opposite directions.

Skipping across the intersecting road they were guiding along and letting a stacking truck pass, she touched up against the chilly corrugated edge of a dark blue container and reflexively glanced straight up to identify a sudden whirling she could hear in the breezy air.

Catching a glimpse of the huge safety-orange quadcopter drone manoeuvring above the dauntingly high stack of containers she was at the foot of, she apprehensively exclaimed, "wow," as a downward gust of cold air whipped up her hair, dried her eyes and slivered down her face and clothes.

Blinking away as one of its widely-spanning coaxial-rotors positioned itself to incidentally blow a forceful freeze down the inside of her coat, she stepped back along the container wall to shield herself somewhat and peek up at the cues emanating from the robot. 'Ash%K X6 GLH, OPsSP&TING,' she read out of the winter air as her equipment struggled to stay online. '#Ber X? HLi, CfoRATING,' she confusingly gleaned after a refresh before her HUD's low share-power icon blinked on. "Dile al Capitán que consiga su propia leche, o estoy caminando," she randomly intercepted from a conversation her kit cleanly plucked from somewhere else inside the jamming before its response corrupted and cut off.

Feeling the tower then drum and creak with the placement of a new heavy container upon its top, she briskly moved on in an eastward direction to avoid being crushed, 'or cut,' she fretted, touching her fingers gently upon her crown.

Immediately giving a wide birth to a couple safety-vested workers in earmuffs and welding helmets in the small gantry bay next door picketed by neon-orange robocones, she crossed the road as they proceeded to make a screaming racket with a pair of angle grinders. She avoided a profuse gushing of sparks and covered her ears and abruptly shut and covered her eyes tightly when one lit up an acutely piercing light with an arc welder. 'I'm glad I don't work here,' she perturbedly pondered.

Cautiously watching through her fingers as the workers muscled through the jagged metal with their thick work gloves and staunchly bore the fluctuating temperatures and noise of their work through the rest of their safety gear, she introspectively opined, 'I wouldn't last a day.'

And so, feeling delicate amidst all the hazards and inadequate amidst all the labour, Jack began her surveillance of the port's radio waves with her struggling kit while searching on the side for some spare safety gear.

She made her way out first to the end of Te Kawau Wharf, the port's farthest point east, where a large sea green ship had begun unloading through its hull, before skimming over a sudden but meagre list of clean interceptions that came up at the wharf's end in the absence of interference.

While keeping clear and ogling disembarking used supercars that were slowly rolling off the ship's ramp, she expanded her feed to include live chat, a process typically reserved for direct spying due to its chaotic delivery, and was unexpectedly dissatisfied, even considering the diminished reception area. All the immediate results seemed to pour in from those riding along Tamaki Drive, across the water, the top interception of which was a video chat between parents discussing their schoolgirl's sore tummy.

'Next,' Jack instructed with a thought for her HUD's software to skip that discussion so she could listen to a gardener take pride in her tamarillos.

'Next,' she thought again as the list of textual interceptions flowed on in the background, and a storm grey supercar with a poor turning circle held up the wharf's operations.

Finding the signal of the following chat to be notably strong and likely from someone within close proximity, she honed her attention with her ears and eavesdropped to hear them set up a dental appointment to rectify an acute pain surrounding a few sensitive molars.

"Oh," she scoffed at herself, discontentedly rolling her eyes.

When several chats more failed to discuss anything describing 'complex jamming', she shook her head dismissively and reverted her filter back to text.

She then turned back around to gaze over the neatly parked supercars and let her thoughts process, but instead peered straight into the face of a curious and rather uncomfortable-looking worker staring at her from beside the ship's boarding ramp.

The worker gawked up and down at his odd visitor's incompliant outfit in uncertainty and frowned sceptically.

Jack sheepishly moved on in response, past the growing car park of supercars, and back to the Fergusson Wharf to where she could conceal herself once more amongst the drabber, stacked steel of the containers.

Upon arriving there though, she found herself tracked down and singled out by the foreman she had accidentally obstructed at the gates.

Very specifically approaching her from the opened driver's door of his little white hatchback with his hands full, the foreman obligingly passed over a reflective orange safety vest and golden yellow hard hat before giving a friendly insider's wink. "These should be good," he kindly expressed with a rough voice, looking over the items on Jack's arms, "they should keep you safe. While you."

Leaving with just a pleasant thumbs up and an acknowledging nod, he returned to his car and promptly drove on.

Jack gratefully waved and stood in uncertainty for a minute before examining the stiff garments and dutifully camouflaging herself in their conspicuous colours.

And so, feeling delicate and inadequate once more, but now in compliant bright colours, Jack had to progress on with her erratic battery and unstable connection, deciding now to stroll around the current yard's watery perimeter while keeping a natural eye out for anything interesting.

"Wow," she expressed after only a few minutes as she came around to view an interesting sight berthed along the western edge of the wharf.

The huge container ship that had been visible from the road was still in port and, from a flanking perspective, it was a massive object to behold so closely. It bore a long, black, three-hundred-metre broadside hull running all the way along the concrete wharf back toward the road. Stretching up a few dozen meters high from out of the slopping water, it sat impressively over the yard with an even higher off-white bridge construction at its rear filling out the ships' width and rivalling the four towering white gantry cranes working over its deck in height.

Jack watched the widely spread claws of the cranes clutch huge twelve-metre-long containers simultaneously from off the deck and parked autonomous trailers on the ground below and hoist them up into the air in genuine fascination. Carted just below the hip-like braces joining the cranes' legs together, the containers were lowered back down at a safely declining pace to be slotted into a gap on the ship or be placed very carefully and articulately onto empty waiting trailers on the wharf.

As Jack dawdled towards the shore alongside the operations, she was further surprised to spot individual humans operating the cranes from within small orange cabins suspended below each set of the cranes' braces. Accompanied only by a couple supervising humans on the ground and the small flock of seagulls still whimsically larking in the sky, the operators worked attentively in relative isolation, and with great skill.

'Maybe I should work with great skill?' Jack subsequently tried to persuade herself, coming back to the busy port's internal main road over the shore.

Ramping up her concentration after a first hour of distraction and relative aimlessness, she finally pulled out her coder and began addressing specifically the interference that had been stifling her equipment ever since she entered into the yards.

While moving on to the next wharf west, she perused from off of her device a strongly broadcasting local network entitled, 'Port Pascoll Security Proxy,' and observed it persistently supplant her equipment's attempts to connect to the regular, 'Auckland City Council Personnel,' network.

Doubling back at the end of Freyberg Wharf's triangular end, up the other side, she responsibly ignored gawping at autonomous cranes rotate stock from off a small vessel to reset her hardware and switch between IP addresses in an effort to try and evade the bollards' superfluous influence.

Coming next to the end of Jellicoe Wharf where tractors were being delivered into the hull of a medium sized ship, she waited with her hands stretched out over the plashing water to recharge her dead coder in a small, somewhat existent patch of slightly accessible internet.

She then ventured on to the sprawl that was Bledisloe Wharf, an effective twin to Fergusson, with all its activity included, to bury her gaze further into her coder's menus and reconfigure her hardware to switch transceivers before trying to isolate and quarantine the overwhelming signals. Once initiating a protracting decryption routine using the council's servers to decipher encrypted snippets of information she difficulty uploaded, she began reconstructing select segments of corrupted gibberish and interceptions she had acquired throughout the afternoon manually.

Bored after another hour and a half of underachievement and walking in the dimming afternoon, Jack found herself leaning back on the red-orange fence, not too far from the eastern entrance, with her right-hand clasping lightly one of its cold metal balusters in relative disappointment. Situated down a narrow passage, abutting the elevated Tamaki Drive, behind some of the port's warehouses and their changing shift workers, she had stopped to relax in a small, shaded space seemingly unaffected by the bollards.

While letting her coder charge and the interceptions from outside list abundantly, she thought over her predicament with a vaporous wintery sigh.

She enjoyed working in Assignments and appreciated the higher pay and mufti, even if it was this time overtly bright and stiff, but she at least expected to accomplish something while she worked.

Usually during these rare episodes, she would go to her location, find her target and surveil. She would obtain some kind of confirmation straight away about some kind of theory about her target and proceed to catalogue their movements, behaviours and internet activity. She would then take her time to laze a bit while her equipment took over.

But today her equipment was generally dysfunctional, or off. She didn't know what to catalogue and after a total of two and a half hours, she could barely even conceive her target.

'Maybe they're just not here?' she had to consider.

Based on the assignment's briefing though, it was to be at least partially expected. But that meant that Jack would end up telling Gerry that nothing had happened during her run on the job, and that didn't sound very good in Jack's opinion, especially the part about barely conceiving her target.

'Because that would mean I go back to Info sooner, rather than never,' she bemoaned.

After a few lonely minutes of listening to the consistent roll of tyres zip by above on the other side of the fence and workers say their pleasantries as they departed or arrived in the warehouses, Jack's coder vibrated and her HUD lit up with a photo of Gerry biting merrily into a jam donut at his desk. 'Gerry Moeke,' she read from between it and a sound graph ready to animate his voice.

'Answer,' Jack thought, noting the time in her lenses to be 4:31 pm.

Hearing Gerry suck the last few mils of a drink he was emptying through a straw, she chortled to herself and exhaled, "hey."

"Jack!" Gerry happily pronounced.

"Hey," Jack responded.

"How's things down there in, I suppose, the docks? You got in?" Gerry energetically asked.

Jack was a little relieved to hear him ask that and pleasantly replied, "uh... Eventually. Yeah. Yeah. But it, it's uh, getting late, a little. You know, um— "

"Yeah, I understand," Gerry allayed her, "it can be like that with assignments like these— Hey, look, they're sending me out of the office to do a job right now and I won't be here when you come back in, and it's going to take the whole night. Sorry about that, you'll just have to report back to Assignments tomorrow."

'That was my plan all along,' Jack reflected with a raised brow and pursed lips.

"Yeah, nah, I was thinking that," she responded, nodding, and stood off the fence to accidentally move her equipment into the port's interference. "I was thinking maybe we— Oh, Gerry?" she said while tapping the side of her HUD and leaning forcibly back on the fence.

"Gerry?" she repeated.

"Yeah, keep going," Gerry suddenly blurted back into her ears, "sorry; I'm outside now moving to the taxi. I think I went through a bit of interference there as I passed through the front doors. Brrr, it's getting chilly!"

"Uhhm," Jack informed him, "actually I think that's me. I've been struggling for the whole time I've been here to maintain a connection to, to *anything*. I seem to be, jammed, like really, since, the whole time. The short time. But, the whole time— You there?"

"Yeah," Gerry told her, "ok, so you've found the complex jamming, or, is this? Is this what we talked about— Hang on."

"Ki te Piggot Way tēnā," he then clearly told his taxi.

After taking a few seconds to clear his throat and sit, he concisely asked, "is that that?" before spottily adding, "we'll have to go over."

Jack waited for a moment for him to finish, unsuccessfully, before responding, "what? Gerry?"

Once hearing a blip from Gerry in her ears, she blurted out quickly, "I think I'm being jammed by the docks in general and haven't found anything strange and— Hmm," she concluded, watching him cut out.

"Hmm," she chortled once more, looking at him bite into his jam donut. "Gone."

Ready to spend one more half-hour at the port searching before going home, she pushed off the fence and took in a deep breath of cooling air before turning up the dial on her coat.

She moved out from behind the warehouses, avoiding direct contact with their workers, and safely crossed the port's main road to tour again along the water's edge where she came across something rather ironic; her internet connection had finally stabilised, though the interference icon continued to blink, but it was also time for an update.

'Update required for Wholscan v3.7,' she read off her notifications and laughed at herself in pity. It wasn't even the coder or HUD or their operating systems that needed an update, but the specific programme Jack needed to do her job.

Noticing, however, the steady internet connection very weak at just two bars showing out of five, she began returning to her good patch by the red-orange fence when she hesitated at the sight of the second bar dropping.

"Ooh," she uttered in caution, preferring to maintain the connection so the update could proceed smoothly.

Deciding to move on, so long as it was further into the network's strength, she gave way to a convoy of trailers and crossed back into the second bar situated around and in between the container towers of Fergusson Wharf.

She obtained another bar heading further east, beneath another freezing draught from the safety-orange quadcopter before finding a fourth bar at the head of Te Kawau Wharf, where there had been a reliable degree of connectivity earlier in the afternoon.

Appearing very different now, however, with the cargo ship and supercars gone, the long stretch of concrete pointing straight into the Hauraki Gulf was quiet, being graced by just two last SUVs in the car park and a red mobile crane at the end standing still over a cluster of leftover containers.

Being content with her four bars and a seat atop a collection of discarded plywood boxes, Jack blithely set herself down at the head of the wharf beside the water and let her mandatory update download.

She watched the night lighting come on around the port one moment and then watched it come on along Tamaki Drive the next. She observed

Devonport glow across the harbour as the sky darkened and held up her coder to take a picture but be declined.

"Rubbish," she said, reading from off a notification, 'UPDATE IN PROGRESS. Please do not turn off your device. Connecting to server...'

Turning her coat up another degree and adjusting her seat on her box, she watched more time disappear in her HUD before deciding to message Ebee that she could be a little late coming home due to an important update that hadn't quite started downloading.

She then watched the message move to her outbox and sit for a couple minutes to her displeasure.

'Why is this taking so long?' she groaned about her lagging software, pulling down the notification to examine again, 'UPDATE IN PROGRESS. Please do not turn off your device. Connecting to server...'

'Well then *do* it!' she gestured in dissatisfaction and groaned, seeing the time in her HUD turn 4:56 pm.

Glimpsing back at the end of Te Kawau Wharf, where her connection to the council network had been adequate nearly three hours prior, she subsequently slipped off her boxes and briskly started back down its length.

She walked to the painted lines of the near-empty car park to find a fifth bar there for her connection and then slowed to dawdle around in circles to ultimately achieve nothing.

'Oh, forget it,' she sighed out in a misty breath, conceding it simply time to leave without a target and an update and go home when something in her peripheral vision caught her attention.

Glancing at the cluster of leftover containers sitting over the end of the wharf to see what it might have been, she scanned her vision over the scuffed orange and maroon corrugated steel flanks, watched attentively the motionless crane and waited for an SUV to start up and drive. She then cleared her throat and leaned back into her hips and rubbed and sniffed her chilling nose.

"Are you lost!?" a man's firm voice directly accused her from behind, making her leap an inch in a fright.

"Oh!" she instantly panted and nervously replied, turning a hundred and eighty degrees to stare at a very broad, shadowy-green wrapped, black fabric chest standing immediately in front of her, "sorry. I, I um." Conjuring up a quick response while her eyes followed the black up between the green's widening lapels to a tight black skivvy neck, she bent her head deeply back to look up at the fair man's chiselled jaw, straight nose and wavy black hair.

Cowering a little below the blinkless, interrogating gaze descending from his steely black irises, she stepped back and hesitantly continued, "I um, I'm looking for my, um. Father. Who, uhm, works here, along the docks."

Attempting to calm her heartrate using a flattening gesture with her hands, she cleared her throat again and stepped another foot back and added, "sorry, I didn't mean to startle anyone. I'll just— "

"I know everybody here," the man staunchly replied without the smallest flinch, "and none of them are your father."

"That's alright," Jack nervously agreed and exhaled with a submissive nod and courteous step right to go around the man's hulking girth, "I'll just return to the office. He's probably back. By now."

Without looking over her shoulder, she concluded, "see ya," and moved swiftly away from the man and his silent, open, darkly coloured Holden SUV to return to Fergusson Wharf's perpendicular road and head left alongside the port's intermittent traffic.

A peek backward a few minutes later, however, across the glittering water between the intersecting landings, caused her to pause in intrigue as her brain involuntarily pieced together a few correlating curiosities.

'That guy was *huge*,' she candidly declared in her mind, 'and he wasn't in any safety gear.'

Unable to see him or his SUV anymore lurking about the grounds, she deduced, 'and my connection to the council was the strongest when over there,' comparing her four bars now with the five she had just a moment ago.

'It's connected but I can't download,' she surmised, 'I can't take a picture. I can't send a message. But it's connected... Like the bollards.'

"It's rubbish," she mumbled about her equipment's struggles, and then considered, "or is it *complex?*"

Unable to see the man and his SUV with another look over the grounds, she candidly repeated, "and that guy was *huge*."

Assuming it safe to stay for another half-hour beneath the security cameras of the port and rule out her correlations as simple coincidences, she depressed the power buttons on her coder and HUD to reduce her digital presence and irresistibly started back.

She counted across the water just the two lone SUVs again outside the leftover containers and their crane and turned onto Te Kawau Wharf one last time where she slipped off her bright safety gear to stuff in between the plywood boxes. She glanced about the adjacent yards for anything human or roaming-SUV and then set off to the end of the wharf.

Adjusting her gait from skip to stroll and then sneak, she passed over the car park to near the unassuming cluster of containers, and upon closer inspection, and a leftward veer, begin to assume them as more of an assembly.

There were at least four twelve-metre-long container units in the foreground, loosely abutting the car park, all lying in various, crisscrossing angles as if to partition and potentially funnel. There were two more visibly alongside the left, that were wrapping tightly along the assembly like a bulking twenty-four-metre-long perpendicular fence or support all the way until, possibly, hanging a few feet off the end of the wharf. Supposing there to be two more on the opposite side of the assembly stretching to the wharf's end, Jack then turned her sights to a slightly misaligned, right-angled rectangular stack of mostly maroon containers in the middle.

Arranged in such a way as to have, presumably, four exterior walls, all two units high and one long, though overlapping perpendicularly at both the front and rear ends, the central stack appeared to be even more deliberate than its surroundings. A twelve-metre unit on top, offset from the front wall by half its width, concealed five six-metre-long parallel units succeeding it to seemingly form a makeshift roof over the middle's narrower width concealing a potential gap running along the ground below.

After a quick double-check to see the two SUVs were indeed identical in all but colour to the one driven by the huge green man from earlier, she postulated further, 'a potential gap running along the ground below, *where a complex jamming node might be hiding?'*

With the containers on the left-hand corner of the entire assembly appearing to be no more dented, scratched and rusting than any other set she had seen throughout the afternoon standing resiliently up to all the port's stress, Jack proceeded to visualise a path up onto the makeshift roof. Planning to peek down through visible gaps in its alignment to examine its interior without overtly searching around it and being spotted by any other huge green men that might be lurking inside, she stepped forward to the nearest orange container end and took a deep preparative breath.

She clutched tightly the unit's cold, damp, vertical locking shafts covering the left-hand door with both her hands and lifted up and placed her right foot atop one of its knee-high latch handles to heave her weight up off the ground.

She then flinched in angst, hearing the mechanisms clang against their corresponding components, and lowered herself carefully down to rest her left foot back onto the ground and silently exhale a nervous breath.

After rubbing her brow in regret and listening out to hear no resulting grunts, gasps or exclamations, she cautiously tried again to scale the end of the container, though, this time employing some of that great skill she aspired for earlier.

She slid her hands up the shafts and gripped tightly before reaching her left foot out to the unit's left-hand edge to plant her shoe's toe onto one of the narrow door hinges barely jutting out.

After flexing her thighs to raise her six-foot frame up straight and set her right foot firmly against the nearer right-hand shaft, she slid her hands up and gripped tightly again.

Planting on the next hinge and setting her foot firmly again, she gripped the top edge of the box and, with more flexing, hauled herself up over the right-angled steel to lay upon and swivel and roll ever so quietly over the very slightly drumming corrugations to get back upright onto her knees.

'I might be in heaps of trouble if I get caught up here,' she rather delightedly told herself, while rubbing her eyes and nose and letting out a pant.

Still intent on investigating the assembly though, she pressed on with a lick of her lips and slightly excited four-limbed glide over the box's damp, uneven width to reach over a short but precarious gap to the next vertical facade on the middle assembly and prepare to begin the next ascent.

Repeating the steps from before, she gripped and planted and set her hands and feet deftly to raise herself up another container and a half to where she reached horizontally left and manoeuvred into a level nook, behind the front twelve-metre roofing unit, to be concealed from the port.

Resting herself at first to listen for any slight, reciprocating drumming and clanging following her up, she peered over the edge of her five-metre-high perch to the ground and then quietly leaned back.

'I'm like a ninja,' she happily assessed of her stealthy reconnaissance thus far.

She was then alarmed to hear something plastic crack behind her, followed by several calmly walking footsteps.

Turning over onto her knees as silently as she could to inspect, she looked for and located an acutely narrow interval between the roofing units and gazed down through them to immediately observe a shadow, and some subtle reflections. With her eyes adjusting a little more to the interior's dark, she then made out heads and shoulders before distinguishing a large central table.

Blinking in irritation at a light that incidentally flashed in her eye, she kneeled back to stretch her eye muscles before deciding to creep further along her level and observe the assembly's quiet interior from a different angle two container widths across.

'One, two... Three,' she subsequently counted of the people shrouded inside, before a small splash of water past the end of the wharf proceeded the entering of a fourth.

Jack shook her head and flexed her shoulder blades to shake off a building nervousness and took off her HUD.

She couldn't see any obvious jamming bollards in the interior, nor anything resembling a complex one, and the people inside were unsettlingly quiet and sedated in the dark.

A small click then sounded from between what she could only really suppose was the hands of the person sitting at the table. She watched a small red light consequently come on along some shadowy device he was fiddling with a few seconds before a bright sky-blue screen of light, a few inches in size, appeared in front of him.

Lighting up the person enough to display his own pair of green lapels covering a black skivvy he was wearing, it also lit up the room enough for her to make out two more green trench coats draped upon the shoulders, of two others right below and their workshop.

'Weird,' Jack opined as she adjusted her stance into a squat while observing them work and stand and wait without even sounding as much as a sniff or sigh.

Tempted to try her equipment again to hopefully take a picture or video, she placed her HUD down very gently upon the steel and slipped her coder out of her jacket pocket. She consequently lost her balance and skilfully rolled sideways flat onto the corrugations of her perch to suppress the noise of her stumble and then exhale steamily in relief.

'Ooh!' she corrected herself with a hush of her breath.

Rolling back up to her knees as her nerves uncomfortably warmed her back and armpits, she put her idea aside for a moment to peer back down and gauge whether she had been heard.

But the room was dark.

'Ok, time to go,' Jack ordered herself silently, preparing to descend her perch, 'but just, one last look.'

Silently pivoting back around to peer down one last time through her misaligned crevice, she leaned in to glean from the subtle reflections and deep shadows when the workshop suddenly lit up clearly to reveal two dark eyes staring up at her from across the interior.

Shocked by their staunchly prosecuting gaze, framed between a head of neatly cut short hair and a Spanish beard atop a black skivvy neck and army-green clad shoulders, she fell back onto her hands and bottom.

She then hobbled back onto her feet to make sure she had in fact been spotted, and cursed below her breath when the prosecuting gaze again confirmed it.

"Hi," she shamefully admitted from her perch before scanning the interior as fast as possible. Leaning obliquely left to right, she mentally noted of the inside, 'internal container doors, storage boxes. Table, paper, open box, green man sitting. Black plastic forearm in his hand, open. *Open?'*

Without stopping, she continued, 'table, open boxes, plastic leg, paper, guy looking at me, concrete, doors, another guy looking at me— *Time to gap it!'*

A huge silhouette then caught her eye as she turned rightward to leave, leaping easily up onto her perch from below to stand boldly in front and tower over her.

"Did you find your father?" it firmly declared.

Chapter Six
Thursday, 21st June 2063

Paralysed between the prosecuting gaze and the trench-coated silhouette fronting her, Jack stood cautiously up to acknowledge her presence atop their corrugated assembly and swallow a nervous ball growing in her throat.

She exhaled aloud with a quiver and reversed a couple steps as the silhouette neared close enough along the quietly drumming steel to reveal itself to be that of the huge man she met briefly down in the car park.

Holding her hands out in caution, she considered, 'five metres down,' of the ground quite far below her perch and silently shrieked, 'really big!' about the broadly set man she hoped wouldn't grab her with his fingerprint-masking, matt black gloves and throw her off.

Glimpsing at the nearest lower container sitting a metre out from the base of her wall for a split-second to plan a better landing spot, just in case, she looked timidly up into the man's steely eyes as he came to within a solid and crushing headbutt away and stammered.

"Ummm. No," she openly recalled about a father she remembered making up, while taking a safe step back from his chiselled jaw and interrogating stare. "I think I'll just drop down here," she conceded with a downward directing gesture to the lower container.

The huge green man, though, and his bloused black pants and seriously treaded hiking boots, made her feel unsafe to try with another heavy step of them forward.

The lower container too then moved with a rather savage, concrete-etching, hollow-drumming swivel of its nearest end out another metre from the assembly at the forceful, body-extending push of the other green man bearing the prosecuting gaze.

Cursing loudly in her mind at the sight of him shifting a massive object like that without so much as a pant before standing straight to gaze up at her again from the concrete, Jack felt a frigid chill tingle up her spine.

'That is *not* normal,' she discerned in fear with a further step back from the interrogating man who was now obstructing the safest path off her perch.

Hoping to appeal, she looked up once more to him and shamefully cowered, "uhhh," beneath his now even steelier stare and stepped submissively back.

"This is uh, I'm the um. An inspection. Person," she stuttered with her mouth and eyes to inform him, raising and lowering her left wrist that contained her legitimate port pass, "of the um, safety... Um. It's my job, and I'm done here."

Assenting her claims with a nod, she quietly pieced in and shook her head disconcertedly, "and my father."

"Sorry," she then assertively allayed and stuttered some more with her hands before directing past him, "ok, we're done here, so let's just get down, and move on."

But the man's chiselled jaw didn't budge for his lips to speak, nor did his straight nose exhale any vapour. He simply stepped forward again and continued to examine her with an accusing brow.

Jack's nervousness consequently began to shift from submission to restlessness and her heart started to beat harder.

The rather robotically behaving man was acting indifferently to her courteous words and was repeatedly encroaching on her air space. The perch upon which they stood was too high to be comfortable dropping from without shocking her feet against the ground, where there was another robotically behaving man seemingly waiting for her anyway. The corrugations too were becoming slippery with the evening dew developing, and Jack was already worried about reversing off and falling or even turning her back to the increasingly threatening man to walk around and find another way down.

'Why does he have to be so weird!?' she whined to herself about his apparent penchant for intrusion. 'Does he expect me to cower down into a ball!?' she agitatedly imagined of herself squatting down in fear. Having done that already once in the past and endured the beating and borne the resultant abrasions and bruises and hated it, she stepped her right foot back to free up the opening to her right pant pocket and leaned back into her right hip.

As her heartbeat started to beat faster in anticipation of action and her lungs ventilate more quickly, she looked reluctantly into his eyes to give him one last opportunity to actually say something or apologise, or perhaps explain that he was blind.

It was then, however, that in his eyes she saw a twinkle, followed by a flicker. And then with a squint, she saw a tiny static image glow outside the area of his irises that his enlarged pupils twitched beneath to glance at and mechanically zoom out to focus on.

'Breachers?!' she thought in alarm before another set of huge boots drummed somewhere else atop the assembly and caused her heartbeat to race.

Reciting the term taught from her youth to describe individuals among the population who toyed with human digitisation or modified their bodies with prohibited advanced prosthetics, Jack stood in dread at the prospect that one of them was standing over her now.

The breachers had always been taught of as being the most extreme and dangerous of the pro-singularity activist factions and typically bore physical, and sometimes mental, bionic upgrades that gave them superior strength, skill and acuity over everyone else in society including the greatest of athletes and mathematicians.

They were also taught of as being by far the most driven to hurt people.

Having argued with the authorities beside their lesser modified comrades to protect their perceived rights and failed, they were the ones who ultimately fought with the police to retain their illegal wears and advantages. They were the ones who unleashed a bloody period upon the nation until the military intervened to crush them and were also the ones who escaped to evolve their factions into terror cells and initiate violent acts of defiance upon the public.

'Like, perhaps, they're about to do now,' Jack gravely judged, deducing the static image loaded onto the breacher's false sclera to be one of her.

Instantaneously clouding in her mind as her heart pumped hot blood into her energising limbs, she took a half-step back with her right foot, reached her right hand down inside her right pant pocket and clasped at her stinger. With unprecedented haste, she ejected the stiff device powerfully out with her hand into the space above her head, sprang the hardened black shaft with a hollow metallic snap, cocked her hand back further and then ferociously pulled it back down towards the man's neck.

The extended pipe clanged loudly against alloy sheathed beneath the sleeve the man instantly raised around his left arm to protect himself and vibrated sharply through the handle to prick Jack's hand like barbed wire.

Recoiling with still no open path in sight, Jack clenched the handle even tighter, stepped a toe back against the side of a corrugated ridge, swung her right arm back to full cock and struck again with as much force as her frame could muster.

The weapon clanged loudly again on the obstinate forearm and stabbed barbs into Jack's hand, but she didn't recoil, forcibly following it up with a lunge of her legs, backward twist of her wrist and forward slide across the top of the extending forearm to shove the weighted tip of the device to within inches of the man's face.

For what seemed like an episode, she resisted his countering grab and depressed the weapon's power button beneath her thumb with paralysing force to cause the electrodes at its tip to light up a bright violet string of electricity.

Jumping vividly for a split-second between its points, the jagged string suddenly arced across the open air to contact the man's cheek where rather than sting, it bit, savagely, pulsating current straight into his bone and facial muscles. The coulombs scrunched the left side of his face causing him to gnarl in agony and his arms to become stiff and impaired in the pain.

The man dropped to his knees and fell sideways against the roofing containers in a heap and battled to claw the weapon and fend off his opponent but growled in anger as the stinger gripped his face like a jaw.

Horrified by the physically crippling violence after a few more seconds, and done inducing it, Jack lifted her thumb off the stinger's power button and unsuccessfully tried to pull the device out from the rigor seizing the man's clenching hand. She quivered at the sight of the severe two-inch burn she caused the skin just below his completely blackened prosthetic eyeball, that was, thankfully, still structurally intact and in its socket, and promptly remembered he had friends.

Without further need to process what the drumming behind her meant or what was causing the containers to savagely etch the concrete below, she stepped away from her rebooting victim and glanced narrowly at the unevenly lit port. Feeling her hamstrings jitter uncontrollably, an onsetting queasiness vanish and her heartbeat cramp under pressure, she audibly concurred with her body, "*run!*" and abruptly sprung into an athletic dash.

Banging the soles of her shoes along the corrugated perch as she overtly fled, she sped the ten metres to the nook she ascended to earlier and threw herself flatly and obliquely off.

She landed jarringly with a resonating thud atop the lower container, pinching and tweaking her innards, and slipped as her feet were clumsily parted by the container being swivelled below her. Dropping uncontrollably off the unattended side, she instinctively twisted her torso and waist to orientate her feet below her frame too slowly and collapsed her side and right elbow onto the concrete.

Ignoring the panging and grazing to scramble back to her feet in haste, she unwittingly then rammed her left shoulder into the rigid end of the next container.

"Ooh!" she steamily winced in pain and frustration and persevered regardlessly to pump her thighs and arms to get moving and swiftly put as much distance between her and the assembly as possible.

Sprinting over the car park in the dark and veering left across Te Kawau Wharf to return to the offices, she hesitated and veered right again at the stressful sight of another darkly coloured SUV abruptly pulling up on the perpendicular road ahead.

Keeping up the pace as its front doors opened, she bolted across the lanes instead to enter inside the intermittent shadows of Fergusson Wharf's container towers and break all the lines of sight.

Precipitately recalling her assignment's double-secret status as her flight brought her towards two curiously alarmed and reflective dock workers who quite possibly knew and didn't mind the breachers openly operating among them, she pivoted her fevered step left to try and escape the entire premises and its evening shift altogether.

She fled past containers and busy stacking trucks, and beneath bright white lights as she ran directly across the port's main road with a mind fixated on the patch of red-orange fence she leant on in isolation earlier. Avoiding colliding into a short convoy of heavy-laden trailers, she came to the warehouses abutting her patch and zipped into a gap with a walking worker to hastily arrive at and leap up onto and smack unskilfully into the ten-foot-high, smooth metal balusters in vain.

"Argh," she mistily expressed, bouncing off and subsequently turning to spot a three-metre-tall stack of empty pallets against the back wall of the next warehouse over.

'It's close enough,' she appreciatively estimated of the several-metres-long space between the highest pallet and the long and steep grassy slope on the other side of the fence.

And so, without any hesitation peradventure she would be caught, she skipped to and immediately began scaling the splintery stack like a ladder.

Pausing for a second near the top for it all to wiggle and then budge, she quaveringly gripped and pressed down the top slats, pulled her torso over and raised her feet onto the highest rickety pallet to queasily stand and doubt.

"No," she resistantly ventilated against her worry and leaned back and then pushed off the warehouse to launch herself over the fence.

Picking up her feet to ensure she clear it, she then fretted when the inclined grass on the other side lunged up at her rapidly to shock her feet and ankles and pop her knees and pelvis with a forceful slam.

"HARGH!" she physically exhaled as her body buckled in the impact.

"Huh! Ergh!" she groaned, as her crunched joints and shoulders sent signals of serious discomfort to her clouded brain.

Fighting a consequential moment of weakness, she determinedly raised her torso off the sloping earth against the will of her pulsating pain receptors and forced herself to push on. She stumbled up the high grassy climb using her enfeebled legs and left arm while holding her right taught against her body, to alleviate a twinge in her shoulder, and looked west toward the glowing CBD.

There, inside the majestic consortium of steel and glass reaching down to Quay Street, she hoped to conceal herself amidst a profuse public or disappear inside a mall. But its kilometre-long distance away was *so* far, while the port entrance, where an SUV or two bearing breachers could exit any second, was still *so* close. Even the urban high-rises of Parnell, located opposite the great widths of Tamaki Drive and the fenced rail yard adjoining it were distressingly far to run and clamber across in the open.

'But it's all there is,' Jack assertively conceded to herself as the sound of tyres whizzing speedily along the Drive towards the CBD presented another option for her to consider.

Hobbling up onto the crest beside the road and moaning as the accumulation of heat from the running, climbing and her coat cooked her, she swung her left arm lethargically and stumbled onto the footpath where she sunk her head back and took in a deep breath of cold air. Beneath the amber glow of the streetlamps, she then stepped out onto the hexagonal tiles of the six-lane road, holding her left hand above her head, and deliberately attempted to slow a pair of headlights coming from the CBD.

Watching them switch lanes and avoid her, however, caused her to groan in frustration.

'Call Gerry Moeke,' she commanded her HUD while walking further out towards the road's reflective median to hail two more pairs of headlights coming from further down.

'Call Gerry Moeke,' she repeated more distinctly before being startled by the flapping wind from two west bound cars passing from the other direction.

Jittering and increasingly worried by her predicament, she felt for her HUD's temple arms to understand why the device wasn't responding and touched her bare articulator, naked brow and nose.

"Oh no," she exclaimed, feeling her empty coat and pant pockets while watching the oncoming headlights turn off Tamaki Drive, "no way."

Realising she hadn't left just her stinger behind with the breacher up upon the container assembly but also her HUD and coder, she moved into the road's median to maximise her chances of triggering the brakes in the next group of headlights and panted shakily, "oh man."

In spite of the pain in her right shoulder, she raised both her hands into the air to enlarge her profile and subsequently tremble when a quick glance over her shoulder revealed another group of headlights coming from the opposite direction at nearly the same rate.

Being lit up all around by the traffic a few harrowing seconds later, she held, and just before their speedy arrival, stepped half in front of one car heading east to obstruct its sensors and cause it to brake and veer, making its neighbour swerve and the next one over dig in its tyres and screech loudly.

The abrupt deceleration and spontaneous reactions caused the following row of cars close behind to defensively skid their own tyres and swing their headlights and incidentally threaten the traffic in the oncoming lanes.

As more skidding and swerving ensued, Jack skipped away from the danger in the east bound lanes to turn a hundred and eighty degrees, deeply gasp, lower her frame, shut her eyes tightly and brace.

Contacted and wrapped two inches around her tucked elbows, clenched abdomen and tensed thighs by a hefty car's bumper, she was instantly belted by a transfer of momentum and shunted uncontrollably back several metres along the median.

Flying, scraping, grazing and then rolling into a dishevelled mess upon her back, she fought against her winded diaphragm to gulp air and subtly shuffled to reinvigorate her stunted senses.

Relievedly feeling friction beneath her knuckles and heat in her shoes, more bumps around her body and now a whole lot more abrasions, she took another gulp of air and rolled over onto her tummy to begin consciously reventilating her lungs. She flexed the few muscle fibres in her tummy still responding to curl with a whimper, and contracted her grazed limbs beneath her torso with a groan. She leaned back to sit on her left side in the patchy light brightening her closed eyelids and twist around her knees so she could lean forward and apply her weight over them. But a sharp, threading sense of pain inside her left knee she felt while erecting herself made her drop from a strained hunch back onto her left side with an exasperated mewl.

"WHAT THE HECK!?" a disgruntled male called into the air.

"What the hell just happened!?" a displeased female somewhere else further away ranted and cursed.

While opening her eyes a crack into the blazing headlights ahead of her, Jack heard a few doors open and more tyres arrive, though calmly, and stop.

"Are they *ok?*" a worried man compassionately asked from a few metres behind.

"*Are you ok?*" the young woman exiting behind the headlights ahead of Jack asked.

"She's been hit," a concerned woman further away stated helpfully, "I'm calling 111."

Jack shielded her eyes from the bright glow with her left hand and lifted her head to look around only to immediately sink it again in weariness. She was suffocating, hurt and stinging all over, including on the left side of her cheek and forehead, and didn't want to talk. She didn't have the air for it, and had incidentally acquired the attention needed anyway to hopefully ward off the pursuit from any breachers.

"Are you ok?" the young woman from the behind the headlights asked again before dimming them.

Jack then flinched at the feel of two warm hands cup her deltoids through her frayed coat and looked over her left shoulder to see a gentle older lady with ash grey hair in a fuzzy, smoky-blue jumper kneeling down to comfort her.

"Are you hurt?" she softly asked as she brought her eyes down closer to meet with Jack's.

As others spoke around them to each other and over their devices, Jack managed to inhale a tiny amount of air and expire, "h-ah."

'Should I tell them?' she hesitated in her mind with genuine concern, 'about the breachers?'

Her assignment was supposed to be of the utmost secrecy, and her standing with the Assignments Department, which was already casual and sporadic, would be in jeopardy if she revealed her findings to anyone but Gerry. She especially wasn't meant to reveal anything to any random people in public.

'But the breachers were real,' she asserted to herself with a pant, 'and dangerous.'

But her memory failed to back up her supposition with any instance of actual danger besides being approached along the perch and being hit with a stinger.

'But that was *me*,' Jack clarified to herself about using the stinger, before ensuring to note, 'but that perch was *really high*, and they were, like, *really dodgy*. And too close. And had those, eyes. And muscles.'

"Oh," she audibly sighed in regret, contemplating quietly, 'what have I done?' What if I'm *wrong* about them, being breachers?'

"Do you need an ambulance?" the gentle lady interrupted supportively.

Jack glimpsed at her sympathetic face in the presence of everyone else, who were mostly displeased and returning into their cars to leave, and then looked back down at the road.

'I discharged my stinger,' she considered with a pained squint as the sensitivity of her skin's grazes and bumps upon her thigh, bottom, hips, back, elbow, hands and face became more apparent, 'and, I, probably, should tell someone. Especially *if* that guy wasn't a breacher. *Very especially if* he was just a normal guy, doing his job.'

'And Gerry's gone,' she added in sore disappointment about her boss who had left the council for the night. 'And so is my equipment,' she regretfully recalled about her expensive council-issued HUD and coder.

Glimpsing again at the gentle lady's obvious sympathy to appeal, she apprehensively entreated as cars began to leave, "I need to go to the police."

The gentle lady charitably obliged, acting first to reassure the young woman behind the headlights that everything would be fine before helping Jack up off the ground. She offered Vaseline from a glovebox in her hatchback and aided Jack in coating the seeping grazes she couldn't comfortably reach herself.

She then delivered her to the central police station without any consideration for cost or lost time and patiently waited with her in the lobby. Asking only for an email address at the end of her service so she could check up on Jack in a couple of days, she amicably left when an officer was finally ready to come out and take over.

Sitting irritatedly back a time later on a cream plastic chair inside one of the station's cold, varnished pine and green moss-painted, two-tone corridors, Jack was ruminating discontentedly over her general state of discomfort.

She had been brought through into the station by one officer and been told to sit and wait for another. During her time waiting, the petroleum jelly all around her antiseptic-treated grazes, but most especially on her back and upper buttocks, had warmed and turned into to a slowly spreading goo. Some of her dulled pain receptors were beginning to scream and she wasn't sure, and didn't want to know, if the drop of Vaseline oozing down the left side of her face was actually blood.

She also felt as if she had a fever somehow, so quickly, and was consequently fidgeting on her creaking chair to move heat from behind her back and armpits while bearing the cold sterile touch of the station's air upon her skin where her clothing had been frayed or torn.

Her coat too seemed damaged and unresponsive from the wear which presented a financial loss, not just based on a few tears that could possibly be stitched or patched. The garment had started out as a selfless present from Ebee that would keep her warm through winter and bring a smile to her reflection in the windows she walked past during the day, but was now a powerless tattered mess with small fibrous heat filaments hanging out from between its layers.

Jack attempted to console herself with a grateful reflection back on the kindness shown her by Sally, the gentle lady, whose promptness of charity was exceptionally impressive but her current negativity got the better of her.

'I hope she's not *a breacher*,' she pondered warily, recalling typing her email onto Sally's coder before they parted in the lobby. A further recollection back though, to the east-facing orientation of the gentle lady's little blue hatchback made it seem unlikely. Sally also had petroleum jelly on hand, which was something only a genuine, older lady would have ready for random scrapes, or random young women lying near-unconscious in the middle of the road. The bitter tinge left from mothballs too scented the interior of Sally's car which Jack couldn't possibly correlate with anyone hell-bent on upending civilisation through violent revolt.

Shifting her thoughts as she leant back and tried to relax without applying more pressure upon the disturbingly slimy grazes of her back and upper buttocks, she began re-summarising her afternoon in preparation for an eyewitness statement. While hoping she could give it to any of the officers occasionally ignoring her as they passed soon, or perhaps to one of their robotic canines that strolled past earlier into an office at the end of the corridor, where a pair of hind legs was still visible, she began:

'I was working in the port and found— '

"Jacqueline Hart," an approaching male suddenly echoed inside the spartan passage.

Jack flinched with a pant and looked left to watch a blond-haired officer in a tucked, light-blue dress shirt and stiff, dark-blue slacks step out from an office across the passage further back and approach her with a rapping march while holding a coder in his hand. She adjusted her posture carefully as he squatted down on one knee, a foot and a half from her knees, and cleared her throat as he read off his device.

"Jacqueline Hart," he re-read, elaborating, "council warden 5-6-2-0?"

"Yep," Jack replied and cleared her throat a little more.

"I'm Constable Scott-Carey and I'll be completing your statement with you. I see here you have some, you say— Well, you've written, 'double-secret', here, whatever that means. I'm just, I'm going to have to ask you some questions." Shaking his head in unfamiliarity, he explained dismissively, "because I don't know how 'double-secret' is going to help you."

"It's for the receptionist," Jack humbly clarified with an appealing gesture of her hands.

"Well, what? She's," the officer contended, pointing to himself in irritation, "you're talking to me."

Jack was suddenly very uncomfortable, but candidly persevered with politeness, "there are possible breachers working down in the docks."

Watching the officer process her words in his head without alarm, she continued on a little less candidly, "and, I didn't want to, alarm, anyone, the um. They were like, um. In a, a thing, like a building from, the."

Jack paused in the officer's stark and silent stare and took a deep breath.

"There was containers," she said, shaking her head humbly, "an uh, they approached me up on a perch, and blocked me, away, from the um, exit— Uh, like a drop."

'Ah, this is already going badly,' Jack's mind managed to distract her as she stuttered.

"And the um," she fumbled on, "and I used a stinger to um, get away— To, to, to um."

'I hate police,' she thought in the fluster.

'No, I hate *talking* to police,' she quickly corrected and nervously swallowed.

After another moment of silence ensued, the officer recited, "you used *a stinger?*"

"Uh, hu-yeah," Jack affirmed with a small nod, "and I lost it— Oh, *he still has it.* And, and, possibly my coder and HUD," she sheepishly recalled.

The officer's brow lowered as he itched the back of his ear and breathed in deeply through his nostrils.

Standing up to review his own coder, he frowned some more and coaxed with an openhanded gesture, "so you're telling me you hit someone with *a stinger?*"

"A breacher," Jack lightly emphasized with another small nod.

Looking down at his coder perturbedly and licking his lips, the constable breathed in deeply again and rubbed his nose and then proceeded to ask, "do you often have problems with transhumanic individuals?"

Perplexed by the big word at first, and then disturbed once recalling it in her memory to be one of those used repeatedly in the news during ugly, heated debates, Jack inhaled half a breath and retorted, *"what?"*

"Well," the officer reasoned in displeasure, "frankly, you've come in here, you're asking us, me, to write down a statement— You should be writing this. Using a derogatory term I find quite offensive. You don't come in here and marginalise an entire community, expecting us, to do as you please to them, who are already oppressed by the authorities of the past; and you said— *After*, you've said, you hit them with a stinger."

Jack was confused, and worried.

She was already inside the police station where people who get arrested for hitting people with things are taken to and the officer was making her feel like she could be arrested.

While the term 'breacher' had been formally adopted by the government in the 2040s, and been consequently taught her in school, 'transhuman' had become the term among the politically correct in recent years, and she thought it was rather stupid. The breachers were a specific group of people who actually maimed and killed people, while the transhumans were spoken off as a group of people infatuated with legal advanced prosthetics who simply confused people.

Jack actually did know the term 'breacher' had become something of a faux-pas due to her work as an information warden recording people's faux-pas and worse, but she didn't think she would ever find herself sitting in disgusted pain below an armed officer of the law who was so easily offended by her innocent attempt to simply communicate.

"I *hope* that guy was not a *transhuman!*" she mumbled to herself about the man she hit with her stinger.

"Excuse me?" the officer retorted accusingly.

"Um, so the guy was in green," Jack very anxiously decided to submit for her quavering statement, "a green coat. A long, green coat."

"This is the *transhuman* you hit?" the officer sternly inquired and clarified, holding the edge of his unfolded rectangular coder closer to Jack's mouth to record, "you are an information warden, 5-6-2-0, and you have pulled out your stinger weapon and discharged it, on him that you have not yet named. What kind of hit? Where did you hit?"

"Oh," Jack submissively responded, letting her eyes wonder as she went, "uhm, on the um. I don', I don't know his name. I hit on the wrist, his left wrist, he had up, he blocked, with. A, um. Twice. And then his, the um, stinger part... Touched his face. And went off."

"*On his face?*" the officer cajoled with his pointed coder.

"By his left eye, below his left eye," Jack said with a wary upwards inflection, "and then I ran, lea, and then I left it there. Or the, the opposite of that. I left it there and ran."

"Cos I's scared," she ensured to add, "he was like, really big, like, seven-foot tall. And had uh— Fair, skin, dark curly, wavy, kinda short, hair, and had uh, three friends all wearing the same; black under, the coat, gloves, hiking boots, skivvy. And green coat. On top."

"And did you record this with your equipment?" the officer inquired further, "do you have any evidence— "

"I don't have any equipment," Jack promptly added, "I left it there. It was all turned off. He was in possession of my stinger when I left. This was all down on Te Kawau Wharf."

"In Port Pascoll," the officer clarified to Jack's affirmative nod.

Leaving Jack for a moment to walk a few paces down the corridor, he called out to a colleague, "Rory," and asked, "do we have jurisdiction over the port? We don't eh?"

"West Port," the colleague replied aloud, opening his door to incidentally reveal his armoured dogs, "Princes, Queens, Captain, I think. There are a couple others. Maritime covers the East Port."

Jack stood up from her seat while watching them converse and attentively watched the blond officer return.

"Ok, so um," he said, itching the back of his head while reviewing and swiping his coder, "I'm going to get you to produce a profile of the person's face on this programme, here."

Handing over to Jack a character creation app for her to sculpt her best recollection of the breacher's three-dimensional face, he informed, "and then this will run your profile though our system to help us identify who this victim might be so we can try and contact them, to obtain a corroborating statement and counsel them, on, government assistance. This could result in a lot of faces though so finding them could be tough."

Jack became very nauseous.

Hearing the officer call the breacher a victim caused a deep hollow pit to open up inside her stomach and press apart her organs.

Sitting back down to stabilise herself with his coder in her hands, she nervously proceeded to colour the default profile's skin fair and chisel its chin and concomitantly fill up her deep pit with poison.

Worrying that the cheek bones she was placing and forehead she was setting was going to materialise in a few days to sue her for money she didn't have or angrily demand the officer throw her in her prison, she strained in her mind and lied, 'he was, uh, *Asian*, wasn't he?'

'Sorry,' she then stressed for the random man she was going to have disturbed tomorrow, who notably now looked very different from the one she hit.

Handing back the coder and taking a deep gulp of oxygen, she stood up stiffly to brace and watch the officer look over the lie with an indifferent frown and fortuitously utter, "good. We'll put that through the system shortly."

"It was dark," Jack remembered to mention so she could cover her backside, suggesting more timidly, "so it might be a little off. You might need to write that down."

"We'll get in touch with your employer," the officer continued, however, without physically noting her suggestion, and elaborated, "the council, tomorrow, and talk with them about this incident. There may be more information that will come in later, based on your statement, and this profile, but for now, keep your stinger in your locker. Don't leave town. Stay away from anyone transhumanic, and don't comment about this, or anyone involved, or about transhumans online. Or we may need to bring you back in. In cuffs."

Jack couldn't believe what she just heard and was slightly incensed by it but easily chose to stay quiet, as was typical of her demeanour. She didn't like getting in trouble and wasn't fond of loud noises and shouting, and had no intentions to offend anyone, let alone hit them. She also didn't do a lot of social media outside of replying with a few short syllables to a work emailing group she disliked being roped into and wouldn't talk about the incident anyway as it was, or had been at one point, double-secret. As far as leaving town went, she had very little money to do so due to the debts she was paying for her last set of damaged equipment; and would now likely have more lumped on to pay for her newest set lost.

Without any real assurance of a favourable intervention by the police, Jack exited the station in a downcast mood feeling in trouble for more than just hitting a green man in the face. She kept her head down, leaving the premises, and turned her coat inside out to change her appearance somewhat and began a moderate walk back to Charterton beneath a softly falling drizzle.

She stuck to the well-illuminated roads as she went, passing colourfully bright advertisements profusely decorating facades and paths, and walked closely alongside crowds and in between pairs of the public.

She arrived safely outside the blue evening glow of her building and entered inside its warm lobby and felt relieved to observe the same regular blitheness still abiding amongst her fellow tenants and their visitors. Watching them read quietly on their devices and play card games as she passed them, she approached Douglas and vaguely warned him about her situation. With an assurance from him that he and his small team would keep a keener eye out for anything suspicious, she entered into the next empty elevator and retreated up to her apartment.

Entering inside with a quiet, exasperated and relieving sigh, she closed and locked the front door noiselessly and slipped her ruined coat from off her shoulders.

She then turned towards the living room and saw Ebee walking perkily from the kitchen into the lounge, licking icing from off one of her fingers. Spotting a large muffin in her hand, she observed her move pleasantly in her sapphire-blue business blazer and skirt and tan winter pantyhose and greeted, "hey," with an involuntary, fragile smile.

"How's it going Jack?" Ebee peppily replied, looking at her from beside the coffee table and then frowning.

"Whoa, you look a bit, uh," she described in concern, squinting, "you're home later than usual. Is everything ok? Are *you* ok?"

Noticing the high degree of scruffiness in Jack's damp appearance and a random smudge of gloss adorning her left temple, she caringly inquired, *"what happened?"*

Walking between the couches towards Jack as Jack placed her coat atop their entry table and stood in disconsolation, she noticed her grazed knuckles and frayed patches and took a closer look at her head. "Uh," she worriedly exclaimed, shifting Jack's hair carefully from her temple, *"what happened? Do you need first aid? Are you, in pain, at all? Do you need a doctor?"*

Touching Jack's left arm caringly above the elbow to express her sympathy, she anxiously counselled, "do you need a plaster-s? Or bandages? *Dettol?*" she earnestly appealed with an upwards inflection, half-quipping, "or *youthesiser treatment?*"

Jack inhaled deeply and exhaled through her lips and moved her arm out of Ebee's gentle grip.

"Today I came across some bad guys, who might know where I live," she pronounced.

"Oh man," Ebee sadly replied, "and, *they*, did this to you? Is this treated? It looks like Vaseline— "

"This isn't them," Jack spoke over her, "this was something else, an accident. Later."

"Is this Vaseline?" Ebee eagerly re-asked, pointing, "has this been treated?"

"Yeah, yeah, yeah," Jack dismissively confirmed, moving Ebee's finger away from her sores to continue, "these bad guys might know where I live, and might know where *you* live. And your name, and where you work, and shop. Your email... *Your muffin.*"

Looking directly into Ebee's eyes in despair, she explained, "they have my um. They might have my coder and HUD. And all my messages and things. Probably."

Listening attentively and then sniggering very lightly, Ebee held up her muffin for Jack to see to make her feel better and reviewed Jack's visible grazes with her eyes.

"It's vanilla," she revealed, looking in her little sister's eyes while holding the bit muffin up even higher to display its raspberry-and-yellow-coloured paper cup, "with a peach centre, a gooey peach centre, and vanilla icing."

Changing to a slightly more assuring tone, she added while examining Jack's head wound, "we should be safe here, uh, from anyone outside. Douglas and Tim and Pin have got it downstairs. You can be comfortable up here. The guys will turn away any stalkers wanting to, *date you*."

Jack wasn't so convinced. Douglas and Tim and Pin weren't seven-feet tall and strong enough to move a huge metal container with just their hands, even as a team.

'And they're not *transhuman*,' she further criticised, as Ebee continued to stand and support her through her glum mood.

"I'm going to have a shower ok," she uttered, pressing her lips dolefully.

Stepping towards the bathroom, she softly warned over her shoulder, "*please* don't answer the door."

Standing below the gentle, persistent spray falling from two oscillating rails horizontally fixed a couple inches below the bathroom ceiling, Jack let her body's bumps and bruises soak beneath the flow of the shower's hot water. Leaning with her hands against the wall and her arms extended, she let it run down her partially sealed grazes to rinse from off her skin and head all the filth and melancholy. She let its heat soothe her pains and strains inside her muscles and joints before becoming paranoid that someone might suddenly burst in the apartment while she was naked.

Drying gently and changing into a new set of comfortable bed clothes delivered through a quick opening and closing of the door by Ebee, she prepared herself with a look in the mirror and tying of her hair. She applied Dettol to her grazes and the last blob of medical gel from a small expensive pottle in the cabinet and apprehensively returned to the lounge.

Choosing to lay along the centre couch of the c-shaped arrangement with her back rested carefully upon the seat cushions and head upon the armrest, watching the entranceway, she readied herself to wind down for the evening while staying prepared for any strangers that might bust through the front door. But the paranoia was quickly boring, and her favourite cerise couch's cushions surface layers too pliable, and relatively stiff hug from their supportive foam, too reassuring.

After a few minutes of fighting her body's tiredness and mind's innate apathy, she bequeathed pleasantly her security to the couch and pronounced, "I'm sure the couch will take care of it," and rolled more comfortably onto her side.

"The couch will take care of what?" Ebee asked kindly from the kitchen, "do you need some more medicine, stuff?"

"Oh, nothing, and no," Jack replied, rolling on to her back again to peer casually over her couch's backrest, "sorry. I was just mumbling. I've already put stuff on."

"I picked up *six* of those vanilla and peach muffins on my way home," Ebee began to chirpily discuss from the kitchen while tidying old food from the fridge, "from that bakery by my work, 'Rebecca's'. They're right here. And they were *really expensive*. I'll have to go back tomorrow to pay another instalment."

Jack chuckled politely. She remembered Ebee complaining about that particular bakery's prices in the past but also remembered how scrummy their food was. Situated almost at the dead centre of the city, barely a stroll from Ebee's work, they required an exorbitant fee for everything, probably, Ebee once deduced, to pay for an exorbitant rent.

"The people I found today were *breachers*, Ebee," Jack then said into the air.

Sitting up to look over the backrest at her friend standing between the kitchen benches, she clarified, "or, *maybe*. But they reminded me of the same type of people who killed that Jonathan Haven guy. You know that park right beneath your work? You know that guy that has the statue?"

She watched Ebee scan a plate of three-day-old beef with her eyes to decide whether it still safe to consume while processing Jack's statement. At first, very serious about the beef, and then less so, about the idea of an old grumpy group of cyborgs likely deceased since a decade ago still running around Auckland's streets in anything but mobility scooters, she questioned, "were they old?" and squinted with a hint of scepticism.

Jack sniggered and pushed her face into her cushy backrest to try and bury her amusement.

"No, I'm *serious*," she continued with a small smirk, "or at least about the, um, the, '*maybe*'." More disappointedly, she continued, "and the police didn't seem to like... Like, that they were going to do anything about it. When I saw them, when I... When I told them who I saw, or, well, *what* I saw, they just brought up that, *transhuman*, stuff."

Realising an incidental omission from her statement, she added, "actually I didn't tell them about the *eyes*. Oh, *man*," but then remembered feeling consternated beneath the officer's offended stare and consequently sculpting the wrong face anyway.

"Wow," Ebee conceded with a hand on her cheek in slight bewilderment, "do you think it's time to leave your job? Those kind of people are dangerous and if you get on the wrong side of them, I think I could imagine the police being slow to act. If they're really, *really?*"

Ebee looked Jack straight in the eye and queried politely, "are you sure the people you saw were like the ones that did all that killing in the forties? It's been a long time. Are these the people; they didn't hurt you?"

Jack flopped back down onto her back and said, "argh," with a pained squint.

"Argh," she more quietly repeated as her grazes screamed out, and added, "ow."

"Are you ok?" Ebee earnestly asked, stepping out of the kitchen.

Jack shook her head and waved Ebee off in agitation and expressed, "I'm fine. Sorry."

'Maybe I should be more reserved,' she then continued to deliberate in her head, matching Ebee's disbelief with her own degree of doubt. 'Do I even know what Breachers are?' she wrestled in her mind for a moment, 'I really did hit that man and truly burn him. And report him and his friends as terrorists.'

"No," she resolutely then decided and sat back up, "it was *really* them. Maybe. Well, not, not *literally*— They weren't *old people*. I wouldn't know that— Oh, well they weren't, but they were in possession of... Well there were *boxes*, and."

Jack cursed quietly to herself and exhaled a frustrated breath.

"And there was a— Oh!" she exclaimed, "I'm not meant to be telling you any of this! Sorry."

"I hope you don't have to kill me now," Ebee quipped.

"No," Jack laughed, deciding to go on despite the potential penalties she may have already earned talking to the police. "There was a jammer, that jams council equipment, and more, and tricks it into connecting to it, like the internet, but it never connects. Because, I suppose, you're always connecting to it, for some reason? And then there was this guy— And it was hidden. And then there was this guy, who I told, I was looking for my Dad."

Ebee dropped half her brow in confusion and wondered aloud, "how *is* your Dad?"

"I don't know," Jack dismissively shrugged, "I don't care."

If Jack's Dad had been in the port with her doing safety checks, she would have gladly left him with the breachers.

"Anyway," Jack pressed on with wide open hands to gesture while Ebee leant against the side of the fridge and listened, "this one guy I confronted, oh with the, *the Dad guy*— There was no Dad though, ok. He had *lights!* In his eyes just like a HUD. And it wasn't those really nice, expensive contacts. There were really lights *inside* his eyes. Like, at the sides, outside of the, iris-s?"

"Ok," Ebee interruptingly acknowledged, "like a prosthetic— "

"And when I hit him," Jack went on, bringing her fingers together solemnly to summarise, "with the stinger," and then point, "on the side of the face, they were gone. The white part went all black as well. And there was a *zoom*, that stopped *zooming*, I guess. It *unzoomed*. Well I didn't see that, after the first zoom; and then *I hit 'em*."

Jack paused for a moment to stop confusing herself, and Ebee.

"I only hit him once," Jack corrected.

"You *hit*," Ebee recited in surprise and gestured with a pointed finger, "you hit someone with your stinger!? What was that like? Did you *hurt him? Are you ok?* What was he doing?" she asked in puzzlement.

With her elbows leaning on the backrest, Jack ran her hands through her hair and cleared her face of a stray lock of fringe. She sat back down on her bottom and inadvertently answered each question, "I don't know... *Yes... Maybe?*" and glumly summarised her entire story, "it was a bad day."

"Are you sure these people were transhumans?" Ebee wondered in serious concern as Jack sat silently and contemplated. "You've got to be careful about those people Jack. It sounds like the police might not be able to distinguish them from the 'transhuman' minority. Maybe they're apprehensive about being sued if they make a mistake?" Gesturing speech marks, she said, "there seems to be too fine a line between 'pro-singularity activist' and 'disabled person who just wants a limb'. Or an eye."

Jack had seen news headlines and speed-read a few quick articles on the subject in recent times but was still bewildered by the cultural shifting in society.

It had been illegal to fit so-called 'gain-of-function prosthetics' for decades but people's attitudes were now changing, and she just couldn't agree with it. Normal human life was to be respected as far as she felt, and recent youthesizer advances had given potential amputees and other patients a new, though, more expensive, avenue to restore themselves. She had even had her own experience in a hospital at age eighteen, when after breaking her leg on Mt Ruapehu, she was brought brochures by a nurse into her room displaying fancy prosthetic alternatives to a cast that she easily rejected in favour of healing.

"What do you know about these people?" she asked, conceding in her mind that she may have hit someone quite a lot more normal than she first thought.

Ebee scratched her head and rubbed her hair back and interestedly explained, "I work with a number of them, *transhumans* that is, at work— Well there's... Four, maybe, in the whole place? But, they say they feel discriminated and just want to be accepted. This one I work with closely, a women named Mina, often brings it all up during breaks and functions with her transhuman buddies and I'm often around. They argue that if a, healthy person without prosthetics can insert chips into their hands or ears, to add functions like, opening doors or, hearing normally inaudible sounds, then a transhuman should be allowed to add things to their parts as well. She also often brings up defibrillators and other electronic organs. Some of those things are really, *really good*," she admitted with an upwards inflection.

Nodding her head, she looked Jack in the eye and stated, "the laws around prosthetics *are* really strict. And the transhumans have been lobbying for years to get the government to relax the laws around it all."

With Jack still listening intently, she stepped into the kitchen and stepped back out, adding, "and currently there is a lot going through parliament about it. They say that by the end of the year it'll be legal to... I don't know, *do a lot.*" After a second to ponder over their discussion in silence, she displayed and insisted happily, *"muffin?"*

Chapter Seven
Friday, 22ⁿᵈ June 2063

Arriving inside the information wardens' quarters the next morning in a mood of uncertainty, Jack put aside her fear and apathy to responsibly proceed straight to her locker and prepare for a normal working day. Expecting to be let go from an assignment that had gone completely awry and be reprimanded kindly by Gerry for breaking protocol, she slipped off an ordinary, light-grey winter jacket she was wearing and exchanged it for her regular black and white uniform.

Having messaged Gerry earlier from home, using Ebee's coder, about losing all her work equipment to a dodgy group of people the night before, she readied herself mentally to pout when he arrived, or go to her happy place when Gelena, currently in her office, poked her head out. She prepared some thoughts that would soon audibly ask Bob to issue her with another, this time complete, work kit and rehearsed some apologetic words she would need to use to rebut his possible decline.

'Sorry,' she stated silently to herself, 'I'm a stupid. I was attacked. The world is ending. *What's that over there?!* '

'I need my kit,' she then solemnly deliberated with a sigh, resting her forehead gently against the locker's cool steel, 'or I'll be unemployed.'

"Is everything alright?" Gerry's cordially concerned voice then fortunately spoke first from behind, "are you ok?"

Jack turned to greet him and pout but was quickly required to think as Gerry determinedly went on in a hushed tone with his head lowered, "you should have been— Oh!" he abruptly uttered, spotting the grazing on Jack's left temple, "you— Do you need a doctor or anything like that?"

"It's not that bad!" Jack disagreed assertively, having assessed it as luckily just a surface wound earlier in front of the bathroom mirror before treating it. "But if you wanna give me sick money, or," she chortled and glanced around at the other readying wardens ignoring them.

"You should have gotten in touch with me as soon as possible!" Gerry sternly counselled with a hushed tone, "I could have gotten the cops out there a lot faster. I might have even gone out there myself!"

Respectfully pointing to emphasise, and irresistibly stare at her wound, he declared, "you know, I told you Jacqueline, you need to take these assignments *seriously*. Sometimes the council will knowingly send us out to bad areas, so you need to be on guard. And most of all, you need to stay out of trouble!"

After sharing his wisdom, he eased off to let Jack reply and stood patiently in his soft-pistachio-coloured polo and white dress pants.

"Are you hurt in more places than that?" he then questioned aloud, pointing and looking her over.

"Nah," Jack replied, pushing his hand safely away, "yeah, well, yeah but nah. I'm gona be fine. I'll tell you about it. But."

Stuttering with her hands and feet, she looked across the quarters and stepped towards Bob's hole in the wall and spoke, "I have to go order a new kit. Is Alex in?"

"You're not taking this seriously," Gerry said more audibly, following Jack through the lounge area. Pointing his thumb over his shoulder, he apprised, "I've just been blasted by a constable and his senior sergeant about sending out wardens who discriminate and run amuck in the city. And then *discharging a stinger?* How am I supposed to deal with that? These officers are warning us about some pretty serious violations."

"Yes, Gerry," Jack responded, rolling her eyes as she approached Bob's faded, pastel-yellow counter to lean over and peer into his cluttered department. She just wanted to get back to work or, more hopefully, catch up with Alex since he was the first to observe the breachers' electronic jamming. She planned to assess some of his data from the day he observed it and discover some intercepts entering and leaving the port's network that could correlate with the innumerous boxes she observed inside the breachers' assembly.

"Alex is off for the next three days," Gerry then informed her, coming to stand on the opposite side of Bob's hole in the wall. "I've been wanting to speak to him as well," he said, itching his back, "why do you wanna see 'em? Same thing? Port Pascoll?"

Standing straight with her uniform hanging over her arm, Jack answered, "if these guys have my HUD and my coder, which they probably do have, then they could find out who I am, and where I live. And all sorts of things. I need to look through Alex's feed from the time he was assigned to, what is it Parnell? Or CBD? To see if I can figure out what the breachers were doing, and find out who they are, and where *they* live, first."

"With your authority," she suggestively clarified and pointed.

Gerry expressed a dubious brow and shook his head in disbelief. Glancing over the others in the space and sighing, he pronounced to Jack and pointed with both hands, "you could get in a lot of trouble. Not from me, but from, the police. *The police*. You understand, right? What, what the situation is?"

"Yes," Jack concisely told him, "the police did tell me, what they told you I suppose. They are crazy. You can't talk to them, or you get arrested. The breacher's are crazy, I mean," she quickly clarified in discontent, "*or* the police? I don't know."

Speaking over Gerry, she continued with a slight shake of her head, "don't hit people, who are a protected species or something. I get it. But *these* guys," she stressed, "really... They probably, *really* have my stuff. They probably, *really* don't like me. Anymore."

Before Gerry could take her words lightly, she asserted, "and I don't hit people! But they were, it was, it was really an operation! They really had a jammer! Well, like re, possibly, most likely it was them. They were, doing things, with— There was boxes! Things are moving! Containers were moving! And they *approached me*, like, real close."

"And then," she spoke again over Gerry who tried to expound, "last night."

"Last night," he repeated, "I got a call from Gelena, who was— She was very upset," he said, animating himself hold a coder away from his ear, "telling me she got a call from the police while at home, around 9:00 pm. She got an email, too, and they told her one of her wardens was, you know, being bad, and that they would hold her accountable, and all this."

Shrugging insouciantly, he went on, "and she calls me, and forwards the email. And repeats it all to me, at about, probably 9:30 pm; I was actually on assignment, just finishing up; and blasts me about *you*. She wants me to deal with *you*."

Jack was starting to worry. Gerry never 'dealt' with her and was her favourite boss because of that fact. 'And he paid better,' she remembered to add.

Taking in a big breath, she pressed her lips together and exhaled relaxingly through her nose and listened.

"And so, I get in touch with Fang later on," Gerry went on, "Councillor Fang, and talk him through what she told me the police told her, and the email etcetera. And Fang talks to Tech. Tech talks to me. And Fang talks to me—

We get in a party," he said with a grouping gesture, "and we establish that, this *is* a problem."

Jack was now worried and opened her mouth to comment but didn't, just pressing her lips together again to listen some more.

Pausing to look up and think, Gerry elaborated, "there is clearly something dodgy going on down at the docks. There is strange jamming. You see dodgy people. You get hurt," he said, pointing openhandedly to her left temple.

"Oh, this was uh, an accident," Jack corrected him, "it was, I got hit by a car."

"You got hit by a car!?" Gerry asked in surprise.

"Yeah," Jack affirmed with a small nod and dispelling look away, "I should tell you everything, write a report, but I gotta work. I mean, I'm guessing I'm off the assignment, you know, cos, I talked to the police? I told my flatmate. I mean it was like, things were *bad*. So, I guess things are over. I can write it in my break, but I would— "

"Yeah, nah, nah, nah," Gerry assured her, waving off her concern, "Gelena doesn't want you," he chuckled. "That's why she's in her office and won't come out till you're gone."

"Are you serious?" Jack earnestly questioned, glimpsing at Gelena's office door and back.

"Oh āe," Gerry persuaded, "i tangohia e koe ōna maikuku katoa."

"Oh, really?" Jack replied with deep concern for her employment, imagining being run out of town by a fiery blaze set upon her by an angry witch named Gelena.

"She think's you've finally taken all your chances," Gerry helped to illustrate, "and she is *furious*. And she's going to go to Mark about this."

"But that's not right!" Jack opined with a frown and respectfully pointed, "I was working for *you!* The cops should have called *you!* "

"Exactly!" Gerry exclaimed affirmatively, "but they didn't, well, not until this morning, but I explained that to Gelena, last night, that the police officers got it wrong and that Gelena should have just passed it along to me. You were on a difficult assignment, for *me*. You were working for *me*. You were my responsibility. And so— "

"So, I'm ok right?" Jack queried, opening her empty palms, "with info? That, that, so, like."

Too lost in her mind to complete a sentence she hadn't thought through, she dropped her hands, catching her uniform before it fell to the floor, and exhaled in despair, not knowing what to do.

She had hurt someone, possibly very dangerous, with a stinger and was scared they were looking to retaliate. The police seemed only interested in building a case against her for assaulting someone with political privileges. And the thin ice beneath her feet at work was being blowtorched.

"Where's Bob?" she then complained to Gerry, "why is *he* not here?"

Easing and appealing to Jack, who was visibly tense, Gerry spoke, "today, I'm gonna get you to write that report, ok?"

"Oh really?" Jack replied a with a degree of relief, "so, I'm still working— "

"Yeah," Gerry nodded, "you'll get half a day to write the report, but um... I don't think it'll be a good idea to hand you back to Gelena right now, anyway."

In a more upbeat attitude, he revealed, "Fang did mention though a desire to keep this going, the assignment and uh. But I won't have you going out on the street, so I guess we'll figure out something for you here, for now. I'll talk to Fang again this morning and see what he wants. He is interested in um."

Watching Gerry struggle to think with his fingers around his forehead, Jack quickly took the opportunity to pitch, "you know, I just want to find these breachers before they find me."

"Yeah, yeah, yeah," Gerry profusely agreed, "and so does Fang. He's convinced there *has* been something going on, and especially now, after this, he wants us to maintain a presence down there somehow. But *you* won't be going down there again please, you're far too special," he tried to woo, clumsily looking over Jack's head in embarrassment.

"But you get it right?" he then refocussed with an inquisitive brow, "the situation with the police. And these... Breachers? Transhuman, types?"

"Oh," Jack groaned and rolled her eyes, "yeah."

"Like, the police are conflicted internally on how to act right now with all the debate going on in the Beehive," Gerry began to enlighten and illustrate with his hands to his left, "on the one side you have, the pro... Going back to pro-singularity type, uh... Whatever that is. And on the other," he illustrated with his hands to his right, "are those who want to keep this stuff in the movies and in videogames."

"Yeah, yeah," Jack informed him, "I've been told. By my flatmate. Last night. After everything went to rubbish. It'll be in the report."

"And so, you have the police," Gerry interestedly continued to share, "who... May or may not have a stake in either side, individually, but are avoiding acting on leads and crimes so they don't run afoul of the politicians, who together, don't know *what* they're doing!"

"Mhmm," Jack mumbled, letting him go on.

"And that leaves people in our line of work in the dark about," Gerry related, "what is worth investigating? Maybe tomorrow we'll be accused of breaking the law by discriminating!"

"Yeah, like last night," Jack commented in boredom and assured, "it'll be in the report."

Not open to believing the police an unbiased or conflicted organisation as much as Gerry was describing, she began looking away in agitation. Bob still wasn't in for her to request a kit that she would need to write on, and Gelena's thickly spectacled, hazel-green eyes were peeking out through her window's blinds into the quarters.

"So uhm," she muttered, looking back to Gerry in discontent, "where's Bob?"

"I don't know," Gerry replied in disinterest and continued to lecture, "look. I uh, have this friend in the force; he was in my batch when I was there and he's a senior constable now here in Auckland, stationed in North Shore. I have lunch with him each week on Fridays and I'll see him later today. I'll see if I can get some help from him, to, understand what we should do to address this, uh, problem. I think I could convince him to take an interest. He says he's a part of an inner circle of officers throughout the region that look into complicated cases where, other police officers have been hesitant to act, and I think he's got some sway with the Armed Offenders Squad, which could be awesome," he buoyed with opened hands. "Anyway, I'll ask him what he thinks and hopefully convince him to guide us on this," he finished, holding up his crossed fingers.

"Gerry!" Bob suddenly greeted from the dim, distal end of the nearest storage aisle inside his den. Approaching and taking a seat at his counter opposite the two waiting, he leaned forward with his arms folded and more contemptuously added, "Jack."

"Bob," Gerry proactively pronounced to alleviate some of Jack's concern, "how long does it take to crack a warden's HUD and coder?"

Bob breathed in and looked up to wonder to himself.

"About," he said clearly before explaining lively though his thick accent, "if you use a code breaking debugger like Octopus, it'll take about thirty days to get through the encryption on a powerful machine."

"A very powerful machine," Jack assumed he repeated after that.

"And Octopus isn't available to just anyone," Bob expounded, "and decryption isn't an exact art, so," he said with a shrug of his round shoulders, "with luck it could be opened up faster. A cracker would be able to access the high-level code with ease and control the device's basic functions but access to all the council information and our servers will be locked away. By the time anyone gets far enough, we would have quarantined the device anyway."

He then spoke unintelligibly, prompting Jack to politely interrupt, "what about messages and things? Personal messages and notes and stuff? And game saves?"

With most, if not all, her personal data being stored on barely a few different cloud servers she logged into the night before on Ebee's devices to update her passwords and biometrics for, she worried about her lost hardware's small memory cache. Therein she could only hope wasn't a record of her typing and communications, or favourite recipes and terrible Space Flight Simulator landings.

Heeding Jack's concern, Gerry looked at Bob for him to answer and coaxed, "how easy would it be to access the warden's personal data? Anything left on the device?"

"We, that depends," Bob discussed to Gerry, "where did they leave it?"

After a quiet pause amongst the three, he added, "any downloaded programmes might not have very high security when compared to the council portal software, but other streaming programmes like Outlook are pretty solid. Any other programmes requiring a brain scan for access should be hard to crack too, similar to the council portal. This isn't about the hardware Tamati was telling me about earlier, is it?"

Gerry nodded his head very slightly and inquired, "Tamati from Tech?"

"Yes," Bob replied, wiping off a drop of sweat developing on his forehead, "he was just telling me we have quarantined two devices. That's where I've just come from."

"I need to order a new kit please, Bob," Jack had to mention, "with the stinger."

After a brief second to process the request, Bob incredulously replied, sitting up in his chair, "sheesh Jack! Is it you!? You were just given a new device! You lost it *already?*"

"What if these crackers were breachers Bob?" Gerry refocused the discussion with an assertive wave to grab Bob's attention.

"Breachers?!" Bob remarked in surprise, "oh sheesh, Jack, you're unbelievable. Maybe now, maybe tomorrow."

"We're not saying they are Bob," Gerry then assuaged him with a calming palm, "it was just a question: how long could it take people like that to break through the hardware's security?"

Not particularly assuaged, Bob glanced at Jack in displeasure and hypothesised to Gerry, "breachers are obsessively good with electronics, and Jack's password is probably 'Jack'. Jack's brain scan signature is probably, 'Jack'. I would assume they're already in. And that's why Tamati has quarantined the devices but it may be too late," he realised in displeasure.

"How long will it really take them do you think?" Gerry asked and urged, "and Jack needs some new hardware to write me a report."

Bob's tone quietened as he proceeded to think to himself about the news with his hands rested on his thighs while a small frown formed on his face. "They'll be already in the hardware," he mumbled and muttered. "Without a brain scan it could take some time before they could access the council servers and other complex programmes but they could already have a brain scan from someone like Alex, who is as smart as a robot; they could probably just guess what his brain scan signature is. It'd be easier than Jack's. *'Robot',*" he mocked.

Both Gerry and Jack rolled their eyes as Bob's belittling did little to console their concerns.

"They could have got it from Julie," Bob then accusingly proposed with a directing nod of his head to Jack's strawberry blonde co-worker sitting patiently by herself on the longest couch in the lounge area, "she's one of them, isn't she?"

Gerry sneered and retorted on Julie's oblivious behalf, glancing at her and back, "Julie's got an electronic liver. Not a missile for a hand."

He then looked at Jack reassuringly and commented, "I'll have to talk to Tamati about re-securing everyone's info on the servers."

"He's already doing that," Bob commented and subsequently ranted unintelligibly.

"You could always just delete my account on the servers?" Jack hopefully suggested to Gerry, figuring it a way to severe her hackable line into the council, "and we could just restart one afresh?"

Abruptly, Bob scolded, "no. It is illegal for the council to delete any information without an ok from the Ministry. And even then," he said with a doubtful shrug of his shoulders, "did you even *see a breacher?* That's a big statement."

"Well, it doesn't matter does it," Gerry critiqued of his scepticism, "anyone could crack the software. And no one necessarily saw any breacher. I was just saying."

"Hey," he then addressed Jack politely, "maybe we'll get you to do that report at home, take the day off here and write it there."

Guiding them both a couple steps away from the counter to chat, he quickly reminded Bob, "hey, we want that new kit now alright. Charge the old one to us," he said to Jack's great relief.

"Oh," she expressed in gratitude, "really? Wow, thanks."

"Nah," Gerry replied reassuringly, "you were on a dangerous assignment. These things can happen to any warden."

"You should stay at my place," he then suggested, putting his foot in his mouth, "for protection."

Jack sniggered and instantly thought, 'no.' She wasn't interested in developing a close relationship with a big-brotherly figure and believed her Charterton apartment to be quite a lot more luxurious than his Henderson flat. There was also a small team of security guards constantly manning her building's lobby while Gerry, despite being six-foot-eight, was only one man who would be absent all the time, and didn't even have a dog.

"How about I come back in when Alex comes back in?" she said, "in three days. I'll have the weekend off and Monday, then come in and catch up with him about his data?"

"I could keep you safe at my place," Gerry tried to persuade and improve his luck a bit more, "you wouldn't always be alone. I could go out and get groceries for you. It would be a *different* address."

Jack's face scrunched up in embarrassment for him.

"It's not *that* bad," she opposed in amusement. "I've got Ebee with me at home, and we've got a security group who operates there— "

"What about when you're out on the street?" Gerry interrupted with open palms, "your apartment security won't be able to help you if these guys come for you outside."

"*You* couldn't protect me outside!" Jack declared with a pointed finger, "these guys were huge! What I'll do is have the weekend off, and Monday, and if anything happens or I get worried, then I might need to stay at your place. Actually, I *will* call you on Monday night so you can tell me where I'll be working, or not. Or how this will go," she said, glancing at Gelena's office windows.

Gerry agreed with her vehemently and glimpsed over his shoulder at Gelena's cold office windows too, before sagging his shoulders in disappointment. "You could be off for a bit," he conceded to Jack.

"Gerry," Bob then called with three small multicoloured boxes rested upon his counter, "your order is ready."

Stepping to retrieve them with a grateful grin, Gerry reminded him, "just charge it to Assignments," and brought them back to Jack for her to hold. "Oh, I could bring them home for you, with you?"

"Oh for— Thanks," Jack said, rolling her eyes dismissively, and clutched the goods, "I'll get that— No, I'm fine. I'll write that report and call you Monday."

Holding the boxes beneath her arms, she turned around and walked back to her locker to rest them atop and hang back up her uniform.

"I should come check on you over the weekend and *see* you Monday instead!" Gerry then tried to renegotiate.

Scoffing a chuckle and shaking her head in amusement, Jack smirked and shut her locker.

"How about later tonight!?" Gerry enthusiastically offered, "after work?"

"No," Jack lipped back at him and shook her head with her new boxes in her hands while walking on to the exit. "I'm going to be fine," she said a little louder and reassured, "I don't need to be babysat."

Gerry persevered, gesturing across the quarters, "I should call you though! Every day! Just to make sure you're ok."

Jack balanced her boxes just before the door and put up her hand to send him a calming wave.

"I could stand outside your door!" Gerry foolishly proclaimed.

"We'll be fine," Jack politely dismissed.

She then turned to exit when she heard Bob jibe, "yes Gerry. Leave her alone Gerry. Handsome Bob will take care of her instead. You're pathetic." Chortling quietly as she started up the stairs, she listened to him lecture encouragingly, "you just take her by the hand, and you slip a ring on that finger. But she'd probably lose it anyway."

Jack returned to her apartment to reconfigure and resync her new HUD and coder and begin writing a report for Gerry but soon became bored by herself and distracted.

Searching out her favourite recipes again and downloading her usual software, she resumed her latest flight back to Earth in the digital cockpit of an SR-78 and almost instantly caused it to disintegrate in the mesosphere.

She then sat around for a couple more hours writing only a few more words before planning a beef lasagne dish she was going to surprise Ebee with for dinner.

Finding out just before five that Ebee would only be returning to pack for a weekend getaway in Taupo to once again satisfy her extracurricular roll as part of her regional manager's constantly absconding entourage, she put her beef lasagne on hold and wilfully crashed another SR-78.

Helping Ebee pack while listening to her talk about her overloaded day, she assured her everything would be fine at home so Ebee could freely enjoy her well-deserved getaway and wished her luck and gave her a tight hug down in the lobby.

She watched her enter convivially inside her manager's black liftback-limo outside and depart before promptly retiring back up to her apartment peradventure the next car to arrive would be a darkly coloured Holden SUV come to pick *her* up.

Spending the drizzly weekend eating cheese toasted sandwiches, playing games and watching movies and programmes on Ebee's account, Jack let the time pass without her until Ebee arrived back home in the early hours of Monday morning and Gerry called her later that afternoon about work.

Learning that Gerry had organised with Mark, the lower council departments' unified manager, for her to have three paid sick days off to avoid her begrudging supervisor, Gelena, a little longer, she went back to flying spacecrafts into the atmosphere and finishing making her beef lasagne.

Learning the following Thursday, however, that Gelena had successfully harangued Mark into suspending her for the entire following week without pay as an accumulative punishment for a generally poor performance caused her to feel sick and give up thinking about work all together.

At the end of a cold and windy, wet day a week later, after helping the vacuum bot clean the apartment from top to bottom for an upcoming inspection, Jack was lying back along her favourite couch with her feet up in the dark, watching the rain pour heavily outside.

Observing large adsorbed drops zigzag down the glass and streams of water streak diagonally with the wind, she bathed silently in just the shimmering light emanating from the bright billboards hanging across the street.

"Hey Jack?" Ebee inquired coming out of her room in her pyjamas, "did you see that announcement about my work today?"

Having arrived home from work a lot later than her usual lateness and a lot more tired, and bearing an apologetic kea burger combo for Jack to gobble down after her long day of cleaning, she rubbed her puffy eyes and approached the end of the couch.

"No," Jack replied, contracting her legs to make room for Ebee. "I hope you still have a job?" she chortled, pivoting on her bottom to lower her feet and lean sideways into her cushions.

"Oh yeah," Ebee reassured while plucking Jack's coder from off the coffee table to turn on the large three-metre lounge screen affixed to the wall opposite them, "are you just watching the rain, are you?"

"Yeah," Jack said, watching Ebee search about her work on the screen.

"It was the fourth of July yesterday in the States, or today or whenever," Ebee spoke pleasantly and sat on the couch, "and last night my work used that afternoon to announce some changes."

"Oh," Jack sadly replied, being less than impressed with the changes happening of late.

"I've been waiting for this for ages," Ebee went on while looking between the coder and the big screen to bring up a video for them both to watch, "and I want you to watch this with me please, this is *really* important for the both of us. But maybe just the last five minutes tonight, since it's kind of late and I've got to start early tomorrow— You didn't see this yet?" she abruptly inquired, pointing toward the screen with the coder.

"No," Jack assumed having done little more that day than follow their robot around the apartment, fail a few spacecraft landings and scoff the kea burger combo Ebee brought home.

"About the thing?" Ebee inquired further.

"No," Jack said with a hint of doubt.

"The big thing?" Ebee inquired even further.

Jack looked across to the pixels glowing on the wall and read, 'RF Space Announces Next Phase,' above an embedded video and guessed, "something about their station?"

"Oh, you did see it?" Ebee said with a degree of deflation.

"No," Jack assured her.

She knew Ebee's employer, RF Space, like the local space corporation, Expineer, was scheduled to launch their great station this part of the century, after being under constant construction for the last ten years, and so easily presumed any news would reflect that. Ebee's job after all, as a human resources officer for RF Space, was to help manage a liaison team here in New Zealand communicate with Expineer about Expineer's own behemoth, the EX-1, lying half-buried alongside Auckland's spaceport. 'They share a common architecture, or something?' she roughly recalled hearing, reading and watching over the years.

"Ok," Ebee conceded, and informed, "well there was a build up and stuff, all this, American stuff. They showed off new mining shafts in Marius— Which is *huge*. A new laser-cutting, thing, on a big drone in space that you could watch, if you wanted. It's for— Are you hungry or anything?" she then queried with an upwards inflection, "want some popcorn?"

"No," Jack told her with an appreciative smile. She was currently on a fast, letting the oil, carbs and sugars from the burger, kumara chips and L&P digest slowly in her bloated tummy. Definitely not keen on delaying that process by adding cholesterol, she assured and gestured for a pause, "I'm still full."

"Ok," Ebee said, waggling closer to Jack to put her arm around her and squeeze. "It's only the last five minutes anyway. Let's just watch!" she exclaimed and whooped tiredly.

Jack sat quietly inside Ebee's cuddling arm in a more neutral mood waiting for her to select a frame containing a tall, dark-grey haired businessman sporting a slate-coloured designer suit on a broad, darkly decorated stage, about to address an out-of-frame audience. Middle-aged and pleasant looking in a light-blue shirt and silver tie barely visible beneath his buttoned jacket, the cleanly shaven man stood ready to speak with his hands cupped and eyes warmly gazing above an overlay introducing him as, 'CEO of RF Space Corporation, Aaron Heslop.'

"That's Aaron Heslop, our CEO," Ebee declared with an awakening pride, "I shook his hand once when he came to New Zealand. He's tall. Handsome, clean, healthy. *Generous.* I think he's actually a bit older than he looks— It can be hard to tell with all the youthesizer therapies out there and stuff. He has a daughter— "

"*Let's just watch*," she then said, scrunching her face.

"Personally apologise for the delay this afternoon," the CEO welcomingly began with an American accent as the corporation's royal blue, bold and italicised impact-font logo, 'RF SPACE,' glowed behind him upon a huge, black digital backdrop, "I was a little too wrapped up in my other responsibilities and enjoying my small family's company this great day... And it has been a great day," he emphasised with an assertive two-handed gesture, "a great day

151

celebrating our independence from foreign governments, who don't share our values, and even just from those of whom we once descended."

Jack rolled her eyes in scepticism as the video was post-processed more into life with a subtle 3D.

"RF Space, since its inception," the CEO more boldly went on as the logo behind blended into a widely spanning, video presentation, "has always operated with that same philosophy of independence since when right at first, RF Earth, began extracting rich ores in Rouyn-Noranda from the deepest depths of this great continent. Halfway through bringing a million tons of silver to the surface to be used in medical applications and electronics, and three thousand tons of zinc to be used in construction and astronautics, it continued to assert that independence when pioneering attritive bore mining in Madison. Co-developing and employing a fleet of autonomous borers, RF Earth excavated more thoroughly and rapidly though hard rock than *anyone* had ever done before, creating wealth for the surrounding community and furthering humanity's technological progression."

Orating a little louder and more confidently as his video demonstration kept up, he stated, "that independence was again demonstrated with the acquisition of Declan and Declan Space and Autokine Systems to evolve RF Earth into to the world's most *capable* Luna excavating corporation, RF Space, to become the first independent corporation to successfully and sustainably, land, excavate, extract, transact, distribute and profit from the rich ores of the moon. All while housing beautiful, breathing, living, playing, loving human families upon its surface in perpetuity."

Jack was moved to hear those words from the grinning man, as was an out-of-frame crowd erupting respectfully in applause.

Already understanding there to be a few handfuls of people inhabiting extraterrestrial pockets on the moon and Mars and a few small stations in orbit, Jack hummed to herself in pleasure and recalled a period in her childhood she spent reading Ebee's space books on Ebee's bedroom floor in her free time. She recalled watching bits and pieces in those books come to life in articles and videos and around the skies above the city's spaceport as she grew through her teens and remembered becoming quite excited about the future. 'Right up until I became an info warden,' she subsequently remembered in disappointment, reflecting unfavourably on her less than stellar, surprisingly sedate adult life since.

'But it's still been good,' she countered, peeking at Ebee in appreciation.

With the camera in the clip switching to show two other smiling executives standing on stage in their business wear fondly observing and clapping with the crowd as they were all regaled, the camera cut back to the CEO.

"Today, on this day," he spoke even louder with his hands up to hush the applause, "it will my pleasure to announce the next phase in this great corporation's story, a story of independence and work. Ingenuity and innovation. A story with a rich history of *people* who worked and endured over the years and months and days to bring us to where we are today."

"A story about a people with *great power!*" he lively remarked to applause, "*you people*, of RF Space, operating at our Marius campus on Luna and various exploration sites throughout the inner solar system. *You people*, of RF Space, working in our mines, plants, offices, hangars and laboratories. And *you people* of North America and abroad," he emphasised, "who helped build our vast infrastructure here in Florida. Who fed our workers, laboured along our concourses and delivered from our mines and associate suppliers the never-ending extrusion of resources needed to build our utopia, with all your hard work, and sweat."

"And blood," he more solemnly included with his hands clasped, "and belief... I hope good fortune smiles upon you all... Because I do."

"Hm," Jack very slightly chortled and shook her head in disbelief. She never expected to hear space jobs be spoken of quite so naturally in her lifetime, even by a space corporation's slightly conceited CEO. She could easily comprehend building, feeding, labouring and delivering because she saw people doing that every day, but hearing 'operating on the moon' and 'exploring the solar system' be mentioned in the same paragraph as 'hard work and sweat' intrigued her.

In all the videos she glimpsed at in recent years showcasing astronauts operate machinery in space and survey subterranean corridors on the moon, she only ever saw unrealistically talented and privileged people feature in them, who all might as well have been created using CGI.

The real human beings she knew personally and had grown around, besides Ebee and her parents, weren't talented or privileged, and were fallible, and didn't know everything, and were stuck working low-paying jobs on the ground, forking out for gouging power and water bills and missing rent payments. A lot of them didn't even actually have jobs, or plumbing, doing their living beneath old discarded, rusting sheets of roofing iron atop a damp dirt floor. She could barely even imagine those she knew from school who were currently working hard and sweating on Expineer's station, still half-buried beside the spaceport, operating in a space suit and drilling holes into the moon.

And the fact too that so many politicians and commentators online, and lessons taught during her schooling, actually linked the world's surging poverty to the so-called 'necessary concentration of wealth' around the space industry caused her no small degree of resentment towards those wealthy elites privileging from it.

'And yet, here I am now being impressed by one of them,' she mused.

"Does RF Space do mining?" she subsequently asked Ebee in genuine confusion.

"*Yeah,*" Ebee replied in surprise with a brief glimpse back.

"Oh," Jack mumbled and humbly returned her gaze back to the video.

"It then becomes my pleasure, at this time," the CEO appreciatively declared directly to one half of his audience and emphasised, "on this great day. To announce that after more than ten years of meticulous planning and full-scale construction," he spoke, turning to address the entire audience, "both here on Earth, at our Cape Canaveral campus and numerous international support offices, and in orbit, aboard our RF-A6 space station, Angel, that we are proud to announce the launch date of our RF-J1 superstation, Hope."

Waiting for a few seconds to let the audience buzz, he then pronounced, "eight, twenty-seven, twenty-sixty-three," as the numbers appeared simultaneously behind him in RF Space's bold and italicised, blue impact font.

The crowd applauded rapturously as he casually communicated and gestured with a smile, "that's in two months," to someone sitting at the edge of the stage. "Two months," he repeated to another further along before strolling on and clapping with the crowd.

"Hope will initially launch with a skeleton crew," the CEO explained over a chant trying to break out, "and once safely in orbit, will immediately manoeuvre into position to begin its reign over the HHC, or Hope Hemispheric Control. Soon thereafter, it will begin receiving the essential operators to switch on its living systems before shortly opening its gates to the rest of the two hundred and fifty thousand staff and guests that will inhabit its wonderful living spaces over the following year."

After waiting and intermittently nodding for nearly a minute for the crowd's joyous applause to subside, he added, "it then becomes my pleasure again, to announce a new title for this new chapter in our corporation's story."

Ebee bobbed and squeezed Jack tighter again to keep her best friend's interest focussed on the proceedings.

"After months of thoughtful consideration and debate among the many executives and specialists at RF Space," the CEO congenially disclosed, "and many meetings with our investors, a decision was reached to once again evolve the name of our company to match our evolved direction and vision."

Jack watched the stage lights fade to black and the backdrop cut to the name 'RF EARTH' overlaying a sped-up series of snippets showing the corporation's founding and early work to a rousing score about beginnings.

Starting with caves and shafts and manned extractions of ore out of the Earth followed by the development and implementation of cylindrical robots, the montage was overlaid with the word 'BECOMES' before switching to 'RF SPACE' atop a boardroom and lifting its melody to inspire a feeling of progress.

Showing technicians fiddling in an astronautical hanger and then workers clearing a runway, the montage ramped up its score to promote a rocket launch before another, and then another. Showing one ascend into orbit above the American continent and dock delicately with a substantial space station, it then presented, to a triumphant score, a moon landing and digging and carving and excavating from its ashy grey surface. 'BECOMES' once again overlaid clips of robots extracting ore from extraterrestrial locations before the score climaxed, championing the company's new name, 'AH HOPE,' above their campus back down on Earth.

Showing a time-lapse of their superstation growing out of the grass between a bulwark of gentries and cranes before parting the bulwark to present the station's luminous silvery lustre, the video then diverted the camera upwards back to the sky and onwards between the traffic of space shuttles into the starry space of the solar system.

'*Wow!*' Jack thought in astonishment and sniffled as a joyous tear slid down her face and the score calmed and quietened.

"We want the world to understand," the CEO's prerecorded voice spoke over the starry background overlaid by 'AH HOPE', "that under our wing, humanity will have a more prosperous place in the future. We want the world to understand, that this will not be Hope for some. This will be Hope, for all."

"I'M GOING TO SPACE JACK!" Ebee exclaimed enthusiastically, throwing her hands up in the air in excitement.

Jack ducked her vivaciousness and watched the video close out while trying to process Ebee's announcement.

"They'll be going up on the twenty-seventh of August," Ebee excitedly informed, "putting the station up in orbit and organising the air and water and heat and stuff, and then *I'll be going up a couple months later!"*

Jack's eyebrows rose with both surprise and concern as she immediately wondered what that would mean for her. The revelation of going to space was *amazing*, as was the deduction Ebee's lifestyle-sustaining income would be going with her.

"I'm getting a job in *immigration!"* Ebee jovially exclaimed.

Joyful to hear it, and worried, and a little guilty-feeling, Jack waited in bewilderment for her sleepy brain to process which of the emotions she was going to concentrate on and elicit. Chortling a contraction and pausing in astonishment, she chortled a contraction again and hummed with an approving smile. "Wow," her brain kindly threw out in the meantime.

"It's going to be full-on," Ebee raved, "there's going to be, like, three hundred, or like six hundred people boarding *a day*, all with various visas and occupations. I'm going to have to follow them up and make sure they're occupied, and *breathing*," she joked.

"Ergh," Jack responded positively while struggling to discard to logical fact that without Ebee, she would have nowhere to live, leading to a lot more unwanted changes, and a potential stop in her breathing.

"Oh, you don't have to worry Jack," Ebee then assured her with a dispelling frown and wave, "I've paid the lease on the apartment till the end of the year, and I'll help you find a new place before then."

"Ergh," Jack responded pragmatically, and cheered as jovially as her befuddled brain could dribble, "wow... This is going to be huge."

"This is going to be *huge*," Ebee repeated with more elation, looking back at the screen while becoming teary eyed and speechless.

"Em," Jack apprehensively agreed, looking back at the screen while becoming teary eyed and speechless too, but not quite for the same reason.

The two barely slept during that night, Ebee being overtired due to excitement, and Jack being extremely alert due to worry.

Jack couldn't stop thinking from beneath her bed blankets that her big sister, who had looked after her since primary, was going to leave, and for good, and that she, Jack, was going to have to start taking on the world as an adult alone. 'I'm not even ready,' she told herself while remembering thinking solemn thoughts about Ebee growing on in the past.

Unable to imagine any other financial path forward without Ebee other than one straight back into the grime and greasiness of the squatters where she would wallow for the rest of her life, she worried until her tummy began to ache. Unable then to imagine the breachers, she had very seriously disturbed, finding it hard to descend upon her where there were no door locks or security guards to deter them, she worried until her tummy began to cramp.

Jack went back to work the following Monday after her two-weeks of sick leave and suspension and resumed her regular duties as an info warden.

She arrived in the council basement fifteen minutes before her day shift began and dressed reluctantly into her dichromatic uniform. She slipped her HUD and coder in her coat, placing her stinger more apprehensively inside her cargo pocket, and submissively sat down for an impromptu team meeting.

Listening to Gelena warn her indirectly, in front of Mark, about the innumerous amount of unemployed people out there ready to take her job if she underperformed, she nodded in humiliation when eyed and pressed her lips together in shame when it was her turn to agree to Gelena's admonitions.

Going back out onto the streets in a mood of melancholy, she dragged her feet between the cold winter crowds to the transport hub and down into the train station to slump onto a train seat and sink back into despondency.

'It's all changing so quickly,' she contemplated while viewing the live ads along the station wall pitch new HUDs and drone-ready lunchboxes as they went backward through the windows.

'Another day, another... Day,' she sighed while disembarking in Henderson to begin receiving the public's scorn.

"Hm," she sighed a moment later, passing a group of genuinely enfeebled poor people in inadequate clothing beg on their bottoms straight outside the suburb's transport hub for money. 'You look like me,' she commented to herself as memories from her time begging around stations, and from in between hotels in her adolescence, came into her mind.

'Right before the police come to take you back behind the walls,' she further remembered and predicted.

Going on to file Henderson's intercepts through the week and triangulate three people within the area planning a protest online with other residents elsewhere regarding some new jaywalking laws being enacted soon, she saw out her week very slowly, barely passing the minimum report ratio. And not just because she didn't enjoy the work and was lazy, or feared the public's scorn and snares and reduced her output accordingly, even sympathetically, but because of a succession of late nights she spent up at home conversing with Ebee about life's mysteries.

Keeping her sane through this serious time of change, and subsequently lethargic the following day, the conversations about anything from the differences between the girls' toenails and eyelashes to the work Ebee's employer, now called AH Hope, did off-world was succouring, even if only until the next afternoon.

But Ebee didn't relent trying to cheer Jack up each evening she was home, persistently enlightening her that space was never going to be very far away and regularly reassuring her that Ebee knew who Jack was, and was never going to forget it.

During one quiet Monday morning deep inside the council basement, Jack was slouching forward on a steel fold-up chair in front of a computer terminal, pouring over an old collection of Assignments Department data. Currently off-duty and dressed in her comfortable pair of grey marl trackpants and a black singlet, and sitting ahead of a black jersey and jacket hanging over her seatback, she was sifting through a cable of messages for anything untoward, or army-green and seven-foot tall.

As something of a mutually beneficial arrangement with Gerry, she was going over his systematically downloaded cache of assignment wardens' intercepts and captures to search for alert words, phrases and people from throughout the city while rebuilding back her ruined reputation by working for free. 'Or at least just building a reputation,' she contemplated, wondering if she ever really had one worth rebuilding.

Planning to benefit mostly, however, by discovering clues about the shady people she encountered at Port Pascoll, the very people she held responsible for ruining her reputation in the first place, 'besides that policeman,' she grumbled in displeasure, she sat quietly by herself inside the mint-cream office and worked.

"Hey," one of her male co-workers meekly greeted from the doorway, "you asked to see me?"

Looking past her left shoulder to see Alex, an unimposing, lightly pimpled and pale twenty-year old with short, wavy, reddish-brown hair, balancing against the door jamb, Jack nicely replied, "hey, yeah," and adjusted her sagging posture on her creaky seat.

"Are you not cold?" Alex asked, stepping in to fetch and unfold a chair of his own to place on the floor beside her. Dressed in a thick woollen silver jumper and black plants, atop a pair of untied basketball boots, he sat down facing the computer terminal and expired, rubbing his frozen hands together, "so are you working for Gerry, for, like, *real?* Or are you just snooping on Aucklanders for fun?"

Jack chortled while cataloguing another completed facial scan, and replied, "um. Emm," in uncertainty. She was definitely doing work for Gerry, but not to the exclusion of snooping on Aucklanders like Alex semantically suggested.

"Well you've been working in Assignments now, eh?" she said, cleverly shifting the moral dilemma to Alex, "so how is the snooping going?"

"It's going very good," Alex admitted with an upwards inflection and sat forward to rest his elbows upon his knees.

"Are you having fun?" Jack probed him further.

"Nah, it's quite boring, really," he stated, and sceptically scrunched his face, leaning back, "I like the mufti, though, wearing anything I want and going unnoticed. It's like I'm normal, and everyone else is spying on me for a change, those scum."

Jack chuckled aloud and pushed herself back in her chair with an amused grin.

Alex was a constant kidder, always possessing a light-hearted sense of humour, and freely dispensed clever jibes wherever life sent him. He was also a nerd and visibly frail for a taller boy, bearing an unthreatening demeanour, and never expressed much pride in himself despite his sharp wit.

Jack figured this was due to a history of being bullied throughout his school years where any arrogant bones he bore had been broken, or bent due to some moment he carelessly stepped out onto a rugby field. However embarrassing it was, though, that he came to be, Jack liked his company and regarded his friendship dearly.

"And I get paid a bit more," Alex dribbled.

Pausing to digest that last comment and contrast it with her experience of being paid *a lot* more when she did paid work in Assignments, Jack lifted a sceptical brow and wondered. While regarding Alex's friendship dearly, she also regarded him as someone who should be getting paid less than her as an information warden, especially as she had been one for much, much longer.

"What are you doing now?" Alex unwittingly moved Jack's thoughts along, pointing to and staring at the computer terminal's monitor, "I hear you're supposed to be working in Otara. Is that a, is that. Are you meant to be there now? I'd hate to get in trouble for, you know. *Being* around you."

"I'm working nights," Jack told him, resuming her work on the terminal, "late nights."

"Wow, that's a little rough," Alex pitied and inquired, "do you have your licence yet?"

Otara had always been considered a dangerous area overrun by gangs, but Jack, in her own experience, had found it to be otherwise. "It's no *Topher*," she opined, opening a list of IRD numbers in front of her to cross-reference her latest facial scan with.

"But you're walking around there at night," Alex cautioned her, "you really should be in a council car. You need to get your licence."

Unimpressed with the requirement for a driver's licence when all the council cars were self-driving, Jack replied, "but it's stupid that I'd need it when I wouldn't ever actually drive. And if it broke down, I'd have to wait with it. I couldn't fix it— Remember what happened to Pierre?"

"You're so stubborn," Alex criticised supportively, "and Pierre was asking for it. Just get your licence and you wouldn't have to stroll around at night in Otara."

Ignoring a debate and sudden wearing of Alex's charm, Jack steered the conversation back toward the monitor in front of her with a directing wave of her hand.

"This is a series of footage from your *other* HUD since you've been working in Port Pascoll," she said, pointing to a paused video occupying the vertical left half of the screen, "and this is the council's national IRD access," she said of a numerical list of tax numbers, pointing to the right. "Under here is a facial scanning programme made by the Wholscan developers," she further showed beneath the windows, "and your list of intercepts you got that day. It's very small— "

"I am being spied on?" Alex uttered in bewilderment and looked at Jack to facetiously tease, "you scum... And that other coder is my *own* other, *personal* coder. How did you get that on here?"

Smiling back at him in mutual appreciation, Jack nodded, and explained, "you submitted it, to Gerry. And so, I've been cross-referencing whichever faces your non-council-issued— Your personal coder, has been recording with the IRD database to find out who they are, and maybe where they're spending their money."

"Oh," Alex remembered in astonishment and joked about the dubiousness of Jack's current work, "you're evil."

"Just doing my job," Jack happily retorted.

"So, you think you've found some bad guys in all these numbers?" Alex sceptically asked, waving his index finger between the video and tax database. "Are they accountants?" he quipped.

Jack breathed out a laugh at his comments and responded, "accountants are only bad to you Alex."

"Yeah, tell me about it," he promptly replied and sat back, "my flatmate's dad is an accountant who thinks I'm a stain."

"Yeah," Alex reiterated to Jack's slightly stunned, and largely amused, glimpse, "a *stain*. He told him I was a stain and needed to be washed out."

The two chuckled for a moment before Jack felt the need to compliment him and lift his spirits.

"You're not a stain Alex, don't worry," she assured him with a cordial brow, "you're more of a blemish."

"Thanks," Alex replied and took a deep unimpressed breath.

"Does Mark know you're doing this, by the way?" he then queried in earnest, "being here right now? On the, IRD thingy?"

Before Jack could respond, he queried further, "does *Gelena* know you're doing this?"

"I don't care," Jack immediately exclaimed about Gelena and slouched back in her chair, "she's not the boss. And I'm off duty. And Gelena's not allowed in here. And I made sure to tell Gerry to explain that to her."

"Have you told *Gelena* that?" Alex incredulously commented, and quickly added, "have you told *Mark* that?"

"It's fine," Jack asserted and giggled about Mark's weak leadership, "he's fine."

"And how do you always get Gerry to do things for you?" Alex questioned with a curious brow, "and how are you always in Assignments? Are you guys an item?"

"No," Jack concisely explained, "we're friends," and looked back at the monitor, "like you and me."

"Hm," Alex muttered.

He then turned his torso to lean his right side against and hang his folded right arm over his seatback and wonder aloud, "does he think you're bossy too?"

Jack grinned cynically and proceeded to explain the reason she had asked Gerry to instruct Alex to come in and meet with her. "There's a lot going on at the port," she proclaimed, with a two-handed assuring gesture, "lots of orders and movement, but some of them are probably happening under the radar. That's why you're here. That's why you've been going down there, for... Four weeks," she added in jealousy.

JACQUELINE HART CITIZEN PART ONE

"Yeah," Alex unenthusiastically agreed, being perfectly aware of the movement at the port after working there for so long, "you know, you're not supposed to know that."

"And so, what I've been doing," Jack spoke, "a bit over the weekend, when Gerry was in, and now, is, using your footage to search for faces and people, and data to search for communications."

"Yeah," Alex unenthusiastically repeated, "there's not much. Data, that is."

"And that's ok," Jack replied, pointing upward and enlightening, "because after these four, um."

Being distracted by their contrasting situations, she then diverted to mutter, "four entire weeks... Of getting paid more. In mufti. In Assignments— "

"Wai, wai, wait, I was listening," Alex told her in slight frustration, wiggling his hand, "and then you went off. You had me there for a second with the data. And then you went off."

Sighing and taking in a deep breath, Jack refocussed with a two-handed gesture, and exhaled. "Does?" she queried, "what did Gelena say, about you working for, four weeks? Are you actually *in* Assignments now, for like, *forever*— "

"Nah, nah, nah, this, this," Alex asserted with a dismissive wave and pointed to the computer, "you've got my attention. Come on, it's really short. Can you get through this?"

"Ok," Jack conceded, deliberately putting aside her sense of unfairness and increasing dissatisfaction, "umm. I've been filtering your intercepts, the few that you have been getting, cos of the bollards, right?"

168

"Yeah," Alex agreed and nodded and rolled his hand encouragingly, "the poles screwing up my connection all day to the council. I think they transmit a stronger, sort of, pirating signal— "

"And I've been filtering out the weak intercepts," Jack continued to speak over him, "the one's received with relatively very low signal strength— "

"Yeah," Alex agreed and rolled his hand again, "coming from distant cell transmitters and such."

"Yeah," Jack stated, "and filtered for just those, likely having been transmitted from nearer your, likely from coders and HUDs, nearer your, *actual* position."

"Uh huh," Alex coaxed, bobbing his head in urgency, "yeah."

"Are you ok?" Jack suddenly paused to ask in irritation and frown.

"I need to go toilet," Alex promptly informed while keeping his eyes forward to encourage her to press on.

"Oh," Jack courteously replied and obligingly pressed on, "well. The um. I did a search through the filtered intercepts— The strong ones, there is about eleven hundred over those four weeks, looking for slang and things, signs of irregular people kind of working there, cos the dock workers, some of them might be in on this, maybe, you know— "

"Ok," Alex said, hurrying her some more.

"Uh, and *I found something*," Jack happily revealed.

"Ok," Alex repeated, hurrying her some more again.

"Random electronic receipts without any titles and stuff," Jack explained, "and some messages possibly discussing their orders."

"Devious," Alex stated and pointed, standing up to prepare to exit, "*you, devious, I mean.* This has got to be illegal."

"And anyway," Jack went on to elaborate with a shrug, "they discuss objects like caps and digits, and here," she pointed out, "*thighs.*" Bringing to the front of the monitor's windows a specific list of cut and pasted snippets, she highlighted, "all being sold with these codes, nearly once a week as shown on these informal receipts. Numbers of B10, B11 and B12. J8, J9, J10, J11 and so on."

"Yeah, ok," Alex uttered with an ungrateful fidget by the doorway, "you nearly done?"

"Yeah," Jack assured him, surmising, "well, I think I recognise, this, like I've seen this type of thing before. When I was in hospital ages ago," she asserted, looking at Alex.

"Yeah, ok," Alex courteously goaded, and jiggled, "do tell."

"When I was eighteen, I broke my leg up at Turoa," Jack told of one of her early snow trips, "and I was in a bad way, bad enough that the doctors were handing me magazines for prosthetic replacements all day, as was the craze. I healed fine though without any plastic, but one of the models that I, decided on, just in case was the J11, by Alternate Reality— A left leg. There were J11 arms," she gestured, "fingers, feet... Kneecaps all through these magazines. Alternate Reality was *huge* then, and still is."

"Yeah, great," Alex agreed and hopped, "is this it? *You're done?*"

"Yeah," Jack said, quickly logging out and standing up, "so, I'll wait for you in the lounge."

"Wai, wait for me?" Alex stated over his shoulder as he went out into the hallway.

"Yeah," Jack audibly assured him, sliding her jersey over her head and singlet, "in the lounge. We're going."

"*We're* going? Where?" Alex curiously called while marching off to the restroom.

"Topher," Jack said to herself.

Chapter Eight
Monday, 23rd July 2063

Disembarking from a bus in Topher's transport station during an early, sunny afternoon, Jack stepped out onto the concrete, buttoning her jacket right up as she walked, and immediately recognised where she was, based on the smell. Though a mini-mall adjoining the station was scenting the air with a concoction of different international dishes from its various ethnically themed shops, there was a slightly pungent odour wafting in from the polluted creeks behind and a weedy, opaque pong profusely expanding around a nearby group of smokers.

"Oh man, even my HUD can smell it," Alex said as he stepped down from the bus to join Jack and lift his woollen jersey collar to cover his nose.

"Oh," Jack reluctantly reacted and pulled his jersey down, "sorry, but you can't do that here, ok? It'll draw us some unwanted attention."

Conceding with a frown, and proceeding to slip on his HUD, Alex read out, "it says: Smelly Garbage Capital of the World," in disapproval and moaned.

Jack reached her hand out to kindly grab the metallic red HUD from off his face and respectfully instruct, "no HUDs. And no coders. More people here go bare than not, so we'll have to go bare as well. We got to try and blend in." Looking at the fashionable device, she then asked out of curiosity, "does this have one of those olfactory things?"

"No," Alex replied, "I just wrote it in the last time I came here. The GPS set it off."

Jack smiled in amusement and examined the HUD's square edges and read the time, '1:16 pm,' from off its lenses before realising, "is this is your personal one? Hm."

Placing the thickly rimed, circular lenses back into Alex's waiting hand, she inquired, "how much was it? It's nice."

"They're Under the Suns," he stated with a smile, and revealed, "I got them for sixteen-eight."

Detecting a small amount of self-esteem emanating from her oft-intimidated friend, Jack complimented, "they're styley," to which Alex agreed, "yeah," while slipping them in his pocket, and mentioned, "my Mum thought so too."

Moving on from the station and its international dishes, pungent creeks and loathsome locals, the two wardens strolled on into Topher's right-angled, suburban streets while keeping their wits about them. They passed groups of truant teens and most probably their parents, indolently sitting alongside the footpaths and partaking in vice, and wandered through the neighbourhood's smell, hoping to quickly discover something there they could connect with the port.

Coming to the head of a T-intersecting street where the two could look down and observe a sample of the suburb's notably uniform, old-American high-rise architecture, Jack slowed to a stop and remarked, "the last time I was here it had been raining. And it didn't smell at all."

"Yeah," Alex doubted and averred in displeasure, "well it stinks now. And I'm not surprised."

Entertained by a knowledge of Alex's rivalry with the residents of Topher, Jack folded her arms in amusement and smirked. Alex was from Charlemont, another ill-talked about suburb further south holding a similar reputation for despair. Like Topher, it was considered an extremely low-end and decrepit part of the city, but unlike Topher, it was covered in low-level cheap housing for students. The edge of Alex's neighbourhood too looked like a bomb site from the motorway, as far as Jack was concerned, which was a big reason why she would much rather live in Topher. But she would never say that out loud as not to upset Alex or jinx herself, or accidentally make some new friends.

"This place looks *so old*," Alex criticised while stepping out onto the cobbled road to cross with Jack.

"Mm," she responded, looking both ways, "it's because of the push they had a few decades back to make Topher a rich kind of, cultural place, or something."

Stepping up onto the next footpath, she shared, "on my HUD once, I read that, the old-fashioned look was part of the design. It was originally a bunch of warehouses and some homes that they bought out to make more condensed housing. I guess they did it to help make the community more, rich, or valuable, or something."

She could see though, that it hadn't worked, or at least hadn't had any lasting effect. To her, the people in Topher seemed as poor and depressed as they could be outside of the squatters, and maybe Charlemont. They dressed either simply or like they were pretending to be successful, and they filled the sidewalks and occasional balconies all day looking outside at everyone else looking outside. The level of unemployment was striking, and numerousness of the unattended children running around in unproductive bands, disheartening.

The depression wasn't just evident in the people, however, as the area had always retained a shabby dampness that endured even in the sun. Rain and dew seemed to soak deep into the concrete and brick, and the tall drab buildings packed together in blocks cast long, soggy shadows over the neighbourhood's narrow streets. With the faux lighting, so abundantly used in the inner city, being either reduced or faulty down Topher's paths, there were many persistently shady corners for mould to grow and a few dark alleys to hide danger.

Even the vehicles packing the car parks along the streets helped to create a picture of poorness, being predominantly a collection of well-used jalopies from the 2030s and 40s, all bearing either dents and rust or fairly placed pink stickers.

'The only thing not depressing are the stalls,' Jack contemplated about the infrequent food carts and random tables hawking fake merchandise.

"What are we doing here, *really?*" Alex moaned with concern as the two slowed to navigate around a wide crowd of locals in the path, "cos I'm supposed to be at the port. With all the people, you know, paying these peoples' incomes."

Jack ignored him to walk between two parked cars and look both ways along the street.

"Because when you spoke about going to Topher," Alex stated as he followed, "I was like, hmm? But now that we're in Topher, I'm like, *damn*... What a way to... *Die*," he considered in jest, "I thought I was going to get crushed by a falling container, or crane or something, but now I'm gona die from, cholera."

Stepping up on to the next footpath, Jack slowed before a group of children swinging a long skipping rope between the parked cars and parallel buildings' stairways and turned to reply, "can you keep it down? Because I don't want to die from, *being beaten.*"

"Oh, yeah," Alex realised, and quietened his tone. "I was just worried. I don't wanna, you know, cark it right here, and," he mumbled, swallowing, "and die and. Make Gerry pay me overtime, for not working... Like I'm doing now."

Jack just stared at him in bemusement for a few seconds to transmit a silent command of submission. Alex was typically very malleable and loyal but seemed to be struggling in the presence of his rivals and their smell.

"This *is* working," she then assured him, pointing both her index fingers at the ground, "*this is* what you're doing today."

"Okay," Alex replied slowly in uncertainty before submissively discussing, "let's just make sure Gerry knows it was under your instruction, and that, you know I finish at four. Cos they're not going to want to pay me overtime."

"You finish at four?" Jack queried with a curious brow. "Did you start early?" she added over him.

"Uh, no," Alex wondered, looking around arbitrarily, "that'd be my normal knock off when I start at eight-thirty."

Jack went to walk on but paused to calculate and sceptically address, "that's seven hours. It's normal for you to work seven hours?"

Having always wanted to work for seven, or even just six hours, to compensate for how boring her work was, she started to become a little jealous. Despite being paid peanuts already and recognising seven hours would equate to a few peanuts less, she always thought a little less boredom and being spat on would result in some better mental health.

Contemplating then about Alex's hours and their current assignment, she tested, "you work nights sometimes, eh, in Info?"

"Yep," Alex told her, "sometimes."

"For seven hours?" Jack questioned with a discerning eye.

"Yep," Alex repeated, "for seven hours too."

"And what about in Assignments?" Jack investigated some more.

"Yep," Alex peppily repeated a third time.

"What time have you been knocking off down at the port?" Jack then energetically interrogated, pointing at him.

"Four o'clock," Alex said.

"*Oh!*" Jack complained immediately out loud, before quietening into a moan and turning to look elsewhere. The breachers as far as she could conclude were operating at the port in the evening during a night shift that started at about 4:00 pm. Remembering and recognising then from Alex's footage that there were no late nights or even early evenings, she deduced, "you know *nothing*," sternly, and then calmed with a constrained wince, "maybe, possibly. And maybe Gerry didn't quite think that one through, or."

Alex stayed quiet for a moment before peppily trying to cheer Jack up by suggesting, "should we keep walking?"

But Jack, who was slouching over her hips in dissatisfaction, couldn't quite let it go yet and randomly asked, "*how much are you getting paid?*"

"I'm not telling," Alex promptly answered and took an interest in nothing particular across the street, "you should talk to Gelena or Gerry, or Mark if you're getting paid too low. But, they might tell you to show up more... I'm just saying," he then clarified, removing himself from Jack's financial woes with some cautious gesticulation, "it's not me. It'll be them. Not me. Them."

"Well, I have been showing up more," Jack solemnly remarked and sagged before straightening herself up to tidy her half-ponytailed hair and get back on task.

Jack had been trying a lot harder to work since her time back from her suspension and had even begun putting in extra hours for free. With Ebee soon to make a leap into space and herself about to be kidnapped by breachers and deleted from society, she had genuinely sought to walk a more productive path so she could somehow avoid that bad future.

Swallowing what small amount of pride she had built up over the last few weeks, she turned to Alex to pat him on the shoulder and compliment, "thanks for coming along Alex. You didn't need to."

Bolstered by the display of gratitude, he gave a big smile back and conveyed, "I just thought you'd need a friend to watch your back. And you also ordered me to come, with no authority whatsoever." He then breathed in as if to take a psychological step up an imaginary worthiness-ladder.

Pleased to see him feel a bit bigger inside, Jack nodded and uttered, "let's keep moving."

Once returning to the head of the street to turn right and tour on elsewhere in the suburb, Jack began to explain the reason for their presence in the area, "a few weeks back Gelena had me working nights here in Topher— "

"Were you walking?" Alex assumed.

"Yeahp," Jack admitted and continued, "and anyway, there were people who didn't want me here, as you could guess, in uniform, and someone eventually threw an *EMP* at me. And it killed my equipment."

"Yeah, that happened to Julie as well," Alex responded.

"Yeah, I heard about that," Jack stated.

"In Greenhithe," Alex added, "but that place is nice. It's all big houses and swimming pools— "

"Yep, yep, let's," Jack exclaimed, interrupting his divergent input, "wait, did that affect Julie at all with her liver and that?"

Alex shook his head as they approached and gave way to a trio of teenage girls coming the other way and answered, "nah, the organ is built to withstand that, but it will have its limits. When I asked her, she said it was fine. She was scared at the time though; worried that it would suddenly cut out and then, she would get tired or sick and collapse but she came away fine. Her equipment died though— Her, you know, *that* equipment," he described, waving his hand to help cycle Jack's thoughts.

After a moment of quiet to pity Julie and her condition, Jack rubbed her chilled and irritated nose and continued to summarise, "well basically, there's that, but in Topher. The people here are, you know, rough," she characterised below her breath, as some of them walked past. "But far more interesting. Implicating, were those messages and informal receipts I showed you, where one of the receipts named a street around here we're coming up to."

"Ok. And why did you need me again?" Alex wondered as he walked.

"I thought there was a chance you could recognise some faces from the port if they're here," Jack began to explain, "or maybe notice some cargo, thing, maybe lying around. Maybe notice a vehicle or, or a badge, or marking. Since you had been there for so long. You did pick up those receipts," she cajoled him further.

Speaking over him, she explicated, "but you probably might not have even been there at the right time to see anything."

"And what," Alex interestedly inquired, "was I *meant* to see?"

Leaning in closer to keep it quiet from a smoking couple sitting on a stairway they were moving past, Jack told him, "breachers."

Alex's head and shoulders bobbed about with surprise. *"Breachers?!"* he declared to a few locals waiting at a traffic crossing before lowering his voice and sarcastically imploring, "oh, sign me up!" to try and allay those glimpsing back at him.

Moving in closer to invade Jack's space and communicate very privately as they went, he aggravatedly proclaimed in astonishment, "you brought me out here with you to find *breachers!?* What on earth are we doing looking for *breachers?"*

"It's our job," Jack replied encouragingly, "it's the assignment. And you came out here by yourself, to watch my back."

"No, yes. No," Alex riposted, pointing, "it's the *army's* job to find breachers. It's *their* assignment. We're supposed to find people who are bad mouthing the mayor and his counsellors."

"Relax Alex," Jack reassuringly expressed over him with two calming palms, attempting to alleviate his worry, "we are just trying to find out where these orders from the port are going. If it's breachers, we'll leave and call the cops. Ok? Now would you stop making us stand out?" she complained.

Settling down quickly at the sight of Jack's perturbed brow, Alex took in two deep breaths and glanced at the interspersed public along the street. "Is this what happened to you a month ago?" he then queried in earnest, "did you find breachers at the— "

"*Oh!*" he then paused in horror, deducing the true target of his assignment at the port that he had been tasked with stumbling onto every day since. "I can't believe you guys would send me there if you thought breachers were hanging out there," he postulated in disapprobation, "you've had me sent there every day for the last four weeks! How could you guys think that was a good idea? That's like workplace bullying or something. Oh!" he then presumed in serious displeasure, "and now you're taking, me to see them *in their house!*"

"*You,*" he expressed, covering his face in disgust, "you're always like this. You, you always get into trouble, and now, and now I'm here, being dragged along, to get eaten by some electronic robot man... With a sick fetish for zeros and ones."

Standing a couple metres on and looking back, Jack rolled her eyes and retorted in embarrassment for him, "oh, go easy. You're not being dragged," she persuaded, "you're being a *gentleman*. I'm just gonna try and find out if they live here or have a hideout and then we'll leave. You might even recognise a few of their goons before they recognise us, and we change course. There were other streets mentioned too," she reasoned, "they might not even be here."

"Argh," Alex uttered in frustration, holding his index finger to his forehead above his tightly shut eyes. He presumed Jack was lying about leaving and felt disappointed in his peers and himself for being duped into such a dangerous assignment and current outing, but couldn't conscionably leave his current post at Jack's side while she waded into danger.

"Argh, alright!" he finally announced, dropping his index finger to surrender to Jack's confidence and boast, "I'll brush off a few goons— Four, but that's my limit. The bodies always leave me a little shaken. And I wouldn't want to change the landscape here too much if any more came out. You know?"

Jack could sense the trepidation in his joke but happily grinned and chortled to reinforce and show appreciation for his loyalty. "You know the real reason I'm here?" she then divulged, "is because they have my HUD, and my coder."

Pausing to let a group of pedestrians pass alongside them, she itched the top of her irritated nose and elaborated as Alex rejoined her side, "my work one. I just wanna make sure um, that... We can find them before they find me."

"The cops didn't even want to do anything about all this," she continued to divulge as they resumed their walk, "they didn't even really believe me that there were any breachers in the first place. So, I'm just making sure that if they *do* exist, you know? They're exposed."

The two wardens continued to roam the afternoon streets, trying to blend in as best they could, but failed to shake off a growing sense of conspicuousness. While avoiding backtracking to hide a semblance of them investigating, they started to notice their mere walking doing a lot to make them stand out. They were moving noticeably faster than everybody else ambling between the stairways and straighter than those staggering along the paths. They were also more visibly determined than those leisurely consuming intoxicants, and bore no obvious prosthetics in a suburb where they were becoming more obvious on the residents as the afternoon wore on.

"You know, I feel like instead of looking around *with* them," Jack remarked about her growing concerns while continuing to walk and stare at a graphite-coloured prosthetic hand hanging from the furry white sleeve of a young woman mincing ahead of them with her friends, "we're looking around *at* them. And it's. I think it's a bit obvious," she perceived, staring next at a strange graphite rectangle horizontally embedded into the shaved right side of the same girl's head.

"I'm getting really tired," Alex dismissively groaned in response from a step back to Jack's left, "and my shins are getting sore again so, are we done yet? Do you feel like you've seen enough? Cos when that sun goes down, we better be out of here," he warned before Jack could reply. "Guys like me are not welcome in places like this after dark... I know addition and subtraction. And you still have to go to sunny Otara after this. *What a day*," he said, raising his brow to feign excitement.

"This was worth it," Jack dismissed his concerns back and elaborated, peering at an idol resident's exposed plastic knee on display at the end of his shorts, "ticking this place off was worth it, I mean." Taking in a deep breath of boredom, she continued, "though we still haven't got to the street I thought we were approaching earlier."

Alex sighed in boredom as he followed unenthusiastically and joked, "these Breachers you met at the port must have been really, really scary... Or *awesome?* For you to want to meet them."

Ignoring his hypothesising to straighten up her shoulders and enliven her senses, Jack double-checked their surroundings and stated, "actually we are nearing the place where that EMP was thrown at me. I think it's the next parallel street over."

"That's, great," Alex wearily uttered and riposted, "they can throw another and wreck my Under the Suns. I've always wanted to find out where these people live who wreck other people's things. Maybe tomorrow we can bring your HUD and do it again."

"I, I, gotta focus, ok?" Jack replied, waving him off.

Coming to the end of the street and crossing with Alex in tow, Jack lead them right, around another corner to split up and pass a large unemployed crowd assembling around something exciting them on the ground before rejoining near the head of the next right-hand, T-intersecting street.

"This way," Jack quietly affirmed to Alex with a backward glimpse before turning right between some more residents heading towards the excited crowd.

Staying quiet for the next few dozen metres as they strolled below the tall, drabby tenements concealing the street from the cool sun, Jack eventually slowed to address her companion and inadvertently inhale a puff of second-hand smoke.

"Huhgh, huhgh, huhgh," she coughed with her fist over her mouth and squinted, offering a peaceful apology to the two locals sitting in their soiled concrete corner beside a stairwell, "sorry. Sorry."

Following her on with his breath held and an amused grin spread across his face, Alex followed her out of the kindly forgiving local's sooty aura and criticised, "you just apologised for inhaling their second-hand smoke. You really need to stop inhaling that smoke Jack. It's insensitive."

"Hurgh, hurgh, hurgh," Jack replied and chortled.

"I mean that smoke contained, like, their own lung tar coming out and stuff. You're effectively stealing," Alex further teased and giggled at Jack's tearing eyes.

"Shut urgh, hurghp," Jack hoarsely retorted, covering her mouth, "there was like ash in that, huhgh!"

Straightening up to recompose herself and identify how much attention she had acquired, she smiled and swallowed with her hand on her chest and coughed again.

"Hahaha," Alex responded, with an upwards inclining pitch, "you, haha, hahaha. Just don't come back to Topher ever again," he suggested with a cancelling wave of his hand. "Or come back with one of those gas masks, with like, an integrated HUD on it. All stealth like, just 'checkin' out the crowds,'" he joked, gesturing quotation marks. "Get some *smokes*, get some *smells*. I think a guy back there was selling, watches, of all things— Get some *watches*," he quipped, poking his thumb backward over his shoulder.

"Shush," Jack instructed while trying to temper her own amusement, "this is the place."

Pulling over beside a fortunately unattended set of concrete stairs at the base of a high, ten-storey coffee-coloured dwelling, she took in a deep, measurably cleaner breath of Topher's air and leaned against a brown painted banister protruding perpendicularly out onto the path to rest.

"See that brick building across the street?" she asked, looking slightly further down to a faded-olive-coloured facade as a small bout of nervousness sprang up in her tummy.

"Yeah? The sort of green one? With the big bricks?" Alex replied as he slowed to turn and lean back against the coffee tenement's adjacent wall and look across the top of parked cars lining the road.

"When I came that last time, working, someone threw that EMP from one of its higher windows," she explained, subsequently looking over the rest of the neighbourhood's windows in caution. "That night, when I was working, I got an alert on my HUD from someone around here about prosthetics, I think. I think. It might have been unrelated but, when I was nearing the spot it was sent from, my HUD got flooded with alerts; like a DoS attack."

"What was the alert for?" Alex asked as he itched his face and adjusted his footing, "the initial one, that is. The one that made you focus."

Jack shook her head and hummed as she pondered for a second to try and recollect. Resting her arms upon the banister, she verbalised, "uh, language?" to try and jog her memory before vaguely recalling, "or, I think the device had already been listed in the past. You know how Assignments does that thing where they can tag a device and you get a special alert when you intercept anything from it? It might have been that, but it was a bit too long ago to remember exactly."

"You know, Jack," Alex politely interrupted, "after a month, you'd think these guys wouldn't be around anymore. That's a long time in terrorist circles to be loitering in the same place. I know Topher is a hole, but do you still think these guys would even be here? Or be here at all? With a great deal of... *Hindsight-relief*, I never found anything at the port."

"You found those receipts and their messages," Jack corrected him over her right shoulder. "But there were," she continued over Alex and then gestured, "oh you."

"No, you," Alex said, gesturing back.

"There were other street names mentioned, I guess," Jack insisted, "I presume based on their, you know their titles, the words, but Topher is the kind of place where if anything bad is happening, the locals all kind of wear it on their sleeves."

"Yeah," Alex agreed, "or on their prosthetic. Do you notice that?" he added curiously.

"The prosthetics?" Jack recited, to which Alex nodded and affirmed, "yeah."

"Yeah, there's heaps," she commented over him about their commonality in the suburb.

"Like, where do they get them?" Alex postulated as some went peacefully past on the ends of people arms. "I don't think that's exactly dole money hanging off their wrists, or elbows, or wherever."

Jack silently contemplated to herself for a moment about the unmarked boxes she observed inside the makeshift shelter the breachers were attending that night at the port and became more nervous. As her hamstrings began to tremble slightly, she recalled spotting an obscured device in the hands of one breacher sitting in the dark right before being approached.

'Is this really worth it?' she apprehensively wondered while watching the traffic go by on the road and numerous residents go about their business in peace.

"Maybe they don't have my HUD anymore," she blurted out, observing some very scantily dressed residents across the street step up and into the entrance of the faded-olive building from whence the EMP that ruined her equipment came. "Maybe they threw it away. Maybe they just didn't care... Maybe I remembered it wrong."

"Maybe there were no breachers?" Alex remarked, successfully reading Jack's mind while peeking at his HUD.

"I know why it would have been tagged," he then read from his own mind, slipping his hands in his pockets, "this is Te Angitu Street. This is where some of those transhuman activists are based. You know those ones that get into trouble for like, *everything*. Protesting, burning bins. Shouting in peoples' faces. Punching them, with their alloy plastic knuckles, that kind of stuff. I bet you the council has had some of those activists tagged, maybe even Gerry tagged them, and you intercepted a message from like... A leader or someone... Yeah, I bet you that's what it is."

"Let's go home now," he abruptly suggested in cowardice, standing off the wall.

"Wait, wait," Jack stated, grabbing Alex's fuzzy woollen arm as he went to leave, "what's the time?"

Pulling his hand out of his pocket with his HUD, he read out, "3:21," and stared at Jack in urgency. "Come on," he tried to cajole her, bobbing his head, "I finish at four. We're in Topher. It's going to get dark. The punching in the face, remember? The knuckles. The shouting."

Jack wasn't quite ready to leave yet but had to agree with Alex's concerns. It was getting late for him, and she wasn't fond of getting punched and shouted at, especially if in that order. Scanning the windows of the surrounding tenements and the people loitering on both sides of the street one last time to spot anything that could clearly justify her anxiety and the need to keep Alex any longer, she saw nothing untoward and relented.

"It's late Jack," Alex told her, gently patting her flexing wrist, "too late to be out around here."

"Sorry, yeah," Jack acknowledged, letting him go, and stood up off the banister. "Let's go."

The following Thursday night, after a fourth consecutive day of spending at least an hour by herself in Topher to investigate, Jack was entering inside the council lobby when she heard Gerry's voice call out to her from beneath the heavy rain pouring outside. Slowing to open the basement stairwell door on the lobby's left, she looked back to watch him skip inside and slow through the vestibule with his hands buried in the pockets of his long grey weaved coat to quickly join her at her side, lower his coat's soaked hood and express an appreciable grin.

"Hey, how's it been?" he asked from atop his coat's collar he was opening, and answered steamily, "it's been wet!"

"Yeah," Jack calmly agreed as the inner vestibule doors cut off the cold breeze.

Proceeding to enter the stairwell behind her and let the side door close gently behind him, Gerry began descending the stairs beside Jack and inquired, "you getting ready for the night shift, are you? It's going to be a wet one. Another wet one."

"Yeah," Jack agreed while swapping her retracted black umbrella between her hands and stepping around the first landing.

"Are you going to be alright?" Gerry queried, "you're in Otara now eh? Going to have a car? You've got a licence now eh?"

"No," Jack told him in relative disappointment as she descended. She had been resistant to the idea of applying for a driver's licence test in the past because she didn't like the risk of failure, and couldn't comfortably afford the tests without Ebee's help. But now, in light of the torrential rain lashing the streets for the last three nights in a row, she was really starting to regret that resistance.

"Oh. I thought you had your licence," Gerry commented in confusion, going around the second landing behind her. "I thought Alex told me that on, a couple days ago. I must have heard wrong," he spoke over Jack.

"Nah, I don't have it," Jack assured him, stepping around the third landing. "That's why I have my umbrella," she said, holding it up to be seen.

"Oh ok," Gerry unenthusiastically expressed, skipping ahead of her to guide her into the car park above the wardens' quarters, "well. I just really wanted to check up on you eh, as a supervisor. And so, I came in late hoping to catch you; you haven't been answering my calls or emails."

"Oh, sorry," Jack cordially responded, following him into the quiet car park to converse more formally and move him along, "I've been working in Topher— Oh visiting Topher, each day this week and some of, I think all your calls came then. Your emails I sort of just didn't reply to," she chortled in guilt, "sorry."

"Oh," Gerry replied in uncertainty, and gestured, acknowledging, "well, Alex did tell me you've been going to Topher each day since Monday, uh, in mufti," he emphasised with a point, "which is good. But you, have you? Have you been watching the news lately?"

"Um, no," Jack honestly replied with a slightly agitated sigh.

"There were *two kidnappings* there last week; *girls!*" Gerry declared, gesturing surprise with both hands, "I didn't actually know that till Tuesday before I had to leave town for a conference in Wellington, but as soon as I did,

I tried to contact you and Alex. Alex answered, and informed me he had moved his attention to Greenhithe, for some reason, but, did you *read* my emails or did Alex contact you?"

"No," Jack answered in the negative for both those questions and looked down to try and dispel Gerry's interest in continuing his discussion.

"Look," he politely said, however, and asseverated, "I'm becoming concerned with this situation with you trying to track breachers at the same time that females are being kidnapped, in the *very suburb* that you think the breachers are operating in. Does that make sense?" he then asked himself before asserting, "yeah. It does, right?"

Licking his lips and blinking, he then pronounced, "it has been a month and nothing obvious has come up. What *is* obvious is that what you're doing, is putting you close to danger. I don't want you jumping headfirst into a barrel."

"You're a barrel!" Jack replied in agitation, looking up at him, "I've been fine. I've been avoiding trouble, only going there during the day— Argh," she then expressed, hunching over to close her eyes, compress her heavy, aching tummy and deeply breathe.

After a second to deduct, Gerry moved half a step back and uttered, slipping his hands in his pockets, "ah... The paracetamol not working this month?"

"Shut up!" Jack replied, squinting with a pant.

Rubbing down her eyes and face after a moment, she straightened up while shaking her head and began stretching her limbs slightly to alleviate a tiredness that had been building up in her muscles. "I've just been playing too much," she admitted about her videogame playing habits at home and explained, "staying up late and playing too long doesn't mix very well with... *Things*. Nothing mixes well with, *things*."

Gerry waited for a moment to let Jack's pains settle before commenting, "I'm more concerned about your time in Topher but. It sounds to me like you should be sleeping instead of going out there, at all. Maybe wait till this night shift period ends?"

Jack exercised a serious level of restraint at that moment, because she liked Gerry and wanted him to be happy and unbruised, and just squinted at him in scepticism instead.

"Well, anyway," he unwittingly protected himself with another shrug of his shoulders and complementary gesture through his pockets, "I really came in to inform about the progress we've made, uh, on our side, with the, the police— And warn you of course."

Swallowing first, he began to enlighten, "I've been meeting up with my friend Maka Parata— That friend I was telling you about in the force, for the past few weeks since your run-in with the, *breachers*, and have been discussing with him the best way to prepare for any future run-ins. And he's told me that as of today, the little committee he's in, that looks into cases of misfeasance— He's not IPCA," he ensured to add, with a single calming palm, "but that committee has been successful in getting a task force up and ready to take on any, *breachers*."

Jack pressed her lips together and raised her eyebrows in pleasure. She hadn't seen any breachers recently to justify notifying a taskforce but was happy to hear one was apparently ready.

Looking rightward out over his shoulder to watch a car silently pull out from its park further inside the complex and leave, Gerry rubbed and itched his nose and continued, "but he's had to keep pushing this as a, these people from the docks as a, potential *terrorist outfit* because, he says, that 'breacher', the word, has become kind of off limits. The word, just the word, has become like a kill switch for them— The Police in general, that is." He shrugged his shoulders and shook his head casually while stating, "it's, politics."

"Yeah," Jack understood, and then looked up with her hand compressing her tummy to caution him, "you know I haven't um... I haven't really found anything yet over there, um. I think I've noticed some things, down Te Angitu Street, but, I don't have anything yet. Uh, mm."

Unsure of the worth of mentioning a single unmarked van she once observed seemingly leave from a delivery to the building beside the one she was focussing on, she just looked up into his eyes to wait for some incidental corroboration he could make as he continued.

"So, those two girls," he did continue, "were abducted in Topher on, *Friday*," he said, pulling out his coder to unfold and read, "it was recorded, the *twentieth*, yeah. This seemed to follow an arrest in, Kunzea Place," he recited, "on the *eighteenth*, two days prior." Searching for Kunzea Place on his device, he then uttered, "which uh. Huh, is in *Greenhithe*. I didn't pick that out. Smart Alex."

Jack wasn't quite so convinced the reason for Alex going over there without being told was because he was smart but agreed that it was definitely a good look for him.

"So, Maka did explain this to me earlier this afternoon," Gerry enlightened further, "that it had been determined that the abduction was indeed in retaliation to the arrest made on one, Ripeka Tunnicliffe, an outspoken transhuman activist. *That* was in Kunzea Place," he made sure to clarify with an attentive palm.

Lowering his coder, he elaborated, "Maka told me that Ripeka had been alienating some of her activist peers lately who decided it time to dob her in. These political groups are usually very tight-lipped, and well protected, but in this case, I think they got fed up with her and hung her out to dry, in police custody."

"Well, what was she picked up for?" Jack softly interrupted, "nothing about breaching I assume. And what was the link to these abducted girls?"

"Ah," Gerry replied in delight, pointing his finger upwards to shake and emphasise, "but this time it *was*, in principle. Seems like you, me, Alex and, most likely, Maka, might have stirred something up. The officers picked her up for housing *a hunting knife in her arm*." Holding up his sleeved left forearm to demonstrate with his right hand, he described, "it's a, it's a full-arm prosthetic and the knife was concealed in a hidden compartment atop her wrist, and was spring loaded. In the past they would have probably ignored it, but given her being hung out by her peers and some recent turbulence out there, and maybe Maka and his committee, they picked her up."

"Oh," Jack admitted with a small surprised nod, "ok. That is a, a thing. And what's the link to the girls?"

"The, you know, masked kidnappers," Gerry said, slicing through the air in front of his face to illustrate, "stated as much in their little video they sent *specifically* to a member of parliament, as a threat I guess. I don't know which politician that was as it hasn't been revealed, but the video did get passed on to the police where it was established as legit. These girls were, taken from Topher— But make no mistake, we don't know where they are now, uh, but they, the kidnappers, do state that this was indeed an act of retaliation for detaining this Ripeka Tunnicliffe activist, and they want her released."

"That's really *extreme*, isn't it?" Jack wondered in disbelief.

"They're *extremists*," Gerry assertively pronounced with a shrug. "They're not smartists."

Before Jack could throw in a supportive quip for Alex, Gerry went on, "these political groups can get really sloppy at times when they infight. We've seen it before in the past. Even when I was there in the force. A gun group once had a big shootout amongst themselves, and well... Now that group is gone."

Jack sniggered to herself in guilty amusement at the few times that happened amongst her similar group while playing team deathmatch online in Dynama X. There were a lot of casualties, and they didn't want to play together as a group anymore.

"These girls were Jenkinses too," Gerry remembered to add, slipping his hands in his pockets and looking down at his shoes, "daughters or nieces of a retired Army general or something. General Jenkins, I guess, or, I don't know. They're weren't *from* Topher, but either way. Whoever they belong to and wherever they were actually from, the kidnapping was, *terrible*, and a predicate was established for the police to take up the case and begin investigating transhuman activist groups."

Openly ruminating, he added, "I mean: you threaten a politician to act in a certain way or you'll kidnap someone? Uh, a General's daughter, daughters, or nieces no less— And you do!? Then you should expect a visit from a counter-terror police unit very soon."

"You know, I never saw any police in Topher while I was there," Jack remarked, and cautioned herself, "but maybe they're operating undercover?"

"Uh," Gerry opined, adjusting his footing and clearing his throat, "yeah. They would very probably be in mufti if they're there, but they would be cautious about staying too long at any one time, unless it was the counter-terror unit. An initial team, in uniform, would have gone in to investigate the crime scene, wherever that was exactly, and then quickly left. Uh, Topher is the kind of place officers can get sued for anything, right up to, blocking someone's view," he described in sympathy. "There is a ton of politically, minded, well, activists living there who seem to have every cop's number and all their kids' names, and there has been a lot of lawsuits. I know the wardens go there but the police and the residents there have a lot of history. Just saying."

Jack wasn't sure what history Gerry was referring to but could imagine some friction occurring if the police showed up in Topher without a valid reason. 'The people living there do seem to be living in a pretty isolated, cultural bubble,' she recognised.

Before she could inquire about their history with the police, however, Gerry conjectured, "but if they could— If the police, could land something really big, something that could outweigh all the lawsuits they would elicit, something worth it; then they would go in there, guns blazing, provided there weren't any kidnapped girls' lives on the line, and take out some of these activist types. Maka's even told me that this terrorist task force he's got going comes complete with a chopper and a few lorries."

"Lorries?" Jack questioned.

"Yeah, I don't know," Gerry replied, shrugging his shoulders, "for holding police, maybe? Holding baddies?"

Feeling less uncomfortable in her tummy and ready to move on now that she was late for her shift, Jack uttered, "so," and shrugged. "So, what now? We focus on the girls, or, let the police do that and we keep going, or, stop?" With the news about the girls creating an even greater reason for her to worry about disappearing, and an even greater reason to discover any shady, cyborg-like groups operating around the city, she became a little perplexed about the situation and hoped Gerry could quickly resolve that with some direction.

Running her right hand through her frizzy hair while shutting her eyes tightly, she breathed in deeply and exhaled to coax him, "so, will the assignment finish and the police take over or are they already out and... What will it take to get this task force out there and catching breachers?"

"Business," Gerry mutedly replied and more audibly clarified, scuffing the sole of his shoe on the toe of his other, "some kind of illegally organised business or faction operating that's related to this kidnapping, you know, organised crime. The predicate is there," he emphasised with a pointed gesture while looking up to think, "but it's not. Not for just *breachers*, of course, I mean, but it is there." Struggling to decipher the complexities of the case, he summarised and gestured, "these girls, were kidnapped by activists believed to be *transhuman* activists in retaliation for the arrest of a known *transhuman* activist; who was illegally armed, if not modified too— But modified doesn't really count anymore. Politics," he stated, waving it off. "The police then, not knowing anything more about these terror-ble people who did this, and knowing their demands and who the demands were too, about releasing a transhuman activist, who was illegally armed, *and loud* I was assured, creates the predicate for them to investigate any, groups, of this description in a counter-terror capacity. Now, would be a good time, to find your breachers."

"Does that make sense?" he then leaned in and earnestly asked.

"Yep," Jack assured him with a single nod before holding up her umbrella to stress, "but now I've really gotta get on with my actual work."

"Yeah, of course," Gerry agreed with his own nod and cautioned as Jack left him to wave her umbrella handle at him and enter back into the stairwell, "be safe out there."

Ruminating on the new information while preparing in the basement and paranoically going back out into the rain to flinch fretfully at the sight of passing SUVs, Jack steered around the soggy shadows of the CBD to catch a bus back out to the residential streets of Otara.

Continuing there to drench her shoes and socks in the suburb's widely spreading puddles and catalogue intercepts, she weighed heavily on the situation happening in the city's underbelly and contemplated giving up her private investigation into the people from the port. She wasn't certain about anything she had found in her digital pursuit of them and could formulate only very little from the various faces she had scanned and questionably cross-referenced using the council's resources. She hadn't seen anything directly implicating during her visits in Topher either and so couldn't see much worth in visiting there again.

While sitting in the front window of one of Otara's local laundromats in her bare feet, waiting for her shoes and socks to dry, she spared a few thoughts for the kidnapped girls and pondered pensively about whether the same thing could happen to her. Topher was clearly a risky place for anyone sporting an authoritarian uniform but, in her experience, didn't seem so dangerous for anyone else, outside of giving them cancer.

'Bad things could happen anywhere,' she told herself at home the next day while distractedly playing more videogames on the holotable instead of catching up with her sleep.

'Helping find these guys could really lift me up,' she then considered about her employment opportunities later that night along Otara's drizzling streets while trying to triangulate the sources of an alert-filled conversation broadcasting from a local, interspersed gang planning a large gathering in Gisborne.

Coming home at the beginning of a torrential rainstorm early Saturday morning, Jack entered into her Charterton building's lobby with a grateful smile and relieved sigh to retract her umbrella, acknowledge Douglas and ride up the elevator to her floor. Planning to spend her weekend off, after drying herself, playing videogames with Ebee and shopping, before perhaps catching up with some recipes, she unlocked and entered into her apartment and immediately sagged her shoulders and frowned.

Ebee's luggage was in the entrance upon the alabaster floor tiles and appeared to be waiting to leave on another weekend getaway with Ebee's employer.

"Come back soon," Jack mumbled to it before feigning a smile and supportive nod at Ebee popping her head out peacefully from the around the living room corner.

Helping the luggage cart itself down into the lobby again so she could place it tidily inside the boot of Ebee's employer's waiting limo, she stood for a moment as the rain battered her sideways to hold her tugging umbrella up over Ebee who approached gracefully, hugged thankfully and entered into the limo's rear cabin through its opened suicide door.

Watching the limo ride off silently beneath the rain on its way to Taupo, Jack predicted for a moment its likely return on Monday morning, an hour before Ebee's work started, like the last time, and moped.

"Come back soon," she mumbled to Ebee's luggage.

Reverting to her reclusive mood for the weekend and altering her plans slightly to accommodate for more time playing videogames, since there wouldn't be any shopping, she went back to slamming spacecraft satisfactorily into the side of the moon and reheating leftovers from the fridge. She spent some time flying directly into the sun too, finding the disintegration effects impressive, and resumed before bedtime both nights her current e-book chronicling a fictional tale about a despondent girl growing up in an ever-changing futuristic world.

Spontaneously winding up in Topher again in the next week after a resurgence of her apathy towards danger, she found herself relaxing back on the drabby suburb's damp wooden benches for a few more sessions of covert staring and eating street food. Ever so slightly enjoying the residents' oblivious company more with each visit, especially as they were ever-present while Ebee was increasingly absent, she started to become a little impartial to the suburb's flavours and growing idea that she could even move in at the end of her current apartment's lease.

Though being quite a bit less exclusive than Charterton, with densely packed blocks and cave-like apartments, and a bit less salubrious, with its trailing moulds, grimy windows, shabby paths and piles of discarded rubbish bags filling some of its alleys, it was at least affordable somehow to the unemployed and presumably affordable to those who were.

With there being no Ebees, however, to distinguish the neighbourhood with grace, nor Douglases to keep the peace, Jack did have a problem. A random guy she watched get screamed at and lightly beaten down the end of the street for cheating sounded pretty sleazy, and a man she heard nearby through the concrete growl at his squealing partner for finishing up their vice was a downright bad guy. Random breakouts of fisticuffs in the middle of the road between the excessively passionate were problematic too, as was the rage-fuelled, and very public, forceable removal of the loser's prosthetics, and subsequent lobbing of them into the path of oncoming vehicles.

'On the whole though,' Jack had to admit about Topher, 'it's better than Alex's bombsite, and slightly closer to the CBD. It's really quite rustic,' she tried to more positively characterise, and incredulously hope that by the time she needed a place to stay, outside of the squatters, the suburb's demographic would have shifted, miraculously, towards the rarer, kindly-saluting elderly couples and their self-walking robot dogs.

While hunching forward on Saturday during a heavy rain saturating the entire city, Jack was staring beneath her profusely dripping umbrella at a bite she had taken out of a battered hotdog she was holding by the stick in her right hand. Having purchased the disturbingly spongy treat earlier at the head of Te Angitu Street from an appreciatively smiley, prosthetically toothed man standing below a sign that read, 'EATS. proteins. cultured.,' in untidy green lettering, she was beginning to regret partaking in the one-hundred-and-twenty-dollar transaction. The very first bite had made her squeamish and the other one hundred and ten dollars didn't look like it would make her feel any better. The white sausage inside the ordinary batter felt and tasted like it was made from silicone, and the gelatinous neon-red sauce on the outside from something transfused inside a lab.

Lowering the treat perpendicularly into the centimetre-high runoff flowing down the steps around her black snow pants and sneakers, Jack audibly expressed, "yuck," and leant her elbows discontentedly into her lap. The rain had thankfully swept Topher's nauseating concoctions out of its air but hadn't swept it out of its food. Jack was also mentally done watching the local residents go about their boring lives, preferring now to just stay home and shoot people online, but persevering anyway to satisfy a serious obligation she felt she had to Gerry and his policeman friend.

Spotting a rubbish bin a dozen meters further down through the rainy white haze battering the suburb's every surface and promptly correlating it with her treat, she picked it back up, mumbling, "disgusting," and skipped down rightwards onto the footpath. 'They should have sickness bags hanging up around here,' she criticised, marching to quickly relieve herself of the battered imitation.

Sneering at the bitten treat one more time as she approached the bin, she deducted, 'I don't think this sausage used to have any legs,' about the perfectly homogenous meat and tossed it into the narrow opening on top.

Turning to dry her fingertips on her black jacket and make her way back, she randomly recalled a giant, fifty-storey tall advertisement she goggled at two nights prior glowing down the side of a skyscraper near the harbour in town. 'High-Protein. Sustainable-Protein,' she remembered reading in solid, canary yellow italics below a photo of a wētā laid on its side upon a wooden chopping board below a selection of colourfully shredded vegetables and curds. 'Or it had *a lot* of legs,' she strained, drily retching, and then drily retching again.

Returning past a sneezing resident traipsing beneath an inadequately small umbrella in gumboots and soggy cotton, she groaned in displeasure and sighed. She just spent one hundred and twenty dollars of her limited money and now had, perhaps gratefully, nothing to show, while a touring hobo she saw a street over rummaging through a pile of black rubbish bags spent nothing and was soon going to have a lot to show.

'One hundred and ten dollars,' she reasoned, climbing back up the stairs to the coffee-coloured tenement she had been sitting below for the last fifteen minutes, 'in protein, that is. Very soiled, high and sustainable protein... That will be puked out all over the street. Because you don't have bags.'

'I should have just given *him* a hundred and twenty dollars,' she figured, turning around atop the entrance landing, 'but it belongs to the vegan now.'

Looking up the street to view the top of the vegan's grimy beige trailer parked on her side of the street near the end, she mocked, 'or the robot?' and incidentally eyed a small crimson van slow on the middle of the intersecting road behind and indicate.

Reflexively reversing inside the tenement's entrance to conceal herself, she retracted and tapped her umbrella's tip on the landing to run out its moisture and assess, 'this guy.'

It was the van she had seen cruising around the neighbourhood thrice before in a conspicuous hurry that she hoped would make an appearance once more before she finally gave up coming. Its driver had been an unusually attentive one, literally holding the vehicle's steering wheel like he was in control of it while gawking purposefully out at all the high-rise windows and their residents lining the streets. He was also the only suspect Jack really had possessing a panel van that could be useful hiding kidnapped girls and carting shady cargo from a port.

Watching it pace down Te Angitu's cobbled road with a unique muffled trill and slow, Jack stepped another foot back into her tenement's darker entryway and stared out incredulously. The van was pulling up almost directly across the road outside the faded-olive brick building from whence an EMP was once thrown at her, making it a key place of her interest, and was double parking with an obvious intent to stop.

'Serendipity,' she mused, watching the driver dutifully communicate through his windscreen with an acknowledging middle-aged resident exiting the faded-olive building's entrance.

"Oh excuse, sorry," a male then startled her from behind.

Jack jumped and twisted to see a much taller, pleasantly smiling teenager in a white baseball cap, white singlet and shorts attempting to exit through the single opened front door she was blocking and obliged, "sorry," in embarrassment. Letting him freely pass before gazing into the leafy-green wallpapered tenement to see no more following, she quietly shifted to the left of the entryway's threshold to peer back out and nervously resume examining the van.

Relatively small compared to the modern living-vans coming in from the motorways to deliver their owners to and from work, and far too dated and basically equipped to be of any sentimental value outside of being a tradesman's backup bomb, it was a very simple cuboidal crimson vehicle with little to make it stand out to an ordinary passer-by. It was clean and lacked dents, suggesting it merely an occasional visitor to Topher, and was inherently far too expensive and clean to be owned by any squatters.

'So, your driver's either an unlucky tradie, or a student, from Charlemont,' Jack deduced, watching a citrine-coloured sedan autonomously move out from its parking space in front of the olive building's entry stairs at the behest of the middle-aged man cooperating with the driver. 'Or a delivery man, making a delivery from the port.'

With descending delivery drones and their jingles being a notable rarity in Topher, Jack was already convinced any shady package deliveries would happen on the ground. She was even more convinced that it would be brought by someone from the outside, since the residents barely ever left, and likely be handed over by a worried guy behaving weirdly behind a wheel. The situation at hand was 'breaching' and nobody, including peaceful, prosthetically assisted people, were comfortable about people breaching serious anti-singularity laws. They weren't comfortable with kidnappings either, even if, like Alex had suggested, they were being undertaken by their transhuman activist next door neighbour friends.

Jack watched the van, from her concealed corner inside, strafe into its park and the driver immediately exit the front cabin in blue rainwear. She observed him move briskly to the van's raising rear door and meet with a taller teenager wearing a wet white baseball cap, white singlet and shorts.

'Oh,' she flinched, recognising the lanky teen from just a moment ago, 'that kid knows I'm here!'

She removed herself a bit more from the cloudy grey light coming in from outside to suddenly leap at the sound of a unit's front door slamming in the hallway behind her.

A pear-shaped man in a ratty singlet, blue stubbies and jandals had exited a unit in the diagonally opposite corner of the dreary hallway and was ambling upon a set of multicoloured prosthetic legs to the front door of the unit nearest Jack. With a set of keys and a wallet in his pale prosthetic right hand, he approached and unlocked before opening and entering without even an indifferent glimpse at the black clad stranger standing outside his home.

'Better finish up quick,' Jack told herself after his door shut loudly behind him.

With a moving creak sounding in the floor overhead, she warily returned her gaze to watch the van and subsequently see its driver trudging a metre-high stack of cardboard boxes up the olive building's stairs. "That is definitely a thing," she lipped silently and started deliberating.

The tall teenager who was soaking without worry in his summer clothing, supported by just a pair of shin-high white socks and canvas shoes was still present and seemed to be manning the crimson van while the driver delivered. The driver, coming back out from the building at a courier's pace, was returning for more cargo while the middle-aged man dallied menially in and out of the wooden double door entranceway with seemingly little to do but wait.

'I could go in,' Jack contemplated about entering inside the olive building to locate and assess the packages, 'once they're gone. But that middle-aged guy looks like he lives there and is a part of the delivery.' Watching the driver heave an even wider stack of more boxes, she more thoughtfully considered, 'or I could come back tomorrow, with my kit, and try and find out more precisely what's really going on.'

After one more round of carting that included a substantial assist from the teenager, the driver exited the building back out into the rain with a load of flattened cardboard that he chucked casually into the rear of his van. Letting the door close by itself, he then scooted alongside his ride back to the front cabin to re-enter, salute the middle-aged man through the windscreen, place one hand on the van's steering wheel and promptly dart off in the opposite direction from whence he came.

"Time to go," Jack decided beneath her breath, observing the tall teenager climb up and encouragingly escort the middle-aged man into his building.

Extending her umbrella as she exited back out into the beating rain to descend leftward into a march back up the street, she rested her canopy just above her crown and tilted it slightly to conceal her rear. She splashed her damp sneakers through the watery depressions in the path and glimpsed over her shoulder to ensure she wasn't being followed.

It was then that she looked forward to see through the rainy white haze battering the parked roofs alongside the road ahead a higher riding navy-blue vehicle coming in the opposite direction. Following it with her eyes as it went calmly past behind her umbrella, she indifferently ignored it and kept on, until her mind calculated its declining speed causing her to slow and look back.

"Oh," she gravely denoted about the squared, navy-blue roof stopping to parallel park in the space left by the delivery van, 'that's a Holden.'

The last time Jack could remember observing a high-riding Holden was in Port Pascoll when she fled from the presence of the breachers on Te Kawau Wharf. The Holden before that, was the one that brought the very first breacher to her just moments before she fled.

Memories from that evening then flooded back into her mind with an angry, stinger-induced, near audible growl causing her to tremble in uncertainty and pause in her tracks.

'No way,' she panted in astonishment.

It had been at least six weeks since that evening at the port, during which time an involved investigation failed to find any trace of the breachers she found there. But now a car like theirs was peacefully parked right in front of her, after a shady delivery, down a street full of people bearing a preference for prosthetics and an activist's aversion to police.

Attentively watching a head of short black hair exit and elevate well above the roof of the Holden and move closer to the olive building's stairs and ascend, Jack quivered as she watched it rise high, atop an army-green collar and broad, trailing army-green trench coat.

'*Breacher!*' she recoiled, staring at the huge man turn one hundred and eighty degrees on the landing to reveal his neatly cut Spanish beard and black skivvy and look up the street with a steely, prosecuting gaze.

Dipping her umbrella as a constricting ball of saliva abruptly grew in her throat, she swallowed and stepped skittishly before attempting to recompose and control her elevating heartbeat. It wasn't night and she wasn't exactly alone. Her umbrella's canopy was opaque, 'and plucking out this ball of lint should make me look boring,' she opined, dropping a small ball of fibres she discovered in her jacket pocket into the top of a rubbish bin she had paused beside. Feigning finding another ball of fibres to fool a pair of residents exiting their tenement further up, she imaginarily added it to the bin before irresistibly peeking back around the edge of her umbrella.

"*Whoa!*" she cowered, spotting another head of short dark hair exit the driver's side of the SUV and tower above the road in army green.

'Time to go,' she asserted, turning her shaking frame to gather herself and collectedly leave, 'it is *definitely* time to go.'

Later that night at home, Jack was sitting upright on her bed with her legs folded while bathing in an electric-blue light pouring in through her un-tinted, wall-spanning bedroom window. Observing it emanate from a new advertisement hanging from the building across the way and glint through the drizzle streaking down the glass, she ruminated in a state of perplexity about a call she had earlier with Gerry.

He had strongly advised her to let him take her place in her investigation into the breachers and had instructed she stay as far away from Topher as she could. He had determined to contact his friend Maka to make plans for an immediate undercover visit and had requested Jack return back to her regular job in Info. He had assured her he would press Gelena to provide her with some safer shifts and persuade Mark to find another way for her to improve her reputation.

But Jack didn't want to stop investigating and just hand over all her efforts to someone else. She didn't want to lose an opportunity to seriously improve her reputation and add something substantial to her C.V. And she most definitely did not want to go back into Info. Getting out of Info had been her truest pursuit this whole time, and she couldn't stand to be so close to something beneficial only to have it be handed off to someone already doing well.

'No way,' she tiredly assured, imagining herself stand with a big, accomplished person's smile in front of Ebee when she came home on Monday. '*I'm doing this.*'

Chapter Nine
Sunday, 5th August 2063

Jack was feeling energised the next morning as she disembarked back onto the concrete platforms of Topher's spice-scented transport station and highly confident after winning a friendly, one-sided debate during a follow-up call with Gerry.

She had had a good sleep and solid breakfast and had successfully argued the reasons why *she* was going to be the one to continue the investigation into the breachers. She had contrasted her readiness with Gerry's, who was soundly sleeping at the time she contacted him, and emphasised the urgency required to visit Topher before the previous day's mysterious delivery completely dissolved into the community's needy hands. She had also proposed a plan she wanted to enact during the day and was looking forward to seeing it come to fruition with Gerry's remote supervision and Alex's material support.

"I hate you," Alex uttered, coming to slouch beside Jack beneath the bright sunlight baking the station's wet pavement.

Having come straight from Charlemont using a different bus so he could reluctantly join Jack on her escapade back into the shabby streets of Topher, he exhaled a deep breath in despair and looked around dismissively at the locals. He wasn't happy about being woken up early on a day off and even less happy about being woken up early so he could spend his day off in Topher.

"We already did this already," he grumbled, scuffing the sole of his shoe across the ground.

"Mhmm," Jack half-heartedly replied while checking her HUD and coder were secure in the pockets of the athletic blue and grey coat she was wearing. Patting the zipped, right-hand pocket of her marl trackpants to ensure her stinger was still inside, she agreed, "we did," and turned right to look over Alex and assess his state of readiness. "But now we're gonna do it again."

Slouching an inch deeper in his thick cream, knitted woollen jumper and fitting black jeans and swaying feebly in his loosely laced white basketball boots, Alex stared back contemptuously and moped, "this is about finding breachers still eh?"

"Yep," Jack concurred.

"*You*, finding the breachers, eh?" Alex said.

"No," Jack corrected.

"Oh," Alex replied in uncertainty.

"It's, *us*, finding the breachers," Jack clarified.

"Oh," Alex conceded in disappointment, "goody."

Encouraging him to move on with her from the station, she gently pushed his left arm and inquired, "you brought your HUD eh?"

"Yep," Alex confirmed as he began dawdling towards the adjacent main road.

"And your coder?" Jack checked, following him from half a step behind to his side.

"Yeah," he assured.

"And your stinger?" Jack queried in more detail.

"Yeah," Alex divulged.

"Wow," Jack then questioned him in surprised, "you brought your, you brought a stinger? *Do you even have a stinger?*"

"Yeah," Alex assured her with a sceptical frown, stopping beside the road to straighten up his posture and wait for more direction. "Why wouldn't I have a stinger?"

'Because you're a wuss,' Jack distinctly thought, gesturing surprise as she came to stop beside him. 'I thought you knew?' she chortled to herself.

Alex wasn't known for his might, or boldness among the wardens, nor was he even remotely scary or tough. Very little about him looked strong, including his untidily curling chestnut hair that was trying at this time to stand up and escape his crown like he was unwittingly dragging it into danger.

More respectfully discussing her incredulousness as she kept one eye on the road for any crimson vans, she postulated, "I just assumed you'd say no, like, cos you didn't have one, like cos they were like scary or— "

"What?" Alex wondered, lowering his left brow to stare at Jack and assert, "it's right here," while patting his right pant pocket. "It's always right here. I don't go anywhere without Little Dorothy."

Bursting out with laughter, Jack panted and giggled, and laughed again, and then lost her balance stepping backward on the dipping splay of the driveway. "Oop!" she exhaled, catching herself with her feet, "sorry."

"Sorry?" Alex chuckled, watching Jack return to his side. "Sorry to the driveway or sorry to me, for making me come out here and protect you from killer robots?"

"Sorry to the driveway," Jack condescendingly quipped with a dismissive gesture before critically remarking, "you named your stinger *Little Dorothy?*"

"Yeah, just now," Alex chortled while noticing a group of older teenagers across the road swagger ostentatiously along their path at the base of some damp high-rises towards another group coming in the opposite direction. "You didn't name yours?"

Jack had never considered trying to name her stinger since it was just an inanimate object comprising a metal telescopic tube, battery, tiny circuit board and some electrodes. "It has a spring," she dubiously remarked.

"Springy?" Alex subsequently suggested and asked, "are these idiots across the street gonna break out in a fight?"

Jack looked across to observe the groups pompously come together and replied, "nah, I like 'Papatūānuku'."

Alex thought in bemusement for a second before bursting out loud in laughter. "Haha, don't you mean 'Ranginui', the sky-dad? Cos, like, *lightning?* Does your stinger spray dirt on people, when you stick it in their face?"

Elaborating over Jack, who started laughing at the image of her stinger spraying dirt onto the breacher from the port's face instead of electricity, he criticised, acting out a forceful encounter, "here punk. Take this detritus! Watch out, it's got bugs in it!"

Managing to subdue her lungs for a moment, Jack reasoned, pressing one hand against her chest, "nah it's like the lightning that goes up, right? There's down-lightning and up-lightning. Isn't that right?"

"Oh yeah," Alex admitted, and then acted out frantically rubbing Jack's stinger on his hair like a plastic comb to build up an electrical charge on it. "Get those ground electrons, down here, to build up an up-lightning charge," he vigorously giggled, and then pretended, "and then WAPOW! Take that punk, I pricked you, on the arm. Hehe."

"Papatūānuku's a *beast*," he sarcastically declared.

"Hmhmm," Jack chortled, calming down as the teenagers across the road began publicly taunting each other, "well, let's just try to keep Little Dorothy and Ground-Mum in our pockets today ok. We better move on."

Pulling out his HUD as they pushed on from outside the station, Alex slipped it in front of his eyes and stated, "yeah let's go find these punks. I'm starting to feel big."

Jack slowed though, to carefully reach and remove his HUD and hand it back to him.

"Oh, right," Alex remembered, receiving them to place back in his pocket, "we gotta go bare or something, eh?"

"Not exactly," Jack explained, looking both ways to cross the road, "that is a thing, but I'm also worried about jamming devices being in range here, that may alert people to our presence. We'll use our equipment, but only once we're in place."

"Ah," Alex unenthusiastically uttered.

"There were breachers here yesterday," Jack disclosed, stepping out onto the road, "really."

"Ah," Alex even less enthusiastically uttered. "Well, can we get something to eat first? Because I'm starting to feel small again.

"Of course," Jack assured him, marching attentively to the next footpath, "just don't eat too much."

After a period of walking along the outskirts of a suburb he was still quite unfamiliar with, Alex picked up his dragging step to walk closer to Jack's right and begin conversing.

"So... How's your flatmate?" he delightedly spoke with a pant, "the hot blonde one. I think I saw her out the other night with a bunch of what must have been her workmates. They were all in suits and whatever. Outside a restaurant, like under the eave. You know?"

Gesturing for Jack to see, he described, "like in the, the place, but really under the. You know? It must have been cold. But they had these, like, table-fires, thingies. It was pretty cool."

Jack dismissively kept up her pace and replied with a diversion. "So where did you get that jumper from?"

"Oh this?" Alex jovially responded, pressing his chest to behold his garment, "thought you might like it. My grandmother made it."

Jack immediately looked at his jumper in disconcert and then him. She was about to take Alex into a shady part of town, to visit a shady building where shady people lived, and breachers had recently visited, and was now beginning to wonder if he understood that.

"My Mum came over to my place this morning and gave it to me," Alex explained as he admired the crossed ribbing down his jumper, "just before I left. She said my grandmother knitted it quickly, when she heard I was dating."

Jack then skipped a step to stare at him with outright concern.

"I only told my Mom there was this girl I liked," Alex elaborated, "and she got all excited and, now, I look like this... A fuzzy cuttlebone," he said, smiling while rubbing his ribbing.

Reaching back over his left shoulder as he kept up with Jack's fluctuating pace, he continued, "my budgie was all over me this morning and I think it's pulled a thread already. Can you see that?"

Noticing then the consternation on Jack's face, he promptly gestured for calm and clarified, "oh, not you; this other girl, a blonde one. And not your friend either," he calmed and clarified further.

"Uh huh," Jack expressed as she came to stop at a crossing and swipe in front of the sensor, "go on."

"She's a friend of one of, well, all, of my flatmates," Alex started to explain, as he came to stop beside Jack. "They're all friends at AUT and, yeah." After a second to look down the intersecting road and at nearby locals waiting to cross in a different direction, he then announced, "I think I'm going to try and get in to uni. Seeing those guys so happy, and busy, makes me feel like. Like."

Proceeding to cross at the sound of the buzzer, Jack interestedly listened in to Alex's word's as he ambled along contemplatively. There was far too much change happening in her life right now, and hearing Alex bring up some more made her wary.

"Like, what?" she coaxed, stepping onto the opposite path.

"Oh, like, *crap*," Alex answered ambiguously, gawking at a trailer up ahead selling street food, "we can't eat that— I can't eat that. It'll make me chunder. And I'm feeling really kinda low already and that'll just make me sick."

Looking ahead to behold a grimy beige food trailer parked on the side of the footpath to the left that they were approaching, Jack reread, 'EATS,' and immediately ignored the rest. "Yeah, nah, nah, let's just," she replied with a quietening voice as they neared it.

Imparting respectfully dismissive nods as they passed the cheerfully beckoning vegan who was leaning over his mobile counter to entice, the two passed in disciplined silence until they put enough distance behind them and the trailer to continue conversing.

"That vegan printed-protein stuff makes me wanna chuck so badly," Alex continued, "it's not even full of sugar, but it still makes me want to get like, an emergency blood transfusion— Or like a whole-body transfusion; it grosses me out that bad. My flatmate eats it, like, every night— He comes home with it from uni or somewhere— Oh, and luckily the other night that blonde girl I told you about, her name is Lucy— Don't tell anyone— She rejected his offer, of it, to her, and I was like: *Whooh!*" he exclaimed pumping his fist into the air, "*nice!*"

"Good," Jack agreed as they approached the next crossing.

"I'd probably have to take a box of these to flush that crap out," Alex expanded, taking out a small plastic jar to inspect and then slip back into his left-hand pant pocket, "but I wouldn't want to overdose."

"What was that?" Jack asked of the jar as they came to stop and wait at the head of the next T-intersection.

"My diabetic medicine," Alex revealed, taking it back out for a second to show before slipping it once again into his pocket.

While watching an elderly local in a fraying green tartan suit and fedora swipe at the crossing sensor repeatedly, Jack blurted out, "what!?" and stared at Alex in surprise. "*You have diabetes!?*"

"Yeah," Alex affirmed with a nod and deep breath.

"But you're not fat," Jack told him in confusion.

Alex looked at her in bemusement for a second and chuckled as the crossing buzzer sounded. Stepping onto the road behind the fraying man, he then frowned and flicked his head sceptically before expounding, "uh. Thanks."

"I though you just had *pimples*," Jack exclaimed.

"Oh," Alex responded with a degree of embarrassment, "um. Mmm. Ok. Sorry. It's not, *on purpose*."

"Nah, nah," Jack reassured his reasonably pimpled face as they stepped up onto the next footpath, "I don't mean you *have* pimples. I was just teasing. Is that not pimple medicine?"

Alex grinned nervously in amusement, "no. I have type one diabetes, which is *way worse*. And it requires me to take medicine with me everywhere I go. I have to take it when I eat and sometimes when I get low. Like, *low*," he said, circling his hand in front of his slender woollen frame, "low energy."

"Man," Jack pitied while noticing a preoccupied local they were passing light something fibrous in the end of his long pipe and relax onto a camping chair at the base of a dingy tenement. "I didn't know. It's like a sugar thing eh?"

"Yeah, no," Alex explained, "it's like an insulin thing. But I'm saving up for a new pancreas so that should, you know. I don't know," he shrugged.

"How much is that gonna be?" Jack inquired, looking ahead again to take a big deep breath of air before it became contaminated, "is that a prosthetic?"

"Uh, about— No," Alex answered while squinting in discomfort, "no, it's not a prosthetic, it's a clone that'll cost about nine hundred thousand, I was quoted. That's a lot cheaper than a prosthetic. And that includes the pig. And it's small pen."

"Ah," Jack pretended to understand, "the pig. Yeah wow. So... So you eat the pig, or?"

"*No I don't eat the pig,*" Alex criticised with a downwards inflection, "well maybe after, but the pig grows that organ. That'd be a gross pig actually; all full of growth hormone, and leftover human pancreas. Yeah, no, the pig will be put down afterwards, or sold, to someone here in Toph— No, no absolutely not," he retracted, "no one is getting a taste for Alex."

"*No one* is eating the pig!" he then spoke over Jack, "that'd be worse than that printed protein, or substitute protein with its big wētā and cabbage ads hanging up around town. Yuck."

Abruptly stopping to cover his mouth and halt a disturbance churning his gut and greening his skin, he leant into a concrete corner beside an adjacent high-rise's entry stairway and convulsed.

"Please don't," Jack appealed, pausing between other strolling locals to prepare for embarrassment, "you've got diabetes. And you'll get your grandmother's jumper dirty. And you'll make me puke," she added, pointing at the damp dirty concrete below Alex's ailing posture.

"I've just really gotta eat," Alex groggily assured between two deeply ventilating breaths, "and take my medicine."

Jack was sitting patiently by herself a time later upon a wooden bench seat tucked between two close entry stairways down Te Angitu Street, watching the mid-morning calmly unfold while waiting for Alex to return from a necessary meander around the corner. She had been waiting for about ten minutes already, hoping for him to pop his head out from between the parked cars any second in a more energised mood when she contemplated in earnest, 'I really didn't know Alex was a diabetic,' and leant back in a state of reluctance.

She had planned for them to venture behind the brick facade of the faded-olive building fifty metres further down the road and across and search around for clues about the previous day's order but was becoming a tad nervous about Alex.

She didn't know he could become so incapacitated so suddenly when he hadn't eaten. She knew he was already a pushover, bearing a feeble frame and pliant personality, but didn't know he needed to pause his life to go and get a snack, peradventure he would turn green and faint. 'What would happen to him if those huge breachers showed up and stared at him?' she wondered critically about his fortitude, 'or if someone called him names?'

"Haugh," she then scoffed, looking arbitrarily at the sandy yellow sedan parked in front of her to reflect on the very notable degree of Alex's weakness and mumble, "I just thought he had pimples."

Spotting him then step out from between the parked cars further up in the left side of her peripheral vison, she observed his nerdy demeanour strut with a degree of nonchalance down towards her with a foam food container in either hand in a much more cheerful disposition than before.

'There is a pretty undefeatable spirt of innocence in that boy,' she remarked, leaning forward to observe him happily, but still warily, return. 'And it is *extremely* conspicuous.'

Reaching out for a white utensil he was holding out for her as he came to sit beside her on her bench, she giggled in amusement and exclaimed, "you got me a spork!"

"Uh huh," Alex affirmed with his own giggle, and shuffled closer to hand across his body one of his foam food containers.

"What did you get me?" Jack gratefully inquired, receiving it carefully to place level on her lap.

"Chicken soup; I got us both chicken soup," Alex merrily replied, placing his container onto his lap. "Careful, it's hot," he cautioned and deeply exhaled.

Taking a moment to taste her soup and ensure the chicken was indeed chicken, or at least convincing, the noodles *noodles,* and the broth not something transfused from something inside a lab, Jack proceeded to consume her soup and pleasantly find it palatable.

"You know," Alex began talking after a few helpings, "it was either this, or fish balls; whatever those are."

Specifically grateful that he chose the soup, Jack hummed and swallowed another serving.

At the end of her small-sized meal, she closed the parcel's clamshell lid and rested her spork on its top. "So is your coder a work one or is it a private one too, like your HUD?" she inquired, as she started to prepare.

"It's my work one," Alex replied, gulping another sporkful of noodles, "I don't have a private one. But this is my private HUD, yeah," he clumsily spluttered, "I think I'm gonna rely more on my HUD though, so I can't be traced so easily, or, like, instantly jammed, like at the port. Just in case— You said that earlier, that *that* could be a thing."

"My HUD's not on the network," he then spoke over Jack as he twisted and served more food into his mouth, "the council one, but I can still join a party chat with Gerry or whatever, so."

"Mm," Jack concurred, inquiring further, "you can take photos though eh? And stream?"

"Yep," Alex said, raising his clamshell to pour its broth into his mouth like a large square cup, "but not to the council. Not stream, to the council."

"You got some on your jumper," Jack then courteously pointed out to his grateful reception before explicating, "we *will* need to get as much evidence as we can of any breaching, and probably faces and stuff, inside the building further down that could be involved in any breaching— "

"You said there were breachers here yesterday?" Alex interrupted, raising his clamshell once again to his mouth, "do you mean like weird robot guys, or people wearing things like guns and stuff in their arms. Or like knife arms, hands. Fingers. Like knife-fingers?"

"It's like super-sharp fingernails they don't cut," he continued distractedly over Jack, lowering his soup to gesticulate and pretend to gut something with his own claw-shaped right hand, "sorry, you go."

"I was just," he went on, however, gesticulating some more, "they have like, microchips on them, the fingernails, and they can change colour— Sorry, you."

"And they can take your *temperature*, of like *your blood*," he couldn't help but continue, "because they're inside your— nah sorry you. I'm, sorry. You."

Jack rubbed her eyes and chortled to herself in bemusement. Alex was feeble, submissive, diabetic and could be completely immature and distracted at times. 'And he's doing it all right here, right now. All at the same time,' she giggled in self-pity.

"You're *so* young," she quipped and commended, "thanks for the soup, though. I'll pay you back."

"Ok," she then uttered with a halting gesture to restart her briefing and let Alex finish his food. "I don't know about any fingernails, that take your temperature, but these guys, these people that we think, might be breachers, are really big, about seven-feet tall-ish, and at least have serious prosthetic eyes and some pretty seriously crazy strength. They also have probably, at least one of them had perhaps a prosthetic, forearm, I guess. At least."

Alex slurped the last of his soup and lowered his clamshell and spork onto his lap to wait patiently for the upcoming part about breaching.

"They wear a big trench coat that's drab green, like they're in an army, and wear black everything underneath and have big boots. When we saw them at first— "

"*You* saw them, right?" Alex interruptingly asked, "not Gerry?"

"Yeah, *I saw them*," Jack agreed and subsequently assured, "but Gerry is in on this too. He knows what I'm talking about. He was a cop! He knows all this stuff."

"Yeah," Alex accepted, shifting his foam down onto the wood to his left so he could lean his elbows onto his knees.

"At that time I saw them at the port," Jack went on, "they had heaps of boxes in their possession, and were the source of the uh, other jamming— Complex jamming! I'm sure of it, *positive*. And one of them even had a *prosthetic* in his hand." Articulating clearly, she revealed, "an *open* forearm, that seemed to have some kind of projection, uh... You know those holograms everywhere, you see them downtown all over the place outside shops, and inside. Usually in glass cubes— "

"Yeah," Alex concurred.

"We have one at home," Jack continued to describe, "but without the glass. You can touch it."

"Yeah," Alex uttered, "like my one at home. Just in my garage," he casually said, pointing his spork elsewhere to emphasise, "next to my Ferrari. I don't use it anymore. It's old. Old hat. Yesterday's— "

"Yeah, yeah, yeah," Jack incredulously responded over him to conclude, "well that prosthetic had some, I think, some kind of *that*, a projection-3D thing, which would be, *usually*, very illegal. Their eyes too were like that a bit but on the inside," she added, pointing to both her eyes. "I can't, it's a little fuzzy now but they were like, uh, just not normal prosthetics, ok? You know."

Comprehending the sudden pause in Jack's briefing to be a time for him to agree vehemently with everything Jack said, Alex attempted to agree vehemently but couldn't.

"So, wai, wai, wait," he summarised, sitting up to list with his fingers, "their strong. They're tall. They've got, at least one prosthetic forearm."

"And their eyes," Jack assertively added, pointing to both her own again.

"And they were in the possession of a prosthetic that could do holograms," Alex added in an unimpressed tone.

"Yep," Jack coaxed him.

"Was anyone *wearing* it?" Alex investigated.

"Well, no," Jack agitatedly replied, "because they were probably just testing it before they would probably put it back in its box and pass it on. We're pretty sure they're being sent into Auckland, to *here*, and possibly other suburbs. That's what we're here to find."

Alex took a deep breath and exhaled in scepticism before leaning back onto the wooden seatback.

"Um, I'm not. I don't know what about that is exactly *illegal*," Alex doubted with a squint of his eyes. "Or, *breaching*; I don't know about these eyes. Considering they're about to change the laws around all this stuff. My flatmates are studying like, law and things, and they discuss this stuff all the time, all this, politics. They don't think *advanced*-advanced prosthetics should be illegal. Er, but right now I think you've gotta be at least wearing them, right, for it to be wrong?"

"There was *more*," Jack irritatedly summarised, "way more, but you just. You're just simplifying it too much. Your flatmates don't know anything. One of these breacher guys was able to push a *shipping container* across the concrete at the port *without wheels*."

"Yeah, ok," Alex concurred obligingly, and relievedly leant forward. "But I thought this would be a bit more, like, *shady*, or *terroristy*. But we're just going to go in there and take pictures anyway, right? You might get some intercepts or something? This is Topher though eh; you'll get *something* dangerous. I just thought when you said 'breachers' it would be a bit *more* dangerous."

"Yeah," Jack agitatedly replied, straightening her posture above the edge of her seat to look down the street, "I get it. Fingernails. You just keep a look out and take photos." Glancing back at Alex, she assured, "those big guys aren't actually usually here anyway; yesterday was the first time I saw them, but. So. We're just here to investigate that delivery from yesterday and look around." Plainly summarising, she concluded, "we're really just trying to get the police off their backsides."

After a moment of silence, Alex commented, "well, you got me off my backside."

After a moment of quiet, he then brought up something far more interesting to him than breachers.

"Hey, did you hear that Expineer was gonna be launching in a few weeks?" he questioned with an upwards inflection, turning his posture more toward Jack, "it's been all over the news. They're going up on the twenty-seventh of August. That's just in a few weeks from now."

Jack didn't want to talk to Alex about Ebee, nor did she want to talk about space, where Ebee was leaving to go to.

"The whole city's going to shut down for the launch so they can watch," he however continued to eagerly discuss. "Apparently though, it's really because there's going to be heaps of electromagnetic interference emitted by the station and its support ships. They're also going to turn off the share-power networks around the city so that all that sort of, radiation, buzzing around won't overheat people's HUDs and coders. It's all to do with how the thrusters work, the station's thrusters. Zi-ol-kowski thrusters. I think I say that right?" he wondered.

"Yeah," Jack replied disinterestedly while scanning the ten-storey roof edges across the street for any odd silhouettes in green. "I've been hearing all about that," she then indulged Alex a little, "my flatmate Elisabeth works for RF Space, er— "

"AH Hope!" Alex corrected, "yeah, they're going up as well. And Solax, but they're going up on the twenty-eighth. The, three countries: us, the U.S. and Switzerland, were all going to make it a public holiday but then the idea just fizzled out in the end when Solax told everyone to get stuffed and, "they'll do things in their own time.""

With a little more energy, he sat up and went on to rant, "did you know that RF Space was named after their founder Ranier Fermia, a French guy? He died like five years back, and now their *egotistical leader* Aaron Heslop has renamed the company after himself. That's the Americans for you," he commented with a roll of his eyes.

After a short pause, he then brought the topic back home, "hey, how did your flatmate end up getting a job with AH Hope and not Expineer anyway? They're based here in Auckland and AH Hope is based in Florida where their station is, Hope."

Jack was in Topher to think about her *own* life going forward and *not* Ebee's, despite the temptation. She had coveted Ebee's amazingly good fortune for far too long already, doing virtually nothing in that time to help herself, and was now looking to improve her own fortune before it became too late and depressing to try. Hearing Alex talk about Ebee's good fortune then was, at least, really surprising, and at most, extremely dampening.

"It's actually really quite jarring to think about it," she respectfully enlightened Alex.

"*I know eh!*" Alex rather passionately replied however, misunderstanding Jack's admonition. "This is a big moment for New Zealand— For Aotearoa; a piece of *Papatūānuku* is actually leaving to go back up, *to meet Ranginui*, I guess, and it's not a big *deal*, to some Kiwis? I see it on social media too, Kiwis championing the Americans but omitting us. It's kinda weird."

"Yeah, well, maybe it's for the best," Jack replied less interestedly, "there's still a bit of a war going on out there isn't there?"

"The Unification War, yeah," Alex filled in, "or something."

"And we've got our own problems," Jack continued to reason, glimpsing down the street. "I don't think we need any attention from the rest of the world's bad guys when we've got our own bad guys getting up to stuff here."

"Mmm," Alex admitted.

"And I guess they wanna get our station up without it being bombed first," Jack propounded, "so maybe directing all that attention to the Americans is a good thing?"

"Mmm," Alex accepted, pressing his lips and blinking agreeably.

After a deep breath, he then spoke, "so do you think your flatmate will try to transfer over to Expineer when everything settles down? When all the stations are up, and everyone is '*unified*' or whatever? Get herself a big penthouse," he quipped, jiggling his hand in front of his face to help illustrate, "right on top of the EX-1."

Jack halted a sad feeling beginning to well up inside her heart by sitting upright to kink her back slightly rearward, press her temples with her fingertips, and take in a deep breath.

Her life was stressful enough without going on about Ebee leaving to go to space and having to worry about losing all the relative wealth and opportunity that would go with her. She currently had breachers to investigate in a suburb that made her feel physically sick, and sometimes fearful, and a supervisor hopefully waiting online to chat that she needed to impress so that she might never have to come back to Topher again.

"Let's just go now," she abruptly declared and stood up.

Speaking over Alex, she held up her rubbish in her right hand and ordered, "let's bin these, go down there, go inside, and look around for signs of breaching, get some intercepts. We're looking for, trails. Let's also keep an eye out for any kidnapped girls."

"Oh," Alex moaned, rolling forward with his body to stand up onto his feet, "inspect peoples' mail, read their messages, deal with possible breachers, and now, help rescue girls from their kidnappers. Sounds like a full morning," he sarcastically put out there in delight while straightening the hem of his jumper. "And I'm not even meant to be working."

Jack ignored him as she moved to wedge her rubbish into the top of an overloaded bin four metres down and dawdle to survey the residents walking on and lingering atop the street's landings. She ignored him some more to gaze up at residents loitering in their open windowsills and stop beneath the clouding sky to let Alex quickly catch up.

"I hate this place," he said, wiping his empty hands together before wiping them on his jumper and asking suggestively, "hey, have you got Gerry on party chat yet?"

"No," Jack replied, gesturing to display a visible absence of electronics on her person.

"Because we could really do with his advice right now," Alex stated, and criticised, "it's not like we're six-foot-eight and had a couple years in the police to prep us for getting punched to death in the face. With a hologram hand." Chuckling shakily, he genuinely questioned, "so why did you have me come in his place!?"

"It was always your place Alex," Jack told him, continuing down the footpath to glance about for anyone green and spot any vans that were crimson.

"Yeah, my place to get *eaten*," Alex decried. "This is like at the port all over again. Where yous sent me for four weeks before telling me yous thought breachers were hiding there. Except now I know. And I'm still going? What the hell? What's wrong with me?"

"You're not gonna get *eaten*," Jack assured him, "we're just gonna look around. We're in mufti; it'll be fine."

Quietening in the presence of a group of locals they were approaching who were sitting in a circle below the damp side of some entry stairs, the two wardens stepped into the nearest gap between the parked cars and looked both ways along the road.

"Are you gonna get Alex on now?" Alex mistakenly asked as he crossed two steps behind Jack, "oh, Gerry! Not me. I'm here already. I suppose you will get me though. Are you gonna start this chat yet?"

"You know, it wouldn't be too late to turn around and go home if you're nervous," he then pronounced, following Jack between the next pair of parked cars to step up onto the next footpath below a grimy white granite high-rise and walk rightwards. "I have a green budgie named Gooseberry. Did I tell you that?"

Jack rolled her eyes at Alex's awkwardly enlivening nerves as she approached a colourfully dressed group of adolescents idling with their bikes and kept her eyes forward as she courteously made her way between them. She then slowed a step to let Alex worriedly stare up at the ten-storey dwellings surrounding them, before staring up at the brick facade of the olive building they were finally arriving beneath herself.

'Eek,' she abruptly exclaimed, making eye contact with a mean pair of eyes looking down at her over the top of a flabby forearm resting in the sill of an open fourth-storey window. 'I hope she stays inside,' she thought, quickly lowering her gaze back down.

Approaching the building's entry stairs at the same rate two young woman were approaching from the opposite direction, she then veered left to skip up the steps as casually as she could pretend to reach the landing and abruptly stop because Alex had already disappeared.

'Get up here,' she silently scolded him with her eyes, spotting him awkwardly stall at the base of the stairs where the two young women were entering into the passenger side of their denim-blue sedan below its opened gull-wing door.

'Ooh, sorry!' Alex's eyes genuinely fretted back, once making contact again with hers.

Staring at him in displeasure as he skipped up to re-join her, Jack cautioned, "don't get lost," and re-turned to briefly evaluate the olive building's immediate innards and enter between the chiselled faces of its widely opened, wooden, double front doors.

Alex couldn't really get lost though, unless he frightenedly exited back out the front. A single, central wooden floorboarded hallway leading to a multiflight staircase at the back was all there was to the poorly lit ground floor, besides six, wooden unit doors evenly spaced on either side along the way that were closed. Being as uninviting as it was, however, with dents and scratches dotting and deeply marking much of the wood, including upon a hip high trim lining both walls along the passage, Jack had to consider that Alex might really do it.

Even the air of the place was off-putting, being increasingly saturated, as they entered deeper, with a mustiness likely originating from a visible film of mildew coating the wood and degrading the adhesion of the green floral-patterned wallpaper peeling from above the trim. Not even two conversing mothers carrying their oddly patchy looking young on the left up ahead seemed to settle the apprehension on Alex's face as he remained close to Jack's side while she delivered them towards the rickety-looking wooden staircase and began climbing.

"Do you know where we're going?" Alex sincerely questioned below his breath as he circled left around the intermediate landing behind her, "or are we just going *up*?"

Jack just gave him a silencing glance and made room for a broad, curly grey-haired silhouette in a translucent, flowery blue dress coming to stand atop the carpeted edge up ahead. Observing an elderly lady then descend out of it upon a pair of sapphire-blue prosthetic feet that clacked with each waddling step downward, she yielded up more room to her right and politely apologised, "sorry," when they brushed shoulders. Subsequently being perturbed, however, to hear a mellow mechanical sound ring out through the lady's wheeze as she listlessly went by, she stepped up onto the carpet of the next floor with a frown and sincerely questioned, 'what, is this place?'

Moving to the opposite end of the hallway so the two wardens could prepare in a patch of grey light breaking in through a horizontal array of windows overlooking the street, she then proceeded to pull out and power on her coder and notice a nervous look in her companion's eyes.

"I, I'm a little worried," Alex uttered above a muffled crescendo occurring behind the nearest unit door to the right of the windows, "about the locals. Catching us going through their stuff, and their messages, and things— "

"Don't worry," Jack told him, pulling out her HUD to synchronise it.

"Because *these* locals," Alex continued, "seem— "

"YOU HATE ME!" an infuriated young women in colourful polished plastics yelled, bursting out from behind the nearest unit door. "YOU ALWAYS HATED ME!" she reemphasised at the top of her lungs, slamming the door so vengefully hard it bounced back open. "TAKE YOUR MONEY," she distressfully groaned into her unit, "AND— JUST GIVE IT TO HER!"

The two wardens abruptly reversed in alarm and very reluctantly gaped as a disgruntled man inside the unit visibly stood behind his couch and reciprocated, "YOU STUPID WOMAN!" They listened to him swear and watched him stomp around the perimeter of his couch and shout, "GIVE MY PARTS BACK IF YOU DON'T LIKE IT— "

"Shut up!" a muffled voice erupted from behind another door across the hallway. "Just shut up already!" it repeated before banging the inside of its door in outrage.

"THEN! FINE!" the infuriated young woman shouted into her unit. "TAKE," she continued, unintelligibly stammering on as she forcefully jiggled her mustard yellow jaw from clean off her face and spread her footing for her to aggressively pitch the prosthetic straight back inside.

"DON'T WRECK THEM!" the man raged, striking a deflective pose.

"I HATE YOU!" the self-harming woman seemingly shrieked through her deformed buccal cavity, proceeding to fidget with her black, white and mustard yellow forearm to remove it cleanly from below her right elbow joint and throw it disgustedly back inside as well.

"I HATE ME!" she seemingly wept while fiddling resentfully with her left thigh to forcefully unclick and completely remove her entire white and black plastic leg from under her black shorts and balance with a hop upon her other.

Raising and slamming the large appendage sideways at the doorway and consequently collapsing into a bawling heap of regret, she hurriedly then began dragging what was left of herself away.

The stunned wardens watched, with others poking their heads out from behind their doors, the woman obliquely worm to the stairs with an amplifying, agonising cry to where she could shuffle onto her bottom and clench balusters to begin lowering her uneven frame down the steps.

"YOU DISGUSTING ROBOT!" the man suddenly growled, picking up the discarded leg to spitefully fling it into the well ahead of his sobbing, disappearing partner. "YOU— GROSS!" he yelled, stomping back into his apartment to swear frustratedly out loud and jarringly slam his door closed behind him.

Being discombobulated by the noise, the rage, the door slamming and flying prosthetics, and completely resistant to the idea of getting involved, especially when undertaking an undercover investigation, Jack just remained in her stunned state and let the locals settle down themselves. She let the agonising cry in the stairwell slowly repress into an agonising moan on the storey below and let all the concerned residents disappear one by one back inside their homes.

Once believing it peaceful enough to resume their day, she then let out a longly held breath with a, "whew," and subsequently let Alex adjust that belief once reading a mortified, 'WHAT. THE. HELL!?' expression from off of his unremitting face.

Recollecting two more storeys up at the end of a quiet hallway in a patch of grey light breaking in through a horizontal array of windows overlooking the street, the two wardens proceeded to pull out their equipment again and restart their preparations.

"I feel like I've been here already," Alex dubiously uttered, pointing to a nearby unit located to the right-hand side from the windows, "and someone comes out that door. And takes their, face off. And then the... Rest."

Jack didn't see the young woman's disfigured face from her angle quite so clearly as Alex saw it from his during that startling interruption, and so gave him a sympathetic moment to share his nightmare while resynching her equipment.

"I saw her tongue," he troubledly revealed, demonstrating it with his hand, "it wiggled from straight out of her throat."

Taking the sympathetic moment back with a disgusted quiver to preserve what was left of her own innocence, Jack inserted, "I saw a fight the other day where that happened in the street. And— Further down. And, they threw a guy's arm, plastic arm into an oncoming car, to get run over."

"Ah," Alex anxiously replied.

"There, there *are*, good people here, though," Jack ensured to inform him of her observations.

"Yeah," Alex disquietly replied, and opined, "*us*."

Letting a descending family comprising two responsible-looking parents and two pleasantly behaving pre and primary schoolers wearing lovely cream dresses demonstrate that good for themselves by circling around the stairwell in peace, Jack slipped on her HUD and initiated a party chat with Gerry's jam doughnut-eating icon. Blocking her left ear to enhance the speaker while watching the pixels in front her eyes animate the progress of her connection, she swallowed and cleared her throat before greeting, "Gerry?" the second his sound graph blipped into life.

"Jump in," she more quietly signalled to Alex.

"Āe," Gerry greeted back to the sound of him unfolding an old metal chair with a screech that he bumped onto the hard council basement floor in his background. "Hold on while I move this, and swap this, for, something bigger. I just got in from after a visit to the bakery, where I bought yous some food, with mine. Are yous gonna come in after this or? What's happening? I got Alex an apple turnover? And I got you a blueberry bran muffin."

Speaking over the rest of his receipt, Jack uttered, "um," and watched Alex's empty icon connect to their party. "I. We've just, gotten, into position to start this party, um. You may need to put our food in the fridge for tomorrow, for now; we've eaten. And we don't know what, how, this is going to— "

"Hey Gerry?" Alex interrupted in a disaffected tone, "do you have your face on?"

"Yeah— What?" Gerry replied, clearing his throat as he sat down in front of a fixed council terminal. "Yeah, I've got my *game-face* on," he energisingly quipped.

"A-oh," Alex responded in a subdued tone, "good... Good." Adding with an upwards inflection, he then further inquired, "hey, Gerry, are you busy? Because I was wondering if we could swap— "

"Don't listen to him Gerry," Jack interrupted with a smirk at her material companion, "Alex is hard. He can take it."

Interjecting quickly before another appearing empty chat icon could successfully connect into the party, Gerry sounded, "uh," before clearing his throat and advising, "here's Maka now; he's going to join our party. Alex, this is Maka Parata, a senior constable in the police so watch what you say."

"Bananas," Alex irresistibly replied before Gerry could warn, "and make sure you're not intercepting while off-duty."

Jack very quickly became nonplussed to hear that, and rather visibly so, to Alex's disaffected delight. It was rare for him to come across Jack at a loss for commanding words and so was amused to see her share in the bewilderment she was causing him this day, most especially just after a moment of such anxiety.

"Hi Gerry," a burly new voice suddenly announced to the party with a timbre of urgency, "have you got those wardens ready?"

"Yeah bro," Gerry instantly replied, "we've got wardens 5-6-2-0 and 7-8-0-1 here in chat with us."

"Hey," the wardens enounced as Gerry continued, "but they are both off-duty, hence we'll be only streaming today; and not even really— It's not even— Anyway, you know. So, Jack and Alex are going to locate products suspected of breaching anti-singularity laws," he declared, taking in a breath, "uh. And there's also these two missing girls... Emerald Jenkins and, Ajes-i-pha Jenkins?"

Cutting in abruptly, Maka re-evaluated, "yeah nah, you can forget about those two. The word now is that they are possible *runaways* who hopped the ditch a week ago with a small group of transhuman activists, in, I guess, some kind of, solidarity with all this... *Mess* surrounding the activists here." Taking a big breath, he divulged, "their group was picked up in Sydney but have since been let go by their authorities, so."

With Alex now gazing out the window in slight disinterest, Jack respectfully questioned, "s-does that mean that that task force thing is, not a thing, anymore?"

"Yeah," Gerry eagerly wondered as well, "so what are we working with now? What's, the situation? How do we move forward with our investigation, into these breachers?"

"At this time," Maka began to explicate, "the Terrorist Task Force remains ready for deployment and is in fact on standby right now, just in case. These girls, may be located now, and have stated that they are safe but investigators here will now need to rule out the possibility of them communicating under duress. They will also need to investigate whether they, with others who we don't exactly all know yet, falsely staged a crime over their kidnapping, which is very seriously illegal in and of itself. There is also still the connected threats sent to Manaia Winiata's Ministry of Health office to coerce a release of an offender and coerce Te Ariki Wright, an opposition anti-singularity politician, to change his stance on an upcoming anti-singularity amendment being brought to parliament— "

"That *does* sound like a mess," Alex said, randomly giving a few cents.

"Which is very, *very* seriously illegal," Maka passionately described. "And so, regardless of the state of these girls, who clearly aren't even in the country anymore, the police are still poised to find others remaining here who were involved, and remain suspects in these cases of political coercion, or extortion— "

"This still counts as terrorism? Doesn't it?" Gerry chimed in.

"In— Yes," Maka agreed, "in twenty sixty-three, as of, or, still up to today, this behaviour does fall under terrorism. It falls on the lighter end— "

"The threats?" Gerry clarified.

"Yep," Maka agreed, "on the lighter end for political coercion, with political extortion being heavier, but regardless of where they fall, these uh, actions, did qualify on the terror scale, and were largely performed and facilitated by people we don't know specifically, but who have declared themselves to be transhuman activists."

"So, we're still on," Gerry figured.

"We are still on," Maka assured.

"Ok then," Gerry redirected, "Jack? Have you got anything yet? Or?"

"W-uh, we are in place," she spoke in uncertainty, looking for support from Alex, who was still looking out the window in disinterest. "We um, don't have anything yet. But we did find some, um, domestic stuff. Nothing um, though, what we're looking for. Or, well, maybe?"

Stepping towards her distracted companion to tap him on the arm and get some input while Maka and Gerry talked between themselves, she waited, and then tapped again because he ignored her. "W-what?" she asked, irritatedly looking out his window to view what it was that was absorbing his utmost attention.

"Did those deliveries from yesterday come in a van?" Alex spoke, pointing obliquely down the pane to a curiosity occurring at the base of their building.

Adjusting her head closer to the glass to look down as straight as she could, Jack leaned forward to examine and behold the crimson roof of a van that may have been parked there the day before.

"Oh!" she expressed in complete surprise about her luck. "That could be the delivery van! Or, some other like it. We gotta check it out!"

Looking out again to confirm the sight of the van being parked directly below the building's entry stairs, she stood back and pressed her HUD against her ear. "Uh, Gerry?" she politely interrupted, "there may be a delivery going on *right now*."

"Sorry Maka," Gerry said, interrupting himself and finally taking a bite of his first jam cream doughnut, "hey, Jack. What's happening?"

"There's a van parked at the front of the building now that may be making a delivery," Jack roughly repeated, walking back towards the stairs, "and we're gonna check it out. We may go quiet," she warned, flicking her wrist for Alex to follow, "don't leave chat."

"Ok," Gerry affirmed through his partially filled mouth as the wardens briskly went to work, "hey Maka? Is there any legal way for us to get a stream going? Where we can— "

"What?" Maka replied with a frown while trying to decipher, "oh yeah. But you would all have to switch to non-council equipment. And at least one of your wardens would have to get a private HUD up and running. Gerry you would probably need to leave the building over there. Are you *eating*?"

"I can start a stream now," Alex offered as he approached and started down the stairs behind Jack. "I have my private HUD on and will set up another party," he explained over Gerry's concurring input, "just so long as everyone keeps their faces on."

"No intercepting," Maka ensured to remind everyone, "no entering exclusively private properties unless clearly invited. Gerry, get off any council equipment. No one declare any authority whatsoever. Actually, turn all council equipment completely off."

"Āe," Gerry replied, gathering his and his wardens' bagged bakery confections into his coat, "switching over now. Alex, you send me an invite. Maka, will *you* need to move?"

"Argh, this never just listens to me," Alex warily complained in a muted tone, circling around the stairs a storey down, "stupid machine. Jack can you slow down? Your pace— I can't— Your moving too fast for my brain to think clearly."

Jack slowed in the next intermediate landing to remove her HUD with her left hand and turn to pluck Alex's metallic red HUD off his face with her right. "Is this locked?" she quietly asked, anticipating an affirmative reply, "what's the password?"

"Uh," Alex mumbled, wondering for a second before quietly confessing, "'Alex'."

"Oh," Jack incredulously responded, "are you serious?"

"I can't do that deep-thinking thing you do!" Alex whined in a hushed tone, "just say it, and I'll change it later. When I don't have to move so fast, or think."

"What does the 'Alex' look like?" Jack asked him, slipping the thickly rimmed device on around her eyes, "any zeros or anything?"

"I don't *do* that!" Alex stressed, "it's just the word!"

"Oh my goodness," Jack reproved, resuming their descent. Adjusting the HUD to contact neatly with her articulator patch behind her right ear, she succinctly thought, 'Alex,' to successfully unlock Alex's virtually unprotected device and intuitively command, 'set up a stream, broadcast. Set up a party. Merge stream with party.' Reading from off the blue digital menu popping up to the left of her vision, she perused, 'Invite, Contacts, Gerry Moeke, Jacqueline Hart. Invite, Recent Contacts, Snr Cons. Maka Parata.'

"Here," she then stated, handing back Alex his device over her shoulder while slipping back on hers, since she didn't have another, and going around another landing.

"Man," Alex commented in awe, clasping and slipping his securely back on, "how do you just do that? With such ease? I need— "

"Shh!" Jack interrupted, gesticulating for him to cease talking as she came down to discreetly inspect the empty second-storey hallway for anything she could correlate with an intermittent talking becoming increasingly distinct as they descended.

Continuing around to discreetly inspect the ground storey to expectedly correlate the talking, she abruptly backed up on the intermediate landing and expired, "whoa," after seeing a man in blue rainwear thank a pair of hands extending a flattened pile of cardboard from behind the nearest, open, right-hand doorway. Peeking repeatedly from her concealed position on the stairs to watch the blue rainwear peppily leave with the cardboard, and the pair of hands start singularly offloading from a twin stack of plain boxes sitting outside their door, she stepped hesitantly and then skipped down onto the wooden floor.

Plucking a sixty by thirty, twenty-centimetre-high tape-sealed box from off the nearer stack beside the left door jamb when the hands weren't looking, she turned a hundred and eighty degrees to whip back up the stairs with a creak and bump into Alex in the landing.

"*Are you crazy?!*" he whispered loudly, animating thoroughly his worry as he reversed, "is that even from the delivery? That could be someone's new kitchenware!"

"Shh!" Jack hushed him, energetically encouraging below her breath, "up! Up! Up! *Up!*" as Gerry and Maka entered Alex's party chat.

Ascending back onto the second storey with another creak so they could get out of the well and privately assess the slightly loose contents of the

Chapter Nine

roughly three-kilogram box, she nodded to a spot further up on the right for them to move into.

"I'm outside now Maka," Gerry conveyed, exiting the council lobby onto the street. "Hey, careful, you two," he warned, watching through Alex's feed Jack pull up and begin examining the six sides of the cardboard box's plain exterior. "Could be brittle."

"Could be explosive," Maka further warned, to the wardens' sudden weariness.

"Uh," Jack expressed, very slowly returning the box to its original orientation.

"Hey Gerry?" Alex spoke in apprehension, "what are you up to now?"

"Umm," Gerry dispelled as he started crossing a busy road in the CBD to keep himself occupied, "just watching traffic dude. You should focus."

Giving Alex half a second to flee while balancing the box in her left arm against her chest so she could grab out her coder with her right, Jack used a slightly sharp edge jutting from one of her device's corners to puncture and slice along the tape's seal. 'No way,' she paused to visibly express some doubt and pocket her coder before resuming pulling open the cardboard flaps.

"*Ee!*" Alex timorously muttered, covering his face as Jack safely opened them wide and criticised, "huh-calm down."

"I can hear ticking," Gerry unhelpfully commented, approaching another pedestrian crossing along his path in town, "but that could be the crossing box thing here. Yeah, it's this. Hey Alex— "

"Hey, Alex," Maka commented over him, keeping the tone of the operation focussed, "mate, you're blocking the camera with your hands, I think. Can you, pull them away?"

"Oh," Alex replied, lowering his quivering hands to the height of his chest so he could guard his face from the box.

"No," Maka firmly stated.

"Alex!" Gerry seconded, "you're blocking— We need to see!"

"Oh," Alex moaned, lowering his guard completely to reveal Jack's hand foraging in an abundance of light-pink packing peanuts. "Fine," he conceded, pulling the hem of his jumper taut, "can you see now?"

"Yes," Gerry said with Maka's, "yep, but can you move in a step. Jack, what have we got?"

"*A forearm!* " Jack disclosed, raising the plastic wrapped prosthetic limb out of the box with some of its foam. "And a hand, attached," she further described, twisting the tanned and black patched object around to goggle over it.

"Oh, gross!" Alex whinged disgustedly, "I hate this place. And also, you got some foam on me," he added, looking down to wipe it from his clingy jumper.

"Wait!" Gerry subsequently exclaimed.

"Alex, can you look up again?" Maka asked in slight irritation, "and keep your eyes on the object. Don't cover your HUD."

"Urgh," Alex whined, letting his audience watch Jack pass him the box and hastily begin unwrapping the plastic from around the forearm.

Discarding the rubbish into the box so she could present the synthetically skinned and hairless prosthetic to Alex's HUD, Jack proceeded to considerately turn it around on its axis while examining for herself its very interesting composition. "It has semi-realistic skin," she described, touching and rubbing the various segments of it with her fingers, before noting the scratchless state of the robotic black knuckles, "and it doesn't look like it's really been used, ever. And it has no obvious fingerprints."

"That's gross," Alex commented.

"There are no obvious bones inside," Jack further described of the skin covered segments, pressing parts of the appendage with both her hands, "and there are all these black seams," she added, running her index finger along a couple of examples bisecting both lateral and medial sides of the forearm. "There are these labelled, patches too," she said, pointing at a trapezoidal, black suede trim containing an uninterpretable red logo wrapping the thumb webbing. Pointing to another located on the distal end of the forearm where it was abutting a three-millimetre-wide metal seam circumnavigating the wrist, she postulated, "I think the hand must separate from here. Or just, twist." Going on to test the flexibility of the limb's joints, she revealed, "they're pretty resistant," jiggling the stiff, nail-less fingers and knuckles, and described, "but that is, *amazing*," forcibly swivelling and bending the black wrist.

"Jack, can you check the back for any key ports?" Maka coaxed, "there is usually an articulation plate on the end, like at the wrist— "

"Oh sorry, Ma'am," Gerry randomly spoke, "my apologies. I wasn't looking properly— I truly apologise. I-It's my fault. Hey guys," he then remarked, looking up past the crisscrossing bridges of Babel to the dulling white sky above, "it's starting to spit. I might head indoors again."

Examining a polished metal plate affixed mostly inside the proximal end of the arm comprising some interlocking latches and a curiously blocked rubber port, Jack affirmed, "uh, yeah, Maka. I don't know about a key, but this may be that." She then displayed the end to Alex's HUD and checked on Alex, "are you alright?"

"Yeah," he hummed and shrugged in an unsettled fashion.

"Jack, typically the keys for those types of port come with the prosthetic in its box," Maka went on to discuss, "could you please look inside the box for a key? It could look like an Allen key with a, a, the uh, pattern, on the long end. The key would usually serve as a battery to unlock and access the prosthetic with a little bit of current."

Jack buried her hand again inside Alex's packing peanuts to swirl around and feel for anything useful and then whip the peanuts up when male voices began echoing in the stairwell. "I can't," she disappointedly panted.

"Is this it?" Alex interjected, holding up a slate-coloured Allen key between his fingers.

Snatching it from him as the echoes continued to casually louden, Jack hurriedly brought the long end of the key to the end of the prosthetic to align and insert and consequentially cause the limb to vibrate and click.

"Did it unlock?" Maka asked, and advised, "they sometimes have a beep— "

"It unlocked," the two wardens replied.

"Ok," Maka stated, positing, "now you should be able to pry parts of it open without breaking them. I don't know if the hand can be removed yet."

Jack gripped and removed the ventral segment clean off the arm by accident, subsequently spinning the limb to reveal a moulded plastic sheath of electrical contact points covering the innards. She placed the segment onto the peanuts and plucked out the sheath with little difficulty, letting it gently hang from its wires, and started her probe into the prosthetic's componentry.

"Careful of any electrolyte leaking out!" Maka remembered to warn, "sorry. That, might be late."

"Nah," Jack relieved him, as a subtle perturbance of chiming and ringing began exciting Gerry's sound graph as he moved indoors, "it's— "

"It's clear," Alex finished her sentence, before wearily looking past her shoulder to the empty stairs and back at her. "Unless you drank it when I blinked."

"C'oh," Jack scoffed, dismissing him to poke at a tension wire-wrapped actuator sitting tidily inside the arm's proximal housing. Running her finger then over a flexible battery contorting beside it and around a two-by-four-inch-longitudinal bulk abutting the distal end, she questioned, "what's this?" about the bulk and spun the arm back over. Keenly pulling the dorsal segment up and forward in an arcing motion due to four rotating braces keeping it together, she then revealed a largely empty black well abutting the wrist bearing only one thick exiting wire sticking up.

"What's this?" Alex commented, pointing at an exposed grey contraption affixed beneath the outer segment the thick wire was leading to.

"What is that?" Jack wondered, presenting the contraption's conjoined cuboidal and cylindrical parts to Alex's HUD.

"That, is a disruptor," Gerry boldly declared and coaxed, "a rudimentary disruptor. Maka, we have seen that before. You have seen that before."

"We have seen that before," Maka less energetically agreed, and disclaimed, "I actually also have one holstered on my chest right now, a nicer, handled one, but yeah... That does look interesting."

"Yes!" Gerry congratulated with a clap, pivoting beneath a turquoise glow lighting the gaming arcade he had wandered into. "That's what we need. That's the one Jack," he praised, letting his eyes explore over the various screens and displays vibrantly throbbing and flashing elsewhere in the noisy establishment, "you got 'em— "

"No Jack, you've got nobody!" Maka forthrightly corrected. "That is insufficient to warrant, any, real response! That is not enough!" Continuing over Gerry, he debated, "there is nothing illegal about having a device of that nature in, simply, a plastic case. The recipient could have a firearms licence for goodness sake. And it could even be just a toy!"

Gerry's praise turned to disappointment as he conceded to Maka's reasoning and complained, "argh, that's true."

Candidly, Maka explained, "you need to get this, on someone, before we can do *anything*." Over Gerry's elevated rhetoric, he clarified, "a licenced disruptor in a case is *not* illegal. A licenced disruptor concealed inside the prosthetic of someone wearing it, *is*."

"Wait," Gerry near unintelligibly rebutted beneath a chime resounding from a basketball shooting game he was approaching, "you couldn't licence this— This wouldn't be allowed. It's concealed in an arm! And even if it were just a pencil sharpener, it'd still be illegal," he said, paying for and starting a round. "And who, in Topher, could even get a licence?"

"Yeah," Maka had to agree, "I know, but it also still could be *a toy*. And that would *not* be illegal. And, let's be honest, nobody is going to be charged for housing a pencil sharpener in their arm."

"Could we ping the receiver?" Gerry then questioned with a hint of concentration and physical exertion as he shot, "if he's not licenced— And the deliverer, if he was not licenced. We could have a case!"

"Just," Maka exasperatedly cut in, "Gerry, just let this play out a bit, it might not be what we think. Could either of you there try powering it?" he then asked Jack, as far as Jack was concerned. "Argh, but the key won't be enough," he recanted to Alex's relief, clicking his fingers.

"What's going on here!?" a gruff male voice then startled Jack and Alex back inside their tenement in Topher, *"what's this?"*

"Swish!" Gerry exclaimed to the sound of cheerful arcade music.

Jack abruptly yanked the key from the arm, dropped both items back into the packing peanuts and peeked over her shoulder to see a shorter, solid-looking Polynesian man in a blue cap, white singlet and cream shorts glare accusingly at her from the top of the descending staircase.

"Man, I should come here more often," Gerry disconnectedly suggested as digital bells rang celebratorily in the background around him. "Jack you would totally enjoy this."

Jack ignored Gerry, who wasn't paying attention to his feed anymore, to pay her attention to the tall teenager from yesterday's delivery stepping up from behind the glaring man to join him at his left side. Noticing him dressed in a white cap, white singlet and shorts again, which was weird yesterday during the cold, but now plainly unsettling in the presence of the similarly dressed man beside him, she deduced, 'that could be a uniform,' and turned back to disappointedly mutter, "Alex?"

"I think Gerry's at Romero's," Alex's loudly whispered, calmly shutting the flaps to his box as Gerry cheered about some newly won tickets.

"I think I've found the box," the unimpressed man in white gruffly told his matching teenager friend and pointed. "And caught these guys going through it."

Unable to ward off a sinking sense of guilt growing heavily inside her chest, and worry clouding her mind, nor really concentrate through Gerry's seriously distracting noise, Jack turned to them again and randomly responded, "hey," with a single non-threatening head nod and took in a deep ventilating breath.

The males looked far too staunch for her and Alex to intimidate and far too focussed to take their missing box lightly. They bore similar segmentation upon their limbs to that seen on the seized prosthetic, with it reaching as high and low on the teen as his deltoids and right knee, and roughly emanated an impression of community enforcement.

Tensing her chest and expiring through her pressed lips to hopefully calm her leaping heartrate and enlivening nerves, Jack continued, "sorry. We um— "

"We thought it was our new kitchenware," Alex timidly spoke louder over her and swallowed. "Some of, a box of, food containers, we ordered— But it was a, a hand."

"Yeah," Jack attested, flicking her wrist to point up at the ceiling, "we're from upstairs."

"What?" the unimpressed man asked in confusion as the teenager shook his head in doubt, and Gerry randomly praised himself for his success.

"And the um, courier guy," Alex timidly went on, "is, urgh, was not our uh... Courier guy. We should have gone with the drone. Option."

"Yeah," Jack agreed, freely offering, "sorry. This is yours."

"*Yeah it's ours!*" the teenager rebuked, before curiously inquiring of Jack, "weren't you in my building yesterday?" and then guessing, "is that an info warden's HUD? I think that's an info warden's HUD," he told his friend.

"Are yous *info wardens!?*" the man gruffly asked in alarm, pulling a flat black rectangle out from his pocket.

"Hey, what is this?" Gerry curiously asked, returning his attention to the real world streaming into his HUD, "what's happening? Jack? Maka— "

"They've got company," Maka disappointedly told him in concern, encouraging the wardens, "you've got to get rid of these guys, Alex. Jack, you better not have a council HUD on."

"Get rid of? What!?" Alex incidentally divulged into the hallway, before awkwardly apologising to the much more physically capable males he disturbed ahead, "sorry. I'm streaming."

"*Oh!*" Maka and Gerry both decried.

"What!?" the man exclaimed, holding his rectangle out in front of him to seemingly scan the strangers.

"Cut them off," the teenager proclaimed, looking at the man's rectangle and pointing to the wardens.

"Hey, that could be a pocket jammer!" Gerry pronounced, holding his HUD closer to his ear to block the surrounding noise and insist, "you two, leave the premises now. Drop the box and just leave. Maka, it's time."

"Time for what!?" Maka critically replied, "for me to send in a patrol to arrest your wardens for stealing someone's mail? They still need more evidence!"

"Oh man," Alex groaned in self-pity.

"Oi, Sale," a young Polynesian woman coming partway down the ascending stairs in brown conveniently interrupted. "Mum wants you to go to the market before it finishes," she conveyed, relaxing her elbows upon the inner banister to address him standing at the top of the adjacent staircase down. "And it finishes soon at twelve."

"Oh, yep," the man in white nicely replied, nodding obligingly over his shoulder and lowering his device a little, "I'm just helping out Sherman."

Jack figured it an opportune time at that moment to change the course of the encounter and relieve Alex of Sherman's box, and so grasped it from him, instructing, "let's go," and hastily moved to dump it into the reluctant hands of the teenager. "Sorry," she insincerely told the teen without looking, "we had the wrong delivery," and smoothly continued up the ascending staircase.

"Hey!" the man beside him disapprovingly exclaimed, watching Jack leave. Tightly grabbing the neck of Alex's jumper as he tried to follow her up, he ordered, "STOP!" and yanked Alex back down off the first couple steps.

"Hey!" Alex whined, losing his rearward footing to tip, fall and bang his back onto the carpet and expel the wind from out of him.

"*Hey!*" Jack disgustedly declared, gazing back to see her companion be manhandled and knelt on by the enforcing males while struggling to refill his lungs.

"Hey! Sale!" the young women halfway up the staircase above her called in displeasure, "get off him and go the market! Mum is waiting!"

Gerry cursed at the erratic blur of pixels streaming in front of his eyes and snarling sounding into his ears and ordered, "Alex! Get Jack out of there!" while capturing warped stills of the ceiling above Alex's head and his primary aggressor.

"Alex is on his back!" Maka conclusively deduced, watching Alex's stream spin as his HUD was flung down the hallway, "Gerry, Alex is down! Jack what's— "

"He's winded," Jack vocally described over the elevating rhetoric while dropping down a few steps to yell, "HEY!" at the assailants and anxiously wait for them to stop physically prohibiting Alex's movement and respiration with their pressing hands and knees.

"You think you're the boss!?" the sweary teenager intimidated while trying to hold Alex's lower body in place, "you think you're the boss around here, little piglet!? YOU PUNK!"

"Alex! Get up dude!" Gerry fruitlessly coaxed from his powerless position in town, "Maka, call it in!"

"They need more evidence!" Maka sympathetically argued back, "Jack! Figure it out!"

"Sale! Josh!" the young woman standing above Jack disapprovingly called, "get off him!" appealing next, *"Mum!"*

"HEY!" Jack repeated from the lower steps as her feeling of guilt was pushed out of her system by a rush of heat filling her limbs and a blur of emotion muddling her thoughts.

"Go find Jeremy, or Kupa," the assailing man ordered his teenage companion while choking Alex with his right hand before slapping him with his stiff left and adjusting his weighted knees on his ribcage.

Immediately complying, the teenager stood to pull his sagging waistline up, incidentally eye Jack, and abruptly point his plastic left fist at her as he turned to leave. "You just stay right there," he threatened, simultaneously springing from his segmented wrist a concealed contraption similar in appearance to the one lying in Sherman's box on the floor by his feet.

"HURRY UP JOSH!" the young woman above Jack disgruntledly shouted, "take Sale and go! The market's gonna close!"

"Maka!" Gerry cajoled, "my wardens are being attacked now! *Call it in!"*

Successfully wriggling out from under and pushing off the easing man, Alex flailed to his feet in a fluster and barked for air, leaning his elbow upon the hallway's wall so he could massage his aching chest with his other hand. His head then hit the wall, due to the assailing man shoving it, causing him to protectively curl and brace for a following assault.

"HEY!" Jack shouted in anger, watching Alex innocently shrink from the violence as the teenager descended out of view.

"SALE!" the young woman above Jack yelled.

"*He's an info warden!*" the assailing man yelled back at her, pushing Alex by his shoulder once more against the wall.

"WHAT'S GOING ON DOWN THERE!" a louder, more authoritative female voice then erupted from the landing above the young woman, causing everyone to either pause or jump and steer their sights upwards to an obese, middle-aged Polynesian mother wearing a blanketing coffee-coloured gown. Garlanded with a head of dark curly hair and a displeased frown while leaning needfully with her hands on the inner bannister for support, she commanded, "SALE! GO TO THE MARKET *NOW!*" as an irate resident began banging the inside of his front door opposite the man below. "I WANT MY MILK!" she demanded over the man's informative response, "MY BREAD! My eggs. My buns. I WANT MY BUTTER— "

"Jeremy's coming home," the returning teenager informed, climbing back up onto the second storey and lowering his coder.

"JOSH!" the mother loudly and distinctly ordered him, "take Sale and go to the market!"

Alex slid along the wall at that point to retrieve his metallic red HUD from off the carpet and slide back past his contesting assailants so he could re-join with Jack up the steps. Bearing the red markings upon his neck, cheeks and chin of one vigorously roughed up, and enfeebled body language of one compressing a sore, swelling abrasion upon his right brow, he looked up into Jack's eyes and supplicated for relief.

Jack didn't hesitate to appease him, grabbing his raised elbow to briskly guide him up past the young woman silently endorsing her mother, and the mother loudly admonishing her begrudging son and his friend. Squeezing by onto the landing to be civilly asked, "are you two info wardens are you?" by the mother and circle around to continue up, she respectfully admitted, "oh, uh. Yes," and picked up the pace.

"Oh man," Gerry moaned, hearing the communication come through clearly on his end. "Maka?" he appealed in disillusion, dropping his head back in the arcade and rubbing his eyes, "dude? My wardens— "

"Yeah, I called it in," Maka bemoaned, flopping discontentedly back in his office chair as Gerry relievedly thanked him. "The chopper will arrive in a few minutes. Jack and Alex, you should get out of there if you can, or prepare." Disappointedly standing up from his desk with a wary sigh, he perturbedly announced, "I've got to go. I hope this is worth it," and abruptly left the party.

"Jack!?" Gerry stated, promptly heading out of the arcade into the accommodating plaza, "where's Alex? I'm just getting noise and blur from his feed. Are you there Alex?" he queried, weaving around a blithe group of elderly women in his path.

"Alex is up," Jack replied, circling with him closely in tow two storeys up from the audibly growing commotion they were escaping. "He'll be fine."

"Where are we going?" Alex sceptically spoke, lowering his right hand and pocketing his HUD with his left so he could press against his thighs and start up yet another flight of stairs behind Jack.

"You two need to leave immediately, alright?" Gerry went on, going back outside onto the street to hail a roaming taxi. "Exit the premises to the street outside and wait there. I'll pick you up. I've just got to catch this taxi coming right now— "

"No!" Jack replied, circling the next landing slowly to let Alex's tiring legs catch up, "we'll meet you at the transport station." Unzipping her pocket to pull out and power on her coder so she could synchronise and bring up a detailed satellite map of Topher in her HUD, she stated, "I'm gonna take us up to the roof so we can drop down a fire escape outside."

"Ok," Gerry concurred, watching an autonomous black taxi slow and pull into the empty car park he was standing over.

"Argh," Alex complained, fatiguing to a near halt on the next floor, "no. Not that. I don't wanna get stuck on a fire escape between these guys... We can use that mum to help us go back down and out the front. We'll just promise to *never* come back."

"Oh," Jack groaned at the base of the next staircase and pointed out, "they're still arguing," about the disgruntled echoes growing in the stairwell. "Just a few more floors, please?" she begged, and resumed climbing.

"Alright, I'm coming now," Gerry informed, sitting comfortably back in his taxi's rear seat as it started driving. "It'll be approximately, urgh, *twenty-seven minutes* before I get to the transport station," he discontentedly revealed, reading off the cabin screen ahead of him. "You two will need to."

Passing residents in the well on her way up to the sixth storey to where she could pull over and wait for Alex, who was lagging behind, Jack asked Gerry, "we'll need to what?" and peered back down to rally Alex with an assertive, scooping wave. "We'll need to what?" she repeated, commanding the map on her HUD to zoom in on her coordinates while walking into the hallway. "Gerry?" she asked once more, returning her party chat window to the front of her HUD to find herself disconnected, and sigh. Wasting no time to reconnect though, with Gerry already on his way and Alex finally making it up, she brought her lagging map back to the front of her HUD to discover their building so tightly packed between its neighbours it couldn't possibly fit a fire escape anywhere but on the facade.

"Oh!" she disappointedly expressed, double-checking out the hallway's windows to confirm an absence of any alternative way down onto the street besides falling. "This place is a death trap," she frustratedly described to Alex as he dawdled to re-join her and glumly signal for a break, "there is no fire escape, except for, maybe, down the road."

"So, we'll go ask the Mum," Alex derisively pronounced, promptly beckoning her to turn back with him.

Jack sighed in dejection and dragged her feet, watching him compress his brow again and adamantly walk off towards the descending staircase. Alex was obviously no match for the brutes downstairs, and couldn't possibly know what would transpire after soliciting help from the mum, but had been loyal to her plan thus far, even to the point of being beaten, and was deserving of some recognition.

'Ok, it's your turn,' she reluctantly acquiesced, and briskly closed the gap between them to follow him four steps down the stairs, and abruptly bump into him because he halted.

"Hey!" she irritatedly rebuked, closing her HUD's freezing software to peer past him and see what the hold-up was.

Shuddering instantly at the sight of an exceptionally large shadow on the landing below bending over to pluck a lone pink packing peanut up from off the wood, she then clenched the banisters on either side of her and recoiled. She could see a long, dark open trench coat draping from its flanks and a big pair of black hiking boots planting its width firmly to the floor. She could discern an unnatural exactness in the way it erected itself high in the well to inspect the peanut between its fingertips, and then glance with an ominous glint directly up at the jumper from whence it came.

"Ohgh!" Alex uttered, promptly wiping the remaining peanuts from his jumper, and panicking when they consequently clung to his sleeves.

"*Breacher!*" Jack lipped, precipitately snatching the rear of Alex's jumper to pull him up and back out of the stairwell.

Tugging her seizing companion five skittish metres back into the hallway to break the line of sight and fussily push him a metre rightward to spread out, she indecisively prepared her footing for a confrontation, and then more rationally, an escape, before simply petrifying because it was too late. The breacher's steely stare was upon her, and rising, above the creaking staircase's crest ahead of a broad, barricade of muscle perceivable beneath the thick, matt-black and green-collared weave of his military-style gear. Beholding it elevate its intimidating entirety up onto the sixth floor to crush the carpet beneath its tread and stand imposingly over the room as a seven-foot-tall, four-foot-wide wall, Jack took a fearful step back and shakily swallowed.

The breacher's pre-eminence was daunting and its powerful frame so very present. Jack could measure the circumference of its biceps and forearms bursting through its green sleeves with her eyes and barely conceive the amount of protein, real or synthetic, it would take to sculpt a set thighs and calves so bulging. Even while noticing two taut, yellow plastic bags of ordinary groceries in its matt-black left hand, enveloping a visible bunch of unwrapped bananas and two blue-topped, white bottles of milk, she could barely contain her awe.

'You look *so* heavy,' she admired of the robotic beast's stature before catching an incidental glimpse of its ever so slightly glistening stare. 'And *so* unimpressed.'

Feeling the stare weigh down on her and transmit the breacher's dominance in relative silence for a long few seconds, she swallowed again and shakily cleared her throat. She took in a deep respiring breath, embarrassingly watched Alex nervously choke on his saliva, and processed the few rational thoughts still swirling around in her beclouding mind.

'How do I act?' she wondered, hoping this moment merely a simple passing coincidence where the breacher could assume her just another mindlessly wandering resident, and *not* an information warden here to somehow investigate him and his peers for breaking serious laws.

'And why did he stop!?' she frustratedly questioned, watching him dip his body left to lower his grocery bags to the floor and then straighten up again, as if somehow holding the bags could impair him.

'And why did he stop here!?' she anxiously whimpered about the inconvenience of him stopping in a short hallway while facing her and blocking the exit at the same time. She'd much rather he stopped with his back to her, and on some disparate storey, or in a prison with a series of white girders dividing the gap between them, or on a rugby field with six, or better, fourteen other teammates looking to smash him and win the day.

"Alex!?" she subsequently moaned at her trembling teammate, hoping he would do more than just quiver and stand fearfully in place with his mouth open.

Resolving then, to just look back at the taciturn breacher and hope he was blind and about to pull out some set of keys from his coat's pocket he would use to unlock the nearest door and just go inside, she peered back to respectfully acknowledge him, and went cold.

He was the breacher from the port, an involuntary recall of her memory attested, the very one she encountered more than six weeks ago with the same short, wavy black set of hair above his small forehead, and chiselled jaw outlining his sedately closed mouth. The same one she tried to fool, who wasn't fooled, and the very same one she violently assaulted, as evidenced by a conspicuous, triangular, red scar emblazoned upon his left cheekbone.

She had to assume that scar half of the reason he was standoffish this time, and why, after such an awkward period of standing idly, he was *still* doing it, and with a rather laser-like focus on her, who he had subtly quivering in disgust. It looked, from across the space, like the aftermath of a small but acutely situated electric bite from hell, with a seemingly veiny, disfigured appearance that probably caused him a very tangible, and likely dangerous, degree of resentment.

The perception of which caused Jack to drop her right hand, unzip her right pant pocket and immediately hesitate, warning herself, *'whoa!'* the split-second she realised it was actually someone else somewhere else in the levels triggering her reflexes with a disgruntled growl at their neighbours.

'Stupid neighbours!' she elaborated with an annoyed blink and roll of her eyes.

An acute shattering of glass somewhere in those same levels then caused her to wince in surprise, and then cringe due to a spine-tingling succession of windows loudly breaking down the facade of the building. Hearing them crescendo into an abrupt, high-pitched pop and burst behind her, she curled to protect herself from the splintering panes at the end of her hallway and shrink below a volley of three black, tennis-sized balls flying in past her. Watching them obliquely contact, smear and adhere to the left-hand wall, forcefully thump Alex in the back of the neck, and land with a sticky stopping roll on the carpet further to his right, she gasped a frightened, "OH!" and dropped to help her collapsing companion. But she couldn't help him for more than a second before irresistibly returning her attention back to the breacher.

The scary robotic sentinel was almost completely unfazed by the tumult continuing down the facade and startling scene unfolding around him. He exhibited merely a small turn of his head to observe imperturbably the substantial wad defacing the wall nearly beside him. Only once reading, 'NZ POLICE AOS,' from off a circular, white logo printed onto a hard black shell residing within, did he break from his steady state to glower threateningly at the information warden who summoned it.

"Oh," Jack fearfully despaired, before a bright exploding light and cascade of hot bursting bangs bleached her vision pure white, slapped her skin with heat, shocked her eardrums, and shoved her backward onto the carpet. "Urgh!" she loudly exhaled, gazing unavoidably into the whiteness from her back.

Instinctively rolling left after a short breath to dig her elbow into the ground's matted fibres, she promptly got up on her hands and knees and returned to her feet in a disoriented condition. She hobbled two hundred and seventy degrees while watching the whiteness recede into a blackness, and bent down to successfully locate with her patting hands the heel of Alex's left shoe. She knelt beside him on one knee while hearing a blaring ring develop from the silence in her ears and leant forward to presumably shout, "ARE YOU OK!?" before sitting back on her heel in bewilderment.

She couldn't help him with so few senses, and still had to cope with a breacher hiding somewhere in the monotone blackness. Her hands were also shaking too much for any kind of slapdash surgery, and she probably couldn't handle looking at any more bruising anyway. Her nerves were in complete shock, and her chest was nauseous. Her mind was distraught, and her heart was sorely stampeding.

A few uncovering grey outlines, though, gave her a smidgen of hope. And then a few developing textures, some bearings. A following pouring in of colour interspersed with hot pink speckles then eased her sense of imminent danger before a very audible, vicious, zapping crackle, barely detectable between the undulating ring in her ears, served her an unexpected boost of confidence. The three black tennis balls that had momentarily blinded and deafened her, perturbed her balance and dried out her skin had also whipped the hallway with an electromagnetic pulsing tail that had brought the breacher to a defensive squat in his spot atop the stairs. They had also coated him and his gears, along with everything else, in a glowing pink splutter, setting him on a collision course with Maka and his arriving task force.

"ARGH! GET IT OFF!" Alex abruptly yelped, erratically sitting back on his heels to rock unstably and grapple with the black wad coating his neck. *"IT'S HOT!"* he repeated, clenching his teeth in anguish while clawing into the black gum and frantically tearing at the AOS shell residing within.

Jack reached out to help but hesitate, again, as she anxiously watched him suffer. She could glean around his working hands that he had been quite badly seared by the device and had lost a significant amount of his chestnut hair. His skin bordering the gum was disturbingly inconsistent and his newly exposed scalp *really* raw. There was something very sadly wrong with his obvious ear canal too. It looked like he was going to need to buy another organ.

"RRRRRGH!" Jack growled, leaping to her feet with an unsteady wobble. Rapidly thrusting her right hand into her pocket, clasping her stinger and ejecting it out into the open, she squeezed mightily to depress the handle and spring its snapping shaft into the hallway with a great metallic note. She absorbed the aggravating pang through her palm, and deliberately threatened the one she held responsible for Alex's agony.

"HEY!" she brusquely bawled with a targeting point of her left index finger. "ROBOT!"

The robot stood, in all its pink speckled glory, turning its gaze toward the source of the bawl, to merely listen with its two dead black eyeballs.

Observing it, and its very fortunately ongoing blindness, Jack leant forward, dug in her toes, and absolutely charged at it. She pumped her thighs, flexed her calves, leant even more, lowered her right shoulder, and lunged with all her weight. Transferring as much force as she could into the breacher's waist with a snapping slam of her shoulder, she barged it powerfully a step back, to where there wasn't quite one, and directly followed through with a strong shove.

The breacher tilted while instinctively planting its back foot, but missed a step. It tipped while grasping Jack's pink speckled arms, but slid down the paint. It fell while haphazardly contacting its back foot upon a lower step's edge, but lost its contact upon the carpet with the other. Gripping nothing but Jack's stinger and yanking it from her pushing possession, it ungainly tumbled backwards down the wood, at first sideways, and then head over heels, until its immense weight was dragged by gravity right back down into the wall of the landing.

Jack gazed down at the breacher from her perch upon the top steps in conflict. She became angry because of Alex's severe injury, and was still so because of his howling. She became somewhat satisfied because she barged the breacher, and was still so because there was now a larger gap between them. But she was mortified, because she had just pushed someone forcefully down a flight of stairs. And she was horrified, because Alex was starting to bleed.

It was then that a second bright light exploded, bleaching her vision and everything else once again a completely blinding white.

Chapter Ten
Sunday, 5ᵗʰ August 2063

Jack re-emerged from the second bout of blackness in no less a horrified disposition than she was in before. Alex was in extremely serious trouble, and not just because he was awfully maimed. The amount of blood visibly exuding from his injury between his tightly pressing fingers and palms was far too copious for any kind of consolation. There was no amount of glowing pink tagging speckles that could alleviate his need for *immediate* medical attention, nor was there any obvious reason to believe that the paint and police helicopter buzzing outside would do anything to deter the breacher Jack pushed down the stairs from bounding straight back up.

"His groceries are still here," Jack anxiously noted about the breacher's pink stippled plastic bags and their contaminated contents. Peering at the graffitied door nearest to where he stood from her spot beside Alex on the carpet, and then at Alex, who was hunching over in increasingly audible torment, she promptly concluded there no time to hunch over and subsequently hauled her companion up onto his feet.

"UNNGGHHH!" Alex grizzled over the ringing in Jack's ears, reluctantly standing to stagger woozily between her steadying arms.

"We're leaving!" Jack distinctly ordered, guiding him posthaste towards the ascending staircase. Darting back for a second to fetch her HUD from beneath the pink spatter colouring the carpet as the surrounding residents began bursting out of their units in alarm, she energised the wardens' escape with a faster dart back and an encouraging shove of her neon-coloured companion up the steps.

"Uurgh," Alex agonised, cautiously resisting the climb.

"Don't worry!" Jack assured him, pocketing her opaquely tagged HUD while supportively guiding him up from behind, "let's just go!" Over an erupting cacophony of shouting and screaming churning up the cold, dampening breeze spiralling down the well, she urgently stuttered, "we'll, we'll get, we'll just get you sorted out— Outside! On the."

Jack couldn't stomach gore, always becoming very queasy when something fleshy and red, or even just icky and foul smelling was within range of her senses, and so wasn't mentally prepared to pull over and inspect Alex's injury. A little blood and bruising was comparatively fine, but gooey exudations and lost organs exceeded her few degrees of gastrointestinal tolerance. Only with the briefest glean did she establish that Alex had been maimed. And only with the utmost certainty did she determine that they both needed to ignore it and flee.

"Oh-urgh," Alex shakily expired while tottering around the landing and lifting his hands from off his face to stare at his blood.

"Don't look at it!" Jack warned him, glaring incidentally at his mangled left ear and becoming queasy herself. "Ugh," she panted, shutting her eyes and looking away as a resultant tingle cantered deeply up the back of her thighs.

"Ee-huhgh!" Alex squirmed, protectively recompressing his wound and whimpering while trudging up the rattling left-hand side of the staircase past a pink splattered number of panicked residents flurrying down.

"Please, *hurry!*" Jack urged him, taking a deep recomposing breath and physically pushing Alex to climb faster.

Clutching the left-hand banister to ensure the flurry didn't whip her off, as a roar of voices elsewhere in the building rallied everyone to act, she then clasped the back of her flexing right thigh and squeezed to try and dispel its enervating tingle. Clasping tightly next her holstered stinger through her pants' fabric to reinforce her faltering confidence, and prevent it from being accidentally caught on those inconsiderately sliding past, she exclaimed, "*my stinger!?*" in surprise and peered back down the steps. "My stinger's— *Oh!*" she stammered, recalling it being yanked from her hands a storey down. "Oh," she lamented, conflictedly hoping to never see it again. "My— *Ohgh!*" she complained about the crippling fee it was going to cost her to replace.

"JACQUELINE HART!" the one holding that stinger thunderously growled up the well, clear above the cacophony for all in the building to hear in a burly, vengeful baritone.

"Oah!" Jack gasped with an intense jolt of her nerves and subsequent vault up the following staircase to re-join with Alex. "Go! Go! *GO!*" she told him, pushing him to squash into a criss-cross of residents filling up the width of the next landing so the wardens could escape their doom.

But Alex wouldn't go so hastily with his left hand permanently pressing his head and right hand reaching across his body to dig into his left pant pocket. It wasn't his name being called to account by a wrathful titan that was going to eat him, and so he wasn't in quite as much of a hurry despite his condition. He also didn't understand the thunder as distinctly as Jack did.

"HEY!" he complained, stepping deliberately back down into Jack to ease away from the panicking residents that could knock him over. "It's— I'm hurt!"

"Sorry!" Jack said over him conveying, "I want my medicine!"

"Argh," Jack anxiously expressed, diving her own hand into his left pant pocket to more coordinately retrieve his jar and put it into his palm. "There! Take it!" she demanded, diving her hand then into his other and requesting, "give me Little Dorothy!"

"IT'S THE POLICE!" a blaring resident suddenly warned his neighbours as more and more of the building's residents became aware of the situation.

"GET YOUR WEAPONS!" another roused over the panic, pointing across the hallway.

"ARM UP!" a built young man in a glowing pink and white singlet cheerily called, circling spiritedly past the wardens and giving three hardy claps with his hands.

"Move!" Jack abruptly ordered Alex, bringing his contracted stinger out and pushing him to continue up now that the way was clear.

Arriving on the eighth storey to watch a resident yell, "here!" and chuck two rudimentary-looking, long barrelled objects to his seemingly crippled peers hunkering down against the right-hand side of the hallway, she reconcealed Alex's stinger in her pocket and fretted.

"They've got guns Jack," Alex privately warned her, stopping irresistibly at the base of the next staircase to pant through his pain and observe with a disoriented squint the same resident throw two square magazines to his peers and load up his own weapon. "This is bad."

"Yes!" Jack assertively concurred over the noise, pushing him again. *"So move!"*

"No!" Alex disagreed, turning to convince her with his paling face, "it might be safer to stay inside!?"

"With the?" Jack responded, clenching her fists in frustration. "With the *big guy?!*" she discreetly argued, gesturing down the well.

"Urgh," Alex grieved with a grit of his teeth, "yeah." Appealing with a full free-handed point to his wound, he stressed, "I'm hurt!" asserting, "and I don't want to get more hurt in the, the *this!*" with a point to the arming residents. "Let's get inside an apartment!"

"Come, come, come!" a middle-aged grandmother holding a carpet sweeper urgently called across the hallway from an open unit on the right.

"They've got trucks coming in!" a worried woman holding a gun on the left declared, poking her head out from a unit closer to the windows, "refrigeration trucks!"

Watching a scared mother tightly embracing a blue toddler against her chest scoot for their lives across the hallway into the grandmother's open unit as their pink speckled neighbours readied for a belated ambush of the helicopter they were surveilling, Alex promptly conceded, "yep, nahp. We're— I don't— Sorry to the kid!" he groggily proclaimed, pointing his open hand at the closing unit door, "but I don't wanna be here when it gets shot. Sorry!"

"Good!" Jack replied, shoving him up the next staircase. "Not good!" she flustered from the next landing, gesturing back down towards the unit the kid disappeared inside.

"HOLD!" an armed male manning the left-hand corner of the broken hallway windows on the ninth floor ordered, peering back at seven others standing at the ready in the open unit doorways behind him.

"Oh man," Alex moaned about their obviously eager state while circling at their rear to abruptly stop in surprise and boggle.

"Move!" Jack anxiously stressed, pressing him to climb the first step up a staircase blocked by a shabby, roughly plastered ceiling. "Ohgh!" she exclaimed, stopping to boggle herself and complain, "wha-wh-uh-who just puts a *roof* in the stairs?!"

"Are you sure there was a way up?!" Alex wearily bemoaned over a roar of instructions coming up the well.

"DRONES! DRONES! DRONE!" the armed residents staring out the hallway's broken windows warned, ducking abruptly below one matt black example swerving blithely in through the central window frame's remaining glass.

"HOLD!" their leader boldly repeated as his subordinates braced beneath the imploding shards and evaded the robot overrunning them. "TAMA! WE'VE GOT A DRONE— "

"Residents!" the one-metre-wide automaton rehearsed synchronously with its mechanical peers invading the other storeys, "your building is being evacuated. Calmly proceed to the exits, immediately." Hovering slowly along the hallway, incognisant of those very residents openly calling to have it dealt with, it promptly fired off five small red golf-sized balls from its sides, hitting the ceiling, the walls, an armed resident hunkering close by, and a flummoxed girl standing idly in front of the stairs.

"*Ow!*" Jack exclaimed, lurching backward onto her heels in pain. "Argh-ow," she dispiritedly expressed, glimpsing down and pulling the left breast of her pink spotted coat taut to read, 'NZ POLICE AOS,' upside down from off the deformed ball that smacked into it.

An ear-stabbing *E* straight out of the eighth octave suddenly blurted throughout the building, transforming its damp breeze into an alarming vibrato that throttled everyone's eardrums acutely with noise.

Jack slammed her eyes shut, fumbled the grip of her coat's zip, and sealed her throbbing ears tightly with her hands. She couldn't cope with the racket freely pulsating into her brain, nor conceive how to react now that every thought training in her mind had just broken.

With one ear being recently maimed, however, and the other still partially deaf from a life spent listening to music so loud it could drown out all the bullying, Alex stood tall and yanked at the ball that had glued itself permanently to Jack's coat. He then more effectively unzipped Jack's coat so he could yank it entirely from off her braced arms and throw it at the ground to stomp on it. But the central component of the sticky ball proved too robust for his vertiginous aim, remaining perfectly intact after four effetely given stomps, and the panicking surge of residents rushing incautiously around him, too intimidating.

It was only the actions of one scruffy man sliding out from a left-hand unit further down that seemed coordinated enough to temper the racket by promptly attaching to his truncated left elbow a peculiar appendage he raised to an inch below the invader. While cautiously leaning away from it as it sprang open lengthwise to reveal a brightening glass tube flanked by two energising electrodes, he shut his eyes and triggered a vividly arcing, bright blue electrical discharge that zapped the carpet, danced up the wall and struck into the invader's popping belly.

"YEAH!" the armed residents visibly celebrated, watching the dead robot collapse onto the scruffy man's head and shoulders.

Observing the drone tip and slide down the scruffy man's side onto the floor as the screaming of babies and children in the top few storeys became intelligible again over the remaining alarms persisting below, Jack stood bewilderedly and rubbed her sore spot beneath her black thermal T-shirt. She couldn't believe the mess developing before her eyes. Alex had been beaten up, blasted, and burnt, and had lost a frightening amount of blood. She had pushed someone down a flight of stairs, and the wardens were both now futilely trying to escape him. The unsophisticated residents in the building were arming themselves, and they'd just rebelliously defaced an expensive piece of police property.

'What have I done?' she contemplated with a self-demoting shake of her head.

"FIRE! FIRE! FIRE!" the leader of the armed residents commanded to her breaking point.

Jack's eyes welled up with tears beholding the residents she was investigating obstinately stand, brandish their guns, and wildly begin shooting bullets into the street. She had never witnessed such a rapid descension into such callous behaviour before, nor experienced such a brutal, sudden bashing of her eardrums by a barrage of explosively deflagrating rounds that were being aimed at people.

For every bullet her twitching eyes could see leave its barrel, there was a vicious flash of flame, and every one her quaking ears hear, a savage shock of sound. For every spent case her narrowing eyes could see eject from its chamber, there went a guilty brassy glimmer, and every one her ears hear land inside, a heinously heartless tinkle. Her heart belted with every explosion of power, and wracked with every pause automatically loading in another bullet.

'*How could this have happened!?*' she lamented, struggling to comprehend how the relatively peaceful morning could have turned into such a pandemonium, and how such a keg of powder could have been exploded from such an infinitesimally small ambition she had just to get promoted.

"I just wanted to get off minimum wage!" she sorrowfully cried above the resounding, ear-beating violence, concluding now there no obvious way to improve her life except through making someone else suffer. For an opportunity to dress more comfortably, there had to be a nasty red electrical scar. For every extra cent she wanted, there had to be a cruelly debased squatter lying disrupted in a dirty alley. And for every small promotion or formal acknowledgement, there had to be a battle, and at least one horribly, almost completely vapourised but fortunately clotting, grossly mutilated bloody red ear.

"THE FIRE ESCAPE!?" Jack read through her refracting tears from off the better side of Alex's distraught face.

"Up," she then made out from the reply being given him by a little unkempt girl that had anxiously approached him in a small dark marl dress.

Being ever so slightly heartened to observe the random little girl stand rather bravely amidst the reflex-inducing reverberation of gunfire with just her hands covering her ears, she kindly leant down with Alex, who tiredly knelt, and aligned the girl's straightening index finger with a right-hand unit along the hallway.

"Eh," the little girl asserted between the cracking and cursing, "there. Have... And *Dad?"* she earnestly questioned, pulling back her wayward fringe to stare innocently up at the responsible-looking lady crying beside her.

Jack leapt a foot back from a crystal-black dead eye gracing the little girl's face from inside a bronze plastic eye socket encompassing it, and straightened up with a haunted gasp. The little girl was another of Topher's curiously altered residents she was here to investigate, and by guilty extension, ruin the life of.

"That way?!" Alex eagerly verified, reenergising enough to stand, pivot and extend his good hand to point at the indicated door he was starting towards.

Starting with him to resume their escape from the danger coming up the stairs, and abscond from the little innocent girl trying to locate her parents inside the turmoil Jack caused, Jack dutifully fled with Alex so that she wouldn't ruin his life too.

'Any more,' she hoped, shamefully slipping away with him through the closing centre-right unit door the little girl kindly pointed out for them.

"SPREAD THEM ACROSS THE FRONT OF THE BUILDING!" a resident rushing out of the unit's darkness directed, sliding past the wardens into the hallway with a black polygonal film they were unravelling from a metre-wide spool in their arms.

"BRING THE POWER BANKS CLOSER!" another embracing a matching spool in some stray light beckoned from behind two huge flat open boxes sitting in the left-hand corner of the starkly gutted dwelling.

The wardens sprinted to avoid obstructing two more residents hurriedly heaving an even huger box from laterally across the space, and darted directly towards an unusually grand-looking, U-shaped staircase built against the building's exterior wall. There upon, they could perceive a continuing chance for their escape in the form of a faint grey path of light that was drizzling down its steps from above.

"What is this place?" Jack dubiously asked, skipping between two inviting volutes up its elegantly laid, almond-marbled slabbing. "And who are these people?" she sceptically wondered, circling its wide forking landing right to follow Alex's vividly glowing pink speckles up to the next storey.

"I don't know!" Alex exasperatedly replied, lunging woozily up onto the staircase's crest. "And I just wanna get away from them!" he dismissively panted, dropping to the floor of a short marble lobby leading forwards to lay against the left-hand wall and thoroughly reventilate his lungs.

Jack let out a flustered sigh and reluctantly knelt down on both her knees beside him. She hadn't climbed this far just to be caught, nor urged Alex on just for him to give up, but could completely sympathise with his desperate need to rest. He had been in need of immediate medical attention for some time now and still wasn't about to get it amidst the gunfire, while she was still trying to breathe out a cramp dogging her heart that felt like it could persist until she collapsed or escaped right back to her home. And so it seemed, this lobby, to be the best place right now to pause since they were already in it, being somewhat concealed by its pink stippled darkness, with all the violence happening downstairs behind and in the next daylit hallway intersecting just five metres ahead.

"URGHH!" someone in that hallway bawled above the chaos.

Jack pressed herself against Alex, spotting a loosely strapped long gun jiggle into view beyond the archway bookending the lobby, and pulled her pink speckled legs in behind the profile of a large marble pot plant in front of them. Spying through the plant's stems the gun move left upon the back of a dreading resident dragging his injured peer desperately away from the danger occurring on the right, she nervously shook and guiltily swallowed. She had caused enough damage already to Alex and the breacher but was now going to be held responsible for *a lot more* damage she hadn't even *remotely* considered when planning her morning.

"Urgh," Alex winced from beneath her oxygen depriving weight.

"O— Sorry," Jack apologised, pushing off the wall to return to her knees and compress with her fingers an acute ache developing between her temples. "We can *not* stay here," she advised, growing increasingly concerned about the knowledge of their occupation, and connection to the turmoil, soon becoming ubiquitous among the residents.

Alex was more concerned, however, about the dried blood coating his left hand he was using to open the lid of his medicine jar he tiredly pulled out with his right. Colouring his skin almost completely crimson from the tips of his fingers to the width of his wrist, and saturating thoroughly the next six inches of his left sleeve he raised into the grey light passing through the stems, it looked copious, like it had come from somewhere where there had been an abundant supply, and rich, like it used to be important to someone trying to stay alive.

"Ogh," he giddily groaned, raising his left arm to stare down at the sticky dregs crookedly streaking his elbow.

"Ugh," Jack panted, glimpsing at them too and becoming nauseous.

"KILL ALL OF THESE TYRANTS!" a bald man appearing beyond the archway furiously grizzled, shaking his rifle indignantly towards the street.

Jack re-pressed herself against Alex and pulled her legs in once more to hide while consciously attempting to divert the nausea inverting her tummy with several deep sequestering breaths. She was sensing it very unsafe to kneel in the sights of a bald man furiously taking cover with his gun inside the archway just ahead, and very imprudent to vomit a mess of cheap chicken noodle soup that was only going to incite the breacher more if he had to stomach it when catching up to them from behind.

"Grrr!" she grumbled, expressing her own indignation with a firm, mentally exhausted slap of her forehead. She couldn't believe how stuck she felt hiding in the dissipating cover of a pot from a violent militia that was soon going to figure her out, while being loyalty-bound to someone so incredibly worn and demoralised that they didn't seem to want to escape the breacher pursuing them anymore.

"We can *not* stay here," she whispered agitatedly, sliding forward to relieve Alex of her weight, rest her back on the convex body of the pot, and abruptly duck beneath a bassy blast ricocheting through the lobby and its flimsy plants.

"KABIR!?" the bald man shouted in alarm.

"ERRGH!" a new casualty in the hallway cried, "MERE SEENE!"

"STAY DOWN! STAY DOWN!" another somewhere between them urged.

Jack cautiously peeked around the curvature of the pot to see the bald man yank up the waist of his raggedy pants, reach out supportively for his moaning friend further up the hallway, and peek around his own cover to aim towards the street and fire two ear-splitting bursts with his rifle. She then snapped back to nervously squint, tightly cover her ears, and ardently re-resolve to escape before the residents could find out who it was that had called in the police in the first place and accordingly turn their guns upon them.

"We *can not* stay here!" she determined with a pinning point at Alex, seriously exhorting, "they will find us out and *end* us; OR WE'LL GET EATEN!"

"WHERE ARE OUR OPERATORS!?" the dispiriting bald man implored above a second bassy blast blowing through. "KABIR! I'LL COME FROM BEHIND!"

Seeing him lunge out to disappear back into the chaos and leave behind a gap that the wardens could push into, Jack opportunely sprung to her feet, springing Alex's right arm with her, and eagerly traipsed backward towards the gap, yanking her fatiguing companion on. "We cannot— "

"I *heard* you!" Alex irritatedly complained, swigging a batch of dry tablets awkwardly from his jar as he resentfully used up all of the energy he had produced resting to bend, push off the wall and feebly follow his arm. "Ah-hurgh-hurgh," he consequently coughed, sputtering out an excess of tablets as he followed onwards past two seductive black settees furnishing either side of the lobby.

Jack very briefly paused at the left-hand side of the archway to lean against the wall, pull Alex in behind her and obliquely view the garrison bellowing at the end of the hallway. She was certain these were going to be the last of the residents the wardens would have to slip by in order to escape, but not certain they were going to be as oblivious to the wardens' presence as the two previous garrisons had been below. They had started taking casualties and their anger at those that had hurt them had been well kindled.

There was some hope, however, in the way that they were struggling to sustain their makeshift battlement against the police. At least three of them Jack could perceive, through a visible fuzz distorting the wet weather falling in from outside, were having trouble re-erecting a parapet they had made by stretching one of their polygonal films stiffly across the base of the hallway's tall arching framework of blown out windows. It looked like it was going to be impossible for them to notice anybody searching for an exit behind them with all of the police's gadgetry keeping them all so preoccupied, especially when also having to work inside a fuzz that was very likely gnawing into their brains.

"What *is* that!?" Jack groaned, backing momentarily off to squeeze the ache intensifying between her temples. *"Argh."*

Alex slid across the front of her to catch his faltering balance flatly upon his foot and curiously peek into the hallway before sliding carefully back to ignore placating his companion since he didn't really care anymore about her whinging. Jack had done nothing but deliver him into danger the whole morning, and so it didn't bother him anymore to see her distress. He had a far more serious problem of diminishing life to hold on to, while she just had a stupid headache.

"Uhh," he deeply inhaled, leaving Jack to indulge in her arrogance alone. "Hough," he deeply exhaled, waiting begrudgingly for his next bout of severe pain to ensue.

"WE NEED THE RIVET HAMMER!" a resident struggling in the fuzz pertinaciously beckoned.

"THEY'RE POINTING IT AT US AGAIN!" his comrade on the other end of the film fearfully warned.

"JUST PUSH IT UP!" the other between them frantically compelled.

Jack leant quickly out from the archway to identify the source of the fuzz gnawing into her brain when a third blast of bass suddenly blew over the garrison, denting their film and deflecting upwards to bash a small dead chandelier it jingled and swung wildly from its elegantly bevelled recess.

"HOOUGH!" she involuntarily expired, being whipped in the right side of her face by a ricocheting blast of bass the strafing helicopter supportively fired into a defensively shutting doorway to the garrison's left. "Ergh," she winced, leaning back against the wall to brace her freshly sprained neck with her hands and seek some sympathy from Alex.

'YOU'RE EVIL!' she read introspectively, however, from off the remaining bits of red clotting cartilaginous flesh she hadn't yet virtually blown off her innocent companion's strained, but indifferent, face.

"SARGE IS GONNA FIRE THE HARPOON!" a sprightly messenger halting near the top of the lobby's stairs informed to everyone defending the top storey. "ELECTRIC HARPOON FIRING! DISTRACT THE CHOPPER!"

Figuring their time to escape the breacher and his neighbours nearly up, and Alex's loyalty almost completely lost, Jack decided it definitely now time to un-pause and disregard all of the dangers growing around them. "Electric harpoon, hurgh," she delicately called out, carefully entering the hallway to crunch beneath the soles of her shoes a few feet of window glass littering a large puddle conglomerating across the marble. "ELECTRIC HARPOON!" she relayed more convincingly, "argh." Holding her neck with her left-hand and Alex's soiled sleeve with her right, she then stared directly at one of the recovering residents she presumed was staring directly back at her and informed, "ELECTRIC, hurgh. SARGE IS GONNA FIRE!"

Identifying incidentally the source of the gnawing fuzz to be an exposed, eighteen-inch-high pine cone-shaped share-power terminal the garrison had deployed upon the floor beside them to power their devices, and probable prosthetics, she promptly reversed the wardens and instructed, "th-uhm DISTRACTION! SARGE NEEDS A DISTRACTION!"

"Get up!" the residents encouraged each other to a backdrop of automatic gunfire going off inside the building across the street. "Sarge is bringing out the harpoon! HARPOON!" they shared with the others posting elsewhere on the storey.

Jack turned to avoid tripping on a casualty lying concussed halfway up the hallway before piteously bobbing down to check on him and earnestly inquire, "are you okay?" and very quickly obtain her answer from his supinely shaking state. "Oh, he's having a seizure!" she stated, looking back at the firmly posturing garrison. "HE'S HAVING A SEIZURE!"

"KABIR!" the furious bald man interjected from the perpendicular cover of a right-hand passage located at the rear of the floor opposite the blown-out windows, "I'M COMING!" Waving then at the fellow resident comforting Kabir, he appealed, "hey!" with a scooping gesture, "bring him here! Grab him!? Pull him!?" he beseeched, lively scooping again.

Jack was *already* busy pulling an invalid and definitely wasn't going to pull another that would shortly come too and re-brandish the metre-long matt black rifle jiggling between his jittering right arm and thigh. He was likely going to be the very first one to kill her once everyone found out who she was. "COME GET HIM!" she instead beckoned beneath a tirade of swearing and another intimidating strafe of the helicopter. "HE NEED'S YOU," she coaxed, hoping to vacate the bald man from the passage she wanted the wardens to escape through.

"PULL HIM!?" the bald man stubbornly pleaded, "PULL HIM!?"

"*Nahp*," Jack abruptly declined, frustratedly standing up to pull Alex beside her and point for the bald man to see one demonstrably maimed ear. "HE NEEDS MEDICAL!" she demanded, chancing the bald man's pity for Kabir by marching Alex adamantly two strides towards him, and accidentally stumbling over a busted police drone in her way.

The bald man fortuitously then vacated his spot, anxiously apprising the wardens, "Kelsie has a first aid kit!" with a lateral point through the adjacent marble before instructing, "bring it to the back here so we can both use it!" and hopping on to get down and examine Kabir.

Jack was already planning to use an *ambulance* to treat Alex, and so forewent Kelsie's meagre first-aid kit, and the bald man's plan to stick around, to just *finally* get Alex out of the direct line of fire and into a laterally traversing corridor running straight through into the next building. "Oh," she subsequently panted, stopping in the passage to support her neck and gawp over a copiously spread, white rubber sealant rudimentarily joining the two elegantly renovated penthouses together.

"SNAKES!" the residents throughout the sprawling storey suddenly exclaimed, "SNAKES!"

Alarmed to feel a chilling wet gale just as suddenly gust into the penthouse and loudly blow glass up the hallway, Jack turned worriedly back to double-check on the residents and watch them all be electrocuted between four tethered harpoons the confronting helicopter had shot into the marble surrounding them. "Ohgh," she puled from behind the cover of the hallway's rear corner, squinting through the dust and moisture churning in the air, 'I can't believe it.' But she had to, while guiltily observing the bald man kneeling in the shimmering puddle agonisingly tense up, kink and convulse inside the searing and snapping field above his helpless friend whose condition was rapidly declining into a nasty electrical possession.

"Oh!" she yelped, watching them successively be bashed one by one by a powerful percussive blast resounding from a weapon suspending from beneath the helicopter's intimidatingly wide, mirrored fuselage.

"Disabler!" Alex wearily exclaimed, leaving Jack's faltering grasp to start opening the corridor's nearest doors so he could find somewhere secluded to hide in.

Shocked to observe the bald man be blown up the hallway into a catatonic, wet glassy heap after swindling from him his position of safety not a moment ago, Jack tearfully reversed to distance herself from another sad scene of her destruction so she could glumly persevere in her effort to help Alex. "HEY?" she inquired about his health, gently massaging her fatiguing heart and sprain while watching him paranoically shuffle along the corridor and grope between its cluttered noticeboards. "Are you ok? Don't get far!"

Reacting sympathetically then to a faint cry emanating from behind the nearest fluttering right-hand door Alex had left ajar, she stepped a foot inside, opening the door by its brassy knob, to find therein a wide man acting urgently to untangle a significant mess of metal tubing built up against the contiguous wall.

"Just stay still bro!" he reassuringly advised, yanking a basic school chair out from the tangle awkwardly burying his mate.

"Ameer?" a distraught lady trembled from beneath a bench running below a long spanning row of tattered blinds and blown out windows opposite them. "Can you help me help him?"

Jack was taken aback by the dozen school chairs and desks remaining in the tangle, and by a strew of soggy A4 paper leading across the wet floor back to a big wooden teacher's desk perpendicularly abutting the wall directly across from her. *'This is a school!?'* she deducted, scanning over a broad, freshly erased blackboard affixed to the adjacent wall to her right for anything that could elucidate the establishment's esoteric existence.

"Ugh, I can't feel my *legs*," the distressed mate uttered from below the tangle.

"Please," the woman begged, bobbing back down from peeking over the teacher's desk to stare remorsefully at Jack and grip the barrel of her long gun she was ruefully standing upon its stock. "He's hurt, and I need help to bring him— "

"Hey!" the wide man called from across the mess. "Help me get this off him before the chopper— "

Jack abruptly swung the door closed and ducked to hide from the helicopter's coaxial rotors howling past the window frames outside before anxiously reopening the door two seconds later to courteously imply, "K-*Kelsie* had-s the f-first aid kit!" and slam it closed before the residents could point to Kelsie further inside, or identify that the distraught woman *was* Kelsie.

'I... Am going to get *hung*,' she dejectedly surmised, backing away from another incriminating exhibit, into Alex.

"Haugh!" he frightfully panted, twisting to gaze over his shoulder at Jack while simultaneously unlatching the child-lock of a well-concealed, marble door standing perfectly flush inside the wall behind a noticeboard.

"O— Yes!" Jack relievedly cheered, giving him room to open the spring-loaded door so she could follow him into the dark exit vestibule and support his lumbering tramp left up the last boxed staircase to an exit on a tiny landing's right.

"Oh, YES!" Jack repeated, eagerly helping Alex unlatch and heave the tenement's last door wide open to reveal the freest cloudy grey sky she had ever had the privilege of being instantly saturated by. *"FINALLY!"* she exclaimed, lunging out into the rain to feel the drops of cold chilling water pelt her face, hair and gratefully rising arms.

"ANOTHER ENEMY!" an armed resident to her left exclaimed, pointing cautiously across the street from behind another stretched film standing stiffly upon the ground. "One, two— SIX WINDOWS FROM THE EDGE OF THE BUILDING!"

"RIVET GUN!" a stocky peer of his taking cover behind a huge, galvanised air vent further along called, chucking his unneeded tool between their cover. "THERE! GET IT DOWN!"

"OH!" Jack exclaimed, watching the nearest resident and his parapet be bashed over by a burst of sound being fired at him from across the road.

"ARGH!" the resident cried, skidding to a gripping halt upon his back, "I— "

"WIRI!" his stocky peer yelped.

"DON'T SHOOT!" Jack proclaimed, waving her arms as she frightenedly leapt out to visibly surrender to the police. "DON'T SHOOT!" she begged, squinting through the rain to spot a black clad AOS officer aim at her from inside the top floor of a tenement across the street, "WE'RE CLIMBING DOWN!"

Getting dizzily up from off his knees to continue on now that he was outside, Alex coughed hoarsely and croaked, "we're info wardens!" loud enough for only the residents in front of him to hear. "We're— "

"WE'RE NOT!" a very seriously jolted Jack corrected, grabbing her invalid for the flabbergasted peer to see, "he's been shot, by the police! *LOOK!*" she stressed, pointing at Alex's dissolving blood and sopping burnt scalp as she marched him towards the distant fire escape she had identified earlier on her satellite map hanging down the side of a very tall, unpainted tenement further up the street. "He's hurt! He's been hit in the head!"

"ARE YOUS *INFO WARDENS!?*" the stocky resident disconcertedly questioned, kneeling up to check the fleeing residents and circumspectly turn his hip-held rifle in their direction. "ARE YOUS *INFO WARDENS!?*" he repeated, observing them pass behind him to frantically wave at the police and approach the northern edge of his building's roof.

"Don't shoot!" Jack pleaded, easing Alex the five feet down onto the grimy puddling roof of the neighbouring building. "DON'T SHOOT!" she repeated, waving to the officers spotting them from the tops across the busy urban ravine.

Dropping into the puddles beside her languishing companion to press him on as the helicopter's howl notably wound down, Jack slid her right arm beneath his armpits to pick him up and jump as a blaring metallic collision screeched upwards into the pouring sky and rumbled the ground beneath the wardens' feet.

"MOVE!" authoritative voices began barking as a terrible shrill of screaming erupted below, "MOVE! MOVE THESE PEOPLE!"

"They brought the helicopter down!?" Jack glumly presumed, glimpsing over her shoulder to hopefully spot the helicopter rotors nimbly manoeuvre inside the ravine.

"Errghr," Alex groaned, taking the moment to force Jack's arm down and kneel upon the concrete to bear his pain. "My— Ungh," he uttered, reaching for another dose of his medicine.

"Why?" Jack heartbrokenly asked about the chaos, letting Alex go to decipher from the new swell of panicking that the vehicle had indeed fallen dangerously out of the air onto a street occupied by many innocent, evacuating people and their cars. "Why?" she tearfully wondered, returning to tug Alex's jumper and keep going.

Tugging her groaning companion again more firmly as he messily unloaded another handful of tablets unwisely into his mouth, she scolded, "w-we can't stop here," to motivate him so that they wouldn't get crushed by some second helicopter likely coming with the next wave of police arriving behind their preceding sirens. "Please!" she encouraged, forcefully pulling his arm to re-stand him so they could conclude their last stretch of escaping before it was too late. "There will be an *ambulance* down there. *PLEASE!*"

"I HATE!" Alex hesitantly protested, letting more of his tablets wastefully fall as he stomped the puddling roof with the soles of his boots to get up, fling his jar and go. "I HATE Y-THIISS!" he angrily proclaimed, subsequently letting Jack speed his faltering pace up between another band of Topher's finest exiting onto the suburb's roofing to battle with the police.

"Just keep running," Jack coaxed, vaulting two abutting waist-high walls Alex clambered over to proceed across the last roof beneath an echo of automatic gunfire reverberating between the shabby scarps of the rigid suburb's sporadically jutting skyline.

"Careful," she warned, sliding up against one last waist-high wall to ensure Alex mount upon it first to jump and drop safely into the structure's closest recessed basket nearly one horizontal metre across a deadly fall.

"Haugh!" Alex exhaled, jarring the basket with his flopping body.

"Give me Kelly!" a grandmother clutching her grandbaby one consequently rattling basket up flustered over the ongoing alarm resounding from inside her home. "Please! *Don't shake it!?*"

"Don't drop him!" the baby's mother earnestly pleaded, anxiously exiting their window to join her baby and reactively bracing mother.

Mounting, jumping and landing to immediately trail Alex's pink dotted descent down the dubious structure between a dozen others hastily descending with them, Jack let her crumbling world's gravity drag her eight consecutive baskets down until the soles of her shoes could finally make contact once again with the real ground.

"Ahgh!" she panted gratefully, grabbing Alex's left arm to keep him from joining a line of residents merging into a larger concourse of their cowering neighbours very slowly moving rightwards along the footpath in front of them. "No, no. The police!" she stated, pushing him to instead continue directly through towards a team of five blue, fully-armoured officers garrisoning between a matching police car and police-marked ambulance in the middle of the street.

"Sorry, please?" she then insisted, pointing her way perpendicularly through the concourse to tread upon some feet, apologise sincerely and leap out between two clear autonomous barricades bordering the path.

"Oh!" Alex abruptly cried, collapsing defeatedly onto the road's skin-ablating cobbles, "HERGH— "

"Alex?!" Jack stated, stopping to reverse and pick him back up, after first rubbing a numbness developing in her knee.

"BACK OFF! BACK OFF!" the five officers the wardens were approaching shouted from behind another clear barricade flanking their garrison. "BACK OFF!" they barked, brandishing their weapons at the two breaking locals while gesturing for them to return into their concourse.

Seeing their helmet visors vividly light up with their commands in cardinal red, to warn the locals about the imminent risk of force they were about to experience, Jack exclaimed, "n-w-hey!" throwing her hands up to surrender and announce, "we're info wardens!"

"BACK OFF!" the officers threatened, suddenly advancing over their robotically collapsing barricade to order the locals to, "GET ON THE GROUND! GET ON THE GROUND!"

"Argh," Alex proclaimed, lifting his newly grazed face and chest from off that ground to bewail his overwhelming pain, "eargh!"

"WE'RE INFO WARDENS!" Jack distinctly divulged, kneeling a step ahead of Alex to submit to the nearest broadly shouldered officer confronting her, "WE'RE *INFO WARDENS!*"

"STAY DOWN!" that officer and his visor ordered, aggressively clutching the back of Jack's frizzled hair to tilt her head back and swap his disruptor for a handheld scanner he used to biometrically verify better her dripping face. "STAY STILL! DON'T MOVE!"

"AARGH!" Alex grizzled while being rudely peeled from his prone posture by another officer acting to verify his face too. "OW, it hurts— "

"STAY STILL!" his officer growled at him, "DON'T MOVE!"

"My name is Jacqueline Hart!" Jack anxiously proceeded to submit, "information warden 5-6-2-0. And he, he's Alex Hazelwood, information warden, 7-8-0-1. He's injured! He needs— "

"Get back in line!" her officer retorted, dismissively shrugging her off to point with his free hand up the street, "and scan in at the end! MOVE!" he and his visor yelled, pointing assertively at the concourse beneath another rattling echo of automatic gunfire and bass bouncing off the facades standing overhead.

"HE NEED'S *MEDICAL!*" Jack argued for her companion, flinching nervously as she arose to limp back and bob down to very necessarily assist her companion. "Alex— "

"GET LOST!" Alex resisted, however, rolling back onto his right side to angrily slap her hands away.

"Alex!?" Jack repeated, appealing for his cooperation as the officers demanded she leave. "You need help— "

"I SAID GET LOST!" Alex rancorously resisted, tearfully rebuking her from his miserably sopping state upon the cobbles, "YOU *ALWAYS* GET INTO TROUBLE, and now *HERE I AM!*"

Realising from the deliberate strain in his voice, dilated stare of his eyes and intense flaring of the veins in his neck his newly developed feeling of scorn for her, Jack retaliated, *"FINE!"* and offendedly got back up onto her feet. She wasn't going to spend *a second* of her already lapsed time debating with such an *obstinate child*, especially when having strived through so much violence and pain to get him to the ambulance he needed, just to find out she would now have to *fight* him just to get him *inside* it. "STAY HERE! *GET WET!*" she criticised, complying with the officers' coarsely restated demands to leave the pitifully pink speckled male rejecting her on the road and get back into line.

But she couldn't go four steps before stopping to really behold for the first time the scale of the chaos that she and her ambitions had caused.

There were at least a thousand residents congesting outside right now along both sides of the street in the rain, being driven from their homes by the continuing alarms and flashbangs that had been shot into their buildings. Having to shield their young with just their drabbest robes while being herded behind the barricades by the police and their robotic dogs, they were being made to squeeze into a fearful huddle as the echoes of gunfire continued to overrun them, and the processes of a barbed checkpoint erected at the head of the street slowly started to suck them in.

'What, *is happening?!*' Jack bewilderedly asked, spotting incidentally across the roofs of three obstructing police cars two mechanical arms extend from the rear of a huge black, opened lorry trailer in the left lane ahead to pluck and insert delicately a turquoise gurney into its silver, rotating compartments.

"GET BACK IN LINE!" one of the armoured officers breathlessly bawled, pointing towards the concourse as he stomped towards Jack with his disruptor gripped tightly in his hand.

"I'm with Maka!" Jack riposted, recalling one very pertinent fact that could help her understand what was happening, "WE'RE WITH MAKA!" Stepping worriedly backward while holding her hands defensively up, she explicated, "WE'RE WORKING WITH SENIOR CONSTABLE MAKA PARATA!" and stumbled over a random white teddy bear that must have popped out with the wardens when they exited onto the road.

"GET BACK IN LINE!" the officer coarsely repeated, bashing Jack's sternum with a stiff open palm to push her awkwardly backwards over the curb and into the concourse roughly between the barricades.

"Haugh!" Jack panted, falling unintentionally upon a trio of consequently tumbling mothers, "eergh! We're with AOS, you idiots!" she frustratedly yelled at the departing officer, flexing straight back up to compress a freshly acquired graze stinging her upper left arm, brace her lightly re-sprained neck, and apologise politely to those she disturbed before boldly stepping back out onto the road to declare, "WE CALLED YOU HERE— "

"WE NEED FOUR GURNEYS!" a desperate officer rushing up from further down pleaded, drawing the immediate support from the five officers ignoring

Alex, and immediate attention of Jack who gazed past him to identify the cause of his desperation and instantly silence herself in shame.

The helicopter, that had hurriedly come to save the wardens from the assailing thugs, and incidentally deliver them from a breacher that was going to finish them off, was now lying in a great crumpled heap perpendicularly across the road that had earlier been teeming with people. After howling like such a beast and firing off gadgets like a playful predator, it had dangerously descended into a teetering wreck upon an unknown number of cars, with its crushed nose pitching upward atop a mound of bricks it had uncontrollably mauled from off the facade of the olive building.

Jack was terrified to see its windows shattered and coaxial rotors suspended only high enough to slice someone's waist and head off, and horrified to observe two risking officers drag a pilot out and very valiantly place him upon a gurney. She hadn't ever even imagined being responsible for someone probably being killed in a helicopter crash, nor even fathomed being responsible for the far more probably-deadly battle that brought it down. And she had *indeed* been responsible for passing along the message to the rebels to prepare for the harpoon, and *indeed* been responsible for calling in the police to engage with the rebels in the first place.

'How could all this have *HAPPENED?*' she solemnly questioned, backing away from the sight of the thick harpoon cable hanging out of the exposed ninth storey, and dusty screaming residents that were having to nurse their head wounds in line while cowering beneath the persistently nerve-wracking rattle of gunfire.

"*Maka,*" Jack then remembered, hoping to figure out a way for everyone to somehow get through this disaster, "where's *Maka?*"

"*MAKA!?*" she called, turning a hundred and eighty degrees to go in search for anyone in uniform that would respond to the name. "*MAKA!?*" she repeated, weaving between two diagonally parked police cars in the way.

Slowing to avoid a fracas that was breaking out in between two civilian cars parked alongside the right up ahead, she then paused to witness a lanky teenager shake out of two officers' grasp so he could determinedly move out onto the road.

"*MUM!*" he cried, striding in a white singlet and shorts before his officers could react quickly to tackle him. "*MUM!*" he eagerly yelled, collapsing to jerk beneath the two bullies trying to manipulate his resistant wrists into their zip ties. "*GET AWAY FROM ME!*"

"*JOVAN!*" his panicking mother cried, leaping out from across the road to be with him, "*JOVAN—* "

"*HEY!*" Jack compulsively barked, irresistibly approaching the fracas to scowl at the unnecessary bullying. "GET *OFF* HIM— "

"Mummy!" a little girl yowled, running longingly out to stay with her mother.

"*GET OFF MY CHILD!*" the mother begged her wriggling son's arresting bullies.

"*HEY!* GET *OFF* HIM!" Jack bawled, leaning down to plant her feet and grip with her hands one of the bullies' armoured bodies so she could wrench him from off of the ruck.

"BACK OFF!" the bully ordered his interferer, springing up to bash her chest backwards with his two bulkily gauntleted hands.

"Aargh, *GET OFF ME!*" the teenager growled, twisting to stab with his freed, mechanically unfolding left hand a short electrode into the remaining bully's insufficiently armoured upper-left thigh.

"Urgh-AAARRGH!" that bully bellowed in a horrible, limb-seizing tremolo.

"*HEY!*" a third officer promptly reacting from behind a police car exclaimed, storming around to help Jack's returning bully swiftly save their convulsing peer and assist in making the arrest.

"*HEY!*" Jack repeated, reapproaching the fracas to order the three bullying officers to, "LEAVE THEM *ALONE!*" before observing her one pull from the rear of his utility belt a small device he powered on and flicked to unfold into an arc and vertically slam onto the blubbering teen's wriggling head.

"*NO!*" the mother cried, watching her son go limp as if he were dead. "*NOT MY BOY!*"

"*STOP!*" Jack furiously said, effortfully wrenching from off the ruck that same police officer once again.

"THAT'S *IT!*" he consequently grouched, standing staunchly up to turn around, swipe off her hands and specifically re-engage her. "GET ON THE GROUND— "

"GO AWAY!" the little girl screamed, kicking the armoured shin of the erecting third officer as he forcefully pressed his gauntlet into her mother's tummy.

"LET THEM *GO!*" Jack seriously commanded, feeling a numbness develop in her lower back as she furiously dipped to lunge and shoulder-barge her re-engaging bully back over.

"GET ON THE GROUND!" a fourth officer ordered, clutching her by the upper left arm to restrain her.

"*LET GO OF ME!*" Jack retorted, bounding a free metre back from him to shield her graze and warn the third officer attempting to sedate the little girl like her brother, "*DON'T YOU DARE!* I'M AN *INFO WARDEN!*" she then informed the enclosing fourth officer, exasperatedly exclaiming to his gurney-summoning peers, "YOU'RE HURTING THE *WRONG—* " before a big rushing blur smashing into her left eye turned everything pitch black and silent.

Jack had calmed considerably after awaking in a recovery position fifteen minutes later upon the lumpy backseat of a moving police car with the right side of her face buried into its smoky white vinyl, and hands zip tied uncomfortably behind her back. It had been a disastrous morning, starting off good, with her spirits high and hope brimming, before declining into a very distressing nightmare, throwing out all sorts of moral dilemmas and carnage she had to endure until finally finding a proverbial cliff to jump from so she could quickly end it all and wake back up. 'In *handcuffs*,' she despairingly noted, rolling onto her back so she could lightly squash her hands into the pit of the lumpy bench and seatback and look up at the mood-soothing, platinum-grey vinyl ceiling.

Breathing out a fatigued sigh, in place of a schizophrenic scream she had no remaining energy for, she then moved her mind on to the tenderness panging her swollen left eye, internal ball of weakness obstructing the left side of her neck, and fiery graze still stinging her upper left arm when she wasn't perfectly pressing it into the vinyl. They were all sore, like her self-esteem, but real, and a lot more tear-inducing. And there probably wasn't going to be any decent treatments for them in jail, where she was probably heading, with a charge of deliberately manhandling a police officer doing his job, while being an information warden, who now *definitely* nobody wanted.

There had been stories she had heard about jail, and prison, where practically all of a prisoner's rights were suspended, that hadn't elicited as much concern in her in the past as it did in others since she had endured such a prison-like experience growing up, on and off, inside the squatters. Inmates would be confined for nearly twenty hours of the day, upon a small, rubbish bed, inside a dinky little box, with little to do but breathe in recirculating mattress and toilet particulates and wonder what it was like to be rich, elegantly walking around inside the bridges and floors of Babel. 'It had been made to sound a lot like the squatters,' she fairly admitted while letting her eyes arbitrarily gaze over the CBD high-rises passing backwards outside the tapered, rain-spotting, rear passenger window, 'though the prison's walls would be sturdier, and its roof actually sealed. And there would also be *more food*,' she added, 'though, *no baking*, from Ebee. Or *kitchen*, to do the baking. Or *apartment*, to do the kitchen. Or, of course, *Ebee* to do it all.'

Now feeling *really* melancholy, and a little hungry for some of Ebee's baking, and a big, reassuring squishy hug, Jack started to glumly descend into a depressed mood and cry. Manhandling a police officer wasn't going be the only charge she was going to face, the various compounding others of which were going to include theft, accessory to manslaughter and manslaughter; and all while being an information warden. 'I'm going to go to prison for *a hundred years!*' she wept, feeling already the binds of imprisonment begin to sever her life-preserving connection to Ebee.

'This is it,' the ponytailed policewomen in the front passenger seat wordlessly stated, pointing rightward out the wiping windscreen before glancing back between the platinum seatbacks and through the protective Perspex to check on Jack. "She's crying," she then audibly uttered to her partner in the driver's seat, looking forward again to wriggle and relax in her chair a moment before the car finally slowed and pulled over.

'Oh man,' Jack whimpered, recognising out the passenger window the glassy aquamarine and blue facade of the high-rise apartment building always standing opposite hers. 'They're gonna parade me through my building in handcuffs, knock on my door and shame me in front of Ebee just to get my *toothbrush*.' Watching the female officer then exit the front to stride past and around the car's boot to open the rear driver's door onto the footpath and let in the cold, she fretted, 'eek,' and braced to be shouted at and dragged out of the car by her hair.

"Come on," the officer uttered, however, flicking her wrist to respectfully encourage her paradee out.

Jack rolled half into the footwell to get onto her feet, balance her right side upon the edge of the backseat's bench and cautiously shuffle her trembling self to the opened doorway. She found it uncomfortably difficult and demoralising to manage herself with her hands bound behind her back, while planning which knee to move first from beneath her cramped and hunching body, but did so, exerting some of the last of her sapped energy to lift herself and step out into the puddling gutter with her left foot, and then up onto the wet footpath with her right. "Aah," she nervously inhaled, proceeding to stand very publicly in her responsibly busy street, outside her very responsibly occupied home in front of the taller officer who was standing two metres ahead of her home's very responsible-looking, azurite-blue uniformed security guard.

"Haugh," she exhaled, acknowledging Pin, who was leaning in a relaxed fashion below the entrance's large eave, with a very embarrassed, trembling nod of her head.

"Turn around please," the officer stated, flicking her wrist past Jack's left arm to watch her paradee pathetically step a foot sheepishly back inside the police car, "no, no. No. *Don't* get back in the car."

"Sorry," Jack mumbled, reversing back onto the footpath to let the officer pull out a pair of safety scissors from her armoured vest and miraculously end the parade only a few seconds after it had started.

Turning around to gratefully bring her freed hands back in front of her to inspect that they were still attached to the ends of her arms, and stand respectfully in place beneath the somewhat soothing rain, peradventure she would be rearrested if she flinched, she *very* patiently pointed her banged-up gaze down and waited. She wasn't sure how to act now that she had been freed, especially while the officer who freed her was still standing steadily in front of her in everything but the helmet and gauntlets of her intimidating blue body armour.

"We'll be letting you off with just a warning, this time," the officer autonomously rehearsed before pausing to recollect for four seconds and counsel, "you're lucky that Maka persuaded those officers not to press assault charges against you, or they would've been dropping you off in jail right now. Not temporary holding. And definitely not at your home... You should be grateful."

"Yes," Jack attentively agreed, momentarily making eye contact with the officer's glazy hazel irises to submit, "I am," before gazing down again and concluding, "thank you."

"Thank Maka," the officer corrected her, pausing again to reflect back on some distant memory, and subsequently attempt to warm the exchange, "I. I tried out being an information warden once, for a day... I didn't like it. It wasn't for me... I was looking to trade down after, a confrontation with some very dangerous people while out one night on the beat... It was hard," she glumly described, glancing down at Jack's inter-clasping hands, and then around at the public, "everyone looked at me funny. Like I was a criminal. The whole time. And so I thought it better to remain in the force," she continued, glancing around again more confidently. "You get more done. People respect you more. Or, well... Well. It was the only employment I could get. But at least it comes with decent medical insurance," she said, raising her right hand to her side to stare at her flexing fingers.

Jack was feeling quite dispassionate about the police, and being an information warden, and getting things done, and so stayed quiet because she didn't want to converse about those things anymore. They had all become a curse on her life, 'or had my life become a curse on all of them?' she melancholically contemplated.

"Stay out of trouble," the officer concluded, proceeding to return onto the road and move around the front of her car to her seat, "and don't forget to thank Maka. You owe him." Opening her door, she then cleared her throat and kindly added, lightly pointing at the swelling and bruising noticeably disfiguring the left side of Jack's face, "you should try *Tumornon* for that. It's what I use."

Jack watched the officer disappear inside the car, and then the car slowly disappear into the pleasantly flowing Sunday CBD traffic. It likely wasn't going to be the last police car she saw outside her home, nor its officers the last she was going to have to converse with about the conflict that was still going on right now in Topher. Based upon the faint sirenic chord still ringing through the breeze from the south, Jack had to believe it, and prepare for a succeeding pair of officers to track her down and deal with her a lot more harshly.

The bedlam that she had brought to their city was deadly, and many of the violated residents of Topher *not breachers*, nor any kind of terrorists, or even criminals, that deserved to have their morning disturbed, their homes vandalised, their children taken, and their lives in a few probable cases abruptly ended. And the police that came to rescue Jack certainly didn't deserve it either.

"What happened?!" Jack questioned, gently covering her tearing eyes and sniffling as she turned to inconspicuously march back inside her own peaceful building.

There had been many questions she had asked herself over the last few years while working, but none that felt like its answer would be so self-condemning. Never, when sombrely crossing her lobby after a shift, did she gaze down at its marble and reflect with so much self-loathing. With a bruised eye, yes, and with a fear of being attacked, but never with such a sense of *self-loathing*. *She* had done the attack and *she* had bruised the eye, but she had also done it to a thousand people who *didn't deserve it*.

"Everything going ok out there?" Douglas, her ever-congenial security guard friend politely asked, as he observed his ever-charming information warden friend walk woundedly past him into the available elevator.

'Uuh?!' Jack could only possibly reply as the doors closed and her mind writhed about everything that was going *horribly* out there.

Finally arriving back outside her apartment door to pause pressing her keycard and practise what it was going to be like standing lonely by herself in prison, she proceeded to unlock her latch, enter quietly inside, close the door behind her, and swallow deep down a billowing mass of acid-refluxing guilt.

"Hey Jack?!" Ebee perkily greeted, glimpsing up from an old love story gracing the screen of her uncompromised coder, "hope you had a good morning. I've just been catching up with some reading. Have you had some lunch?"

Sitting quietly at the dining table against the window, with her silver bath robe wrapped around her body, while holding a maple syrup-dripping waffle in her free hand, she then read on, adjusting her posture upon her wooden chair before swapping her waffle for her steaming RF Space branded mug of rich hot chocolate.

Jack too hoped she had a good morning, but she didn't, instead having one of the worst mornings in the city's recent history. "Aah, haughhh," she labouredly replied, clearing her sickly burning throat as she dawdled on from the entrance pretty aimlessly.

Noticing in the corner of her eye Jack's arms dangle lethargically beside her and neck hunch over like she had no purpose, Ebee lowered her book onto the table and carefully placed her mug down onto its matching coaster. "Hey? Jack?" she repeated, standing up to stretch her legs, brush the crumbs from off her robe and walk towards her depressed, or very fatigued, sister who was stopping to hesitantly unload her effects onto the dark wooden entry table. "*What* on Earth are you *covered in?*" she questioned in astonishment, gaping at the glowing pink spatter marking Jack's soggy shoes she was slipping off, damp pants she was loosening and hair, "is that tagging paint!? *Oh!*" she expressed in alarm, gaping next at the unsettlingly long weeping wound lining Jack's upper left arm, "*what happened?*"

"Mm," Jack concurred, bewilderedly staring into her memories of her morning as she bore 'what happened's' pain upon her body.

"What happened, to your eye?!" Ebee inquired on, turning Jack by her shoulders toward her to carefully shift her fringe from off her face and behold one very seriously swollen, blued and bloodied left eye. *"Ooh!"* she subsequently proclaimed, "ooh. Wha-what is this, Jack? Does it *hurt?"* Scanning over it to assess the inflamed, broken skin, light clotting and bruising occurring around her socket before assessing the same problems disfiguring her arm, she stepped a quivering half step back and wrapped her fingers around her forehead to help her think. "Has it been disinfected?" she asked, jumping into the kitchen to fetch the first aid kit, "do I need to disinfect it? I'll disinfect it anyway."

Jack didn't need disinfection as much as she needed her stinger, which was now currently missing from off the entry table along with a coat that might have had her name written clearly inside its collar. And she also didn't need that squishy hug, calculating now it a bad idea since she had become such a stain on society, and would likely stain anyone hugging her, or even being her supportive friend. 'Like Alex,' she remembered of him supporting her moments before angrily slapping her hands away, 'who is *not* a stain.'

"I'll, do it," she then told Ebee, weakly clasping the first aid kit with her left hand as she blocked the attempt to clean her wound with a disinfecting wet wipe with her right. "I'll. I'll do it."

"What *happened* Jack?" Ebee insistently inquired, letting Jack take from her the kit and wipe as she went on to describe what she could see. "This is *bad*. It looks like you were hit with, a brick! Like, did like, a brick, hit you and, like, run-roll down your arm? Or was this from, like, ugh, a dagger or, *a cat!?"* Ebee piteously surmised, holding Jack's left elbow to stare at her arm wound before returning to her eye. "Did *a person* do this to you?"

"It's ok," Jack dejectedly said, tugging her elbow from out of Ebee's concerned hold while shaking her throbbing head, "the police know about it."

"Well they *better* know about it!" Ebee exclaimed, subsequently deciding it critically important to encourage them to act on their knowledge. "I should ring them, and then I'll call Terrence, my parents' lawyer. He's really good," she persisted, moving back to her coder. "He's dealt with all sorts of things like this. Oh, no, first, of course, I'll call the doctors— "

"*Ebee*, please," Jack less-energetically interrupted as she followed her three steps from the entry table, "just, stop." Watching her eager champion halt beside her late brunch and book and stare back, she beseeched, while trembling tiredly and disappointedly, "just wait. I need to do this," she said, gesturing about her disinfecting, "and have a sleep."

"Oh. Yeah," Ebee sceptically conceded, touching her fingers keenly to her coder, "alright." She had seen Jack come home bruised and bloodied several times in the past few years from her work, and could remember how complicated it was to follow up with Jack's superiors and the police about her woes. Pretty much everything Jack did was either concealed beneath a bureaucratic veil of secrecy, or an obstinately thick layer of repudiation. And if Jack wasn't even ready yet to talk about these recent woes then she would just have to wait. "But I am definitely going to call them all by tomorrow morning."

Walking between the couches towards her bedroom, where she would indeed disinfect her wounds and hopefully have that sleep, Jack assured her persistent champion, "I'll talk to you about it all when I feel better," before begging, "don't look at the news," and gently shutting her bedroom door behind her.

Ebee put aside as much time as she could for Jack over the following days, making an early big breakfast for her each morning, booking multiple home visits by a doctor from their clinic, and advocating for Jack with her employer to secure some indefinitely unpaid time from off of work. But she couldn't secure some indefinitely paid time from off of work for herself, nor convince the police to enlighten her about Jack's growing police record. But then neither could she convince her lawyer to take an interest in her case, which forced her to go ahead and put to one side Jack's concern about looking at the news.

"This is bad," she recognised, watching from her couch the aftermath of a police raid in Topher be argued about throughout not just what could be found on every front page of the nation's controversy-gluttonising news. Every known activist was angry, and an endless leak of prohibited private footage about the incident, gushing. She could see Jack had gotten herself into serious trouble, but could also tell Jack could have never known just how explosive their society in general had become. "I can't believe it," she sighed, seeing the images of two information wardens be illegally leaked and deleted repeatedly over and over during the next few intense, near-riotous days while trying to heal the mind of one of those people the angry were aggressively trying to start a destructive riot about.

On Thursday morning, after the angry had been suppressed, and the police had publicly taken all of the raid's blame, Jack was preparing herself quietly in her room to finally go back into her regular work. She had emptied out all of her tears and rested from her wounds, and was now ready to think about responding to the least probing of Gerry's worried emails. She had ignored him for long enough and needed to probe him reprovingly back, and then cajole him to help her respond to the worrying emails and calls she had been ignoring from three different police investigators and some dodgy journalists. After all, it had been *him* that had solicited the support from the terrorist task force and so it *should be him*, Jack determined, to sit down and endure all of the interrogation. And it would likely be *gruelling*, having to sit there and be incriminated by the twists of some breacher-sympathising investigator, for at least up until it was Gerry's turn to incriminate the investigator back.

So far all of the unfortunate deaths had been attributed exclusively to the surprise militia that Topher had sprung up, while the police's demonstration of non-fatal force was increasingly being described by the public as *exemplary*. But there were a lot of questions still to be answered and a lot of details yet to be revealed, and at least a dozen officers' families who were permanently now without a family member. But there were also an innumerous number of Topher's families without a member, their many missing of which were either lying in a coma in a guarded ICU, or confined inside an electromagnetically pulsing jail cell awaiting their chance to be granted an affordable bail.

It didn't please Jack to know any of this, or make her feel all that much safer in the short term, but for now, at least, a judge had issued an injunction to stop just about everyone from doxing her. Along with Alex and every police officer in the country, they could all now go back outside into the public without having a random bottle with their name on it be thrown at the back of their head, or a crude bomb be maliciously thrown through their home's front living room window.

But it wasn't really any legal relief that got Jack out of bed this morning, being it instead her need, like it always was, to desperately make some money. Ebee was still going to leave her life to go to space, and Jack couldn't afford to lose her job due to her absence, and consequently end up back in the squatters. The smell in those places was sickly, and the spirits of anyone dwelling there, persistently compressed. And it was probably going to become a lot more dangerous now that a few hundred new souls from Topher and its gangs were going to have to move in. And so Jack felt it important to get up and resume all of the suffering until the raid had been forgotten, or the last of the respiring breaths she had left in her life had been used up.

"Ahh, haughh," she discontentedly exhaled, staring into her bedroom's tall door-mounted mirror. While the swelling on her face had subsided and the bruising lightened, there could still be seen a C-shaped laceration around the outside of her left eye from the armoured knuckles that had viciously punched it. Besides the much more obvious scraping, cat-clawing cut lining her upper left arm beneath her grey thermal sleeve, it looked like it was going to take months for her foundation to effectively disappear. "Aah, when I'm rich," she anxiously told herself, leaning incredulously back onto her hips, "I'll get it smoothed out."

Exiting into the lounge of her typically empty, mid-Thursday-morning apartment, she then noticed Ebee had left powered on the holotable. And the smell of a loving, though now overbearing, big breakfast had vanished in place of something sweetly and addictively barbequed.

'Space Flight Simulator?' Jack identified inside a holographic box to the left of a holographic waterfall descending opaquely down upon a mouth-watering combo of realistic Jonburger being kept warm inside its foil. "Mmm, hm," Jack genially contracted, realising that Ebee had tried to read her like a book, by setting up what she thought was Jack's favourite videogame upon the table, and treating her to *definitely* Jack's currently favourite, kea-flavoured junk food.

Ebee evidently still believed in Jack, and hoped that a little bit of a treat from the continuing world outside would help reenergise her.

It did.

TO BE CONTINUED...

JACQUELINE HART
CITIZEN
PART ONE

Thanks for reading!

www.ingramcontent.com/pod-product-compliance
Lightning Source LLC
Chambersburg PA
CBHW032242010726
47494CB00002B/600